Katherine's lips were soft and warm...

Vic ached to take possession of first her mouth then all of her. When she parted her lips and tightened her arms around him, he groaned deep in his throat. He covered her mouth with his and marveled when she responded with an eagerness as primal as his own.

He tore at the tangle of blankets between them and allowed himself the fantasy of her silken skin beneath his fingers.

He was amazed at how strongly he felt about this woman. And how determined he was to keep anything bad from happening to her.

ABOUT THE AUTHOR

This is Alice Orr's ninth Intrigue novel. It is set in Albany, New York, where Alice spent many memorable years and had many wonderful experiences, including the birth of her son. She brings that sense of place, along with her love of the Christmas season, her fascination with suspense and a flair for romantic passion to this very special story.

You can write to Alice at Alice Orr Agency, Inc., 305 Madison Ave., Suite 1166, New York, NY 10165. She'd love to hear from you.

Books by Alice Orr

HARLEQUIN INTRIGUE

Dear Santa
Alice Orr

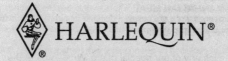

HARLEQUIN®

TORONTO • NEW YORK • LONDON
AMSTERDAM • PARIS • SYDNEY • HAMBURG
STOCKHOLM • ATHENS • TOKYO • MILAN • MADRID
PRAGUE • WARSAW • BUDAPEST • AUCKLAND

To Jonathan—who will be my romantic hero forever.
And to my friend Gayle, who helped make Albany
accurate in this book and meaningful in my life.

ISBN 0-373-22494-X

DEAR SANTA

Copyright © 1998 by Alice Orr

All rights reserved. Except for use in any review, the reproduction or
utilization of this work in whole or in part in any form by any electronic,
mechanical or other means, now known or hereafter invented, including
xerography, photocopying and recording, or in any information storage
or retrieval system, is forbidden without the written permission of the
publisher, Harlequin Enterprises Limited, 225 Duncan Mill Road,
Don Mills, Ontario, Canada M3B 3K9.

All characters in this book have no existence outside the imagination of
the author and have no relation whatsoever to anyone bearing the same
name or names. They are not even distantly inspired by any individual
known or unknown to the author, and all incidents are pure invention.

This edition published by arrangement with Harlequin Books S.A.

® and TM are trademarks of the publisher. Trademarks indicated with
® are registered in the United States Patent and Trademark Office, the
Canadian Trade Marks Office and in other countries.

Printed in U.S.A.

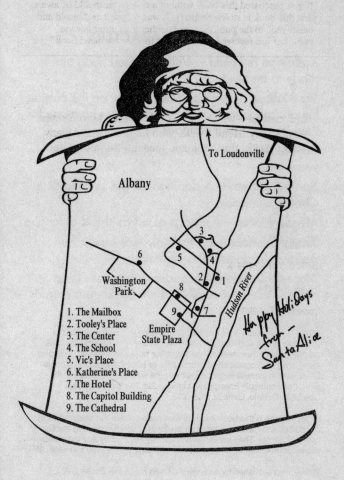

To Loudonville

Albany

Washington Park

Hudson River

1. The Mailbox
2. Tooley's Place
3. The Center
4. The School
5. Vic's Place
6. Katherine's Place
7. The Hotel
8. The Capitol Building
9. The Cathedral

Empire State Plaza

Happy Holidays from - Santa Alice

CAST OF CHARACTERS

Katherine Fairchild—With a bruised heart that is ready to be filled.

Vic Maltese—Tough as black leather on the outside, full of dark secrets on the inside. But is he ready for the love of a good woman?

Coyote Bellaway—The man of his family at ten years old.

Sprite Bellaway—A darling little girl in need of a Christmas miracle.

Megan Moran—As sharp of wit as she is of tongue.

Tooley Pennebaker—The only real family the Bellaway children have right now.

Mariette Dugan—A reporter with a nose for a holiday tale—especially if there could be a murder involved.

Chapter One

For Christmas this year, Coyote Bellaway wished he would come awake one of these mornings all grown up. Maybe then he'd be able to figure out what to do for his little sister, Sprite, and for himself, too. He was only ten, but he could pass for eleven or sometimes twelve. That made him already more adult than kid most of the time. At least, he had to act like he was. Otherwise, somebody might come nosing around and get wind of the truth, that he and Sprite had a roof over their heads but not much more. He wasn't sure how long they'd have the roof, either. Tooley Pennebaker was a very nice lady, but even working every overtime shift she could pull, she was just barely supporting herself. Besides that, she was trying to feed and take care of two kids who were no blood relation to her—though, as far as the school authorities and everybody else knew, she was their aunt. When the real story came out, Coyote had to have a backup plan ready to go or he and Sprite could be out in the cold, and that wouldn't be smart this time of year in Albany, New York.

Worse yet than the threat of freezing their tails off on North Pearl Street, at least from the way Coyote saw things, was the possibility of foster care. He and Sprite would be sure to get split up if that happened, sent off to separate

homes, maybe even different towns. That was exactly what
their mom made him promise about last time he saw her
in the hospital, before they sent her off upstate to that place
that was supposed to be good for her lungs. She'd been
sick so long, Coyote could hardly remember what she'd
been like before or what it was like to be all together—his
mom, Sprite and himself. They'd had last Christmas with
each other. He felt his eyes sting from just thinking about
the little tree on the table with a star on top and how he'd
wished on that star but his wish didn't come true. A week
later, right at New Year's, his mom was worse instead of
better and they'd come for her in the ambulance to take her
away again for this last, longest time.

When they finally let him see her, there in the big hospital on New Scotland Avenue, she'd grabbed his hand.
"You and your sister stick together," their mom had whispered because she didn't have enough breath left to talk
out loud.

"We'll stick together, Ma," he said. "I promise."

His eyes were stinging then, too, mostly because he
could feel she wasn't strong enough to hang on to his hand
very tight anymore. He promised also to do what Tooley
Pennebaker said and not to give her a hard time. Coyote
didn't tell his mom Tooley was so busy working double
shifts at the sewing factory just to pay the rent that she
wasn't around to tell them much of anything. Coyote was
the one in charge. He had to be mother and father to Sprite,
especially since they had no idea where their real dad might
have gone to when he ran out on them after their mom
came down so sick. Coyote wasn't afraid to admit, if only
to himself, that all of this was getting to be more than a
kid could handle. He and Sprite needed a Christmastime
miracle super bad about now. He still believed in such
things, though he'd never tell anybody he did, so the news-

paper sticking out of a trash can on the corner of State and Lodge Streets seemed to Coyote like it could be the answer to his prayers.

"Most Needy Cases Fund Works Miracles," the front-page headline of the *Capitol District Chronicle* said.

Coyote fished the newspaper out of the trash can and hurried into a nearby doorway so he'd be out of the straight line of the fierce cold wind howling up State Street hill from the Hudson River. The frozen snow cover from last night's storm crunched under his feet. The sidewalks hadn't been taken care of yet this morning, and he was careful not to slip and fall down on one of the icy patches. Mostly though, he concentrated on the word he'd seen in the headline. *"Miracles."* He'd just been thinking about exactly that. He told himself this had to be a sign, a good omen like Tooley talked about sometimes. Maybe there could be some Christmastime magic for him and Sprite after all.

"YOU GOTTA LET me do this, Sprite," Coyote said for about the millionth time that night while he tried to work on his letter to the Most Needy Cases Fund. "This is real important."

"I'm 'portant too."

She knew how to say the word right. She was almost eight and very smart. Still, Coyote didn't correct her like he might have done another time. She did this more often lately, talked baby talk to get him to pay attention to her. Coyote didn't need to be a grown-up to understand there was something not quite right about her doing that. Luckily for them, with other people—teachers and even Tooley— Sprite never talked baby-cute. Unlucky for them, sometimes she was anything but cute. She'd pout and refuse to do what she was told. Sometimes she'd refuse to talk at all. She did that more and more often lately, too. Coyote figured he should be glad to have her shut up for a while after the way she used to babble her head off all the time before their mom went away. Instead, he wasn't glad at all. He worried that Sprite acting bad and refusing to give answers in class could bring on a home visit by somebody from the school. Then the truth would come out about how the two Bellaway kids were really living, and they'd be shipped off to foster homes for sure.

"I have to write this letter, Sprite," he said even more strongly than before. "It could mean everything to us."

"Is it a letter to Santa Claus?" she asked.

Coyote was half-surprised to think she still believed in that part of Christmas. Part of him wished he did too, though maybe believing in miracles like the one the newspaper article talked about could be enough.

"It's something like a letter to Santa Claus," he said.

"Can you ask him to bring me a bicycle?" she asked.

She was so pretty even her brother could see it. She had light brownish curls all around her small, pale face that was probably a little too small and a little too pale to be really healthy. She had on a T-shirt and jeans like always. She'd grown out of all her dresses since their mom got sick but he couldn't take Sprite shopping. Now, there wasn't enough money for new dresses. There wasn't enough money for new anything.

"Will you write down that I want a bicycle for Christmas?" Sprite repeated in that whiny voice that meant he'd better answer or she'd ask the same question over and over till he did.

"Yeah. I can write that down," Coyote said.

But, he knew he wouldn't do that. He'd read the article in the newspaper lots of times to figure out just what kind of letter he should send to the Most Needy Cases Fund. They were handing out money, what the article called grants, for the holiday season. Coyote had to get one of those grants for Sprite and him, and Tooley too if he could. They'd be able to make a new start that way, maybe even pay for a nurse. Then their mom could come back from that hospital upstate they called a sanitarium and stay at home again.

So Coyote had read most closely about the woman they were talking to in the newspaper article. The one asking the questions was called Mariette Dugan. The one answering the questions was named Katherine Fairchild. She headed up the committee that did the deciding about who got one of those Christmas money grants and who didn't. She was the one he had to write just the right things for. He read what she'd said all the way through from beginning to end. Then, he read it through again, and again, till he knew it just about by heart.

Coyote'd had to make himself good at figuring out adults, especially this last year. He'd learned that in order to get what you needed out of grown-ups, you had to tell them what they wanted to hear. So far, he'd been real lucky at doing that with Arbor Hill School, where he and his sister both went. Otherwise, the school people might have checked more closely and found out it wasn't Coyote and Sprite's mom signing the report cards and permission slips, no matter how good he'd learned to write her name just like she used to. Nobody understood better than Coyote how his luck could run out any time. Which made it even more 'portant, as Sprite would say, to write the words in his letter that this Katherine Fairchild would like to hear. No matter what he'd said to Sprite just now, the crumpled and stained newspaper page he'd spread out on Tooley's kitchen table told Coyote he'd better not write this letter about anything as unserious as a bicycle.

COYOTE HAD HIS HAND on the mailbox, ready to open the hinged door. He'd waited till Sprite was asleep before he slipped out of the house to hurry the couple of blocks to this post office on Broadway near the corner of Livingston Avenue. He'd been rereading his letter in his mind all the way. He hesitated now with his hand on the box. Was the letter good enough? Everything depended on what he had written. He pulled the envelope from his pocket and bent forward over it to protect the inexpensive paper from the wet snow that was turning the shoulders of his thin jacket more soggy by the minute. He was crouched that way when the long, black car came down Broadway toward him and pulled over to the curb just up the street. Coyote peeked around the blue-painted metal mailbox to watch. Big, fancy cars like this one didn't drive through this neighborhood very often. He had never seen one stop before, except maybe down by the theater at North Pearl Street and Clinton Avenue when rock stars or some other big shots came to perform there. The car's engine purred silently, but he could tell it was still running by the cloud of vapor that lifted from the hood in the dull, gray light.

The front door opened on the passenger side of the car, and a very large man stepped onto the wet street. Coyote was thinking he should stay out of sight, though he wasn't sure why. Something in his head told him that was true. He'd learned to listen to that voice, which had saved him more than once from the bad things that can happen to a kid in the street. He kept himself behind the mailbox where he couldn't be seen from the car, but he didn't stop watching as the large man walked to the trunk of the car and opened it. The gloomy night hid the man's face. All Coyote could tell was that he had on a long, dark coat and some kind of hat. He leaned over the open car trunk and looked like he was wrestling with something that must be pretty bulky in there.

The driver's side of the car opened. The large man must have seen it, too, because he shouted out loud enough for Coyote to hear, "Get back in there. I'll take care of this."

Just then, the man pulled something long and a couple of feet around out of the trunk. He hoisted the long bundle to his shoulder with a grunt. The large man stooped a little under the weight. That meant the bundle had to be pretty heavy. The big man started walking up the old driveway next to the deserted building where the car had stopped. He continued into the alley between the deserted house and a metal fence. He disappeared into the shadows for a minute when he got near the end of the driveway. Then he moved into a small pool of light from a bulb above a doorway almost at the back of the deserted building. He bent down when he got to the back of the building and let his bundle slip to the ground. Coyote was having bad feelings about what might be in that package.

The large man straightened up and shook himself, maybe to get the snow off his coat, maybe to loosen his shoulders after carrying the heavy load. Coyote saw him glance up at the lit bulb above the alleyway door. The man put his hand in his pocket and pulled something out. He reached up in a swinging movement in the direction of the light-bulb. He was going to break it. That thought came to Coyote in just about the same minute he recognized what the man had in his hand. The light from the bulb was glinting on the barrel of a gun.

Coyote crouched lower behind the mailbox when he saw that. He'd been watching the alleyway so hard he didn't really know how tight he had hold of the handle of the hinged door of the mailbox. He didn't even know he had dragged that door partway open. Before he could think what he was doing, his fingers let go of the handle so he could clap them over his mouth to cover up the scared sound that was about to jump out of his throat. He did keep that sound from getting out, but the mailbox door slammed shut with a clang.

Coyote understood how big a mistake he'd made even before the large man's head snapped around to turn his face full into the pool of light from the bulb he'd been just about to break. What Coyote saw there froze him colder than the snow soaking through his jacket could have ever done. The large man had an ugly face, maybe the ugliest Coyote had ever seen, but not from a deformity or anything like that. The only way Coyote could describe it, then or later on, was that the man's face had been pulled out of shape by just plain meanness. A flash of fear shot like a really sharp knifepoint straight to Coyote's stomach. He was in bad trouble, and he knew it.

He took off then, running as fast as his sneakers could carry him, back toward the corner of Livingston Avenue and around the side of the post office, across the parking lot where they kept the mail delivery trucks at night and between two of those trucks to the back of the post office. He skirted backyards, climbed over fences and streaked down alleys, through this neighborhood he knew by heart. He was glad that, since moving in with Tooley Pennebaker, he'd done so much poking around. He knew just where to duck in and when to climb over.

He could hear the large man in the long coat crashing along hot on his trail. Coyote told himself he was too street-smart to let the man catch up. Coyote kept himself crouched low as he ran. His heart pounded as he waited to hear the crack of a bullet from the gun he'd seen in the light from that bulb in the alleyway. He was almost back to Tooley's place when he realized what he'd done that was not street-smart at all.

He'd dropped the letter—the letter with his address written in extra big print on the envelope so Katherine Fairchild couldn't possibly miss knowing exactly where he lived. He'd dropped the letter by the mailbox, directly in the path where the large man had been headed the last time Coyote glanced over his shoulder to see just how hard he was being chased and just how hard he'd better run to make sure he didn't get caught.

Chapter Two

"You didn't plan on any of this happening, did you, Katherine?"

Katherine Fairchild smiled, despite the fact that smiling didn't come very naturally to her these past several months. Megan Moran, on the other hand, could make almost anybody smile. For one thing, she was about as direct as a person could be, and Katherine loved her for it. Still, she wasn't comfortable with being so closely questioned. Too many areas remained too sensitive to bear the light of inquiry even after a little more than a year from the day sorrow had been planted in her heart. Her escape halfway across the country from Chicago, Illinois to Albany, New York hadn't changed that as much as she'd hoped it would.

"I know you don't want to talk about it," Megan went on.

"But I should," Katherine was surprised to hear herself say.

Megan nodded her cap of sleek, red curls so unlike the thicket of unruly dark-blond waves Katherine had spent what felt like several lifetimes trying to tame.

"That's what we've been led to believe," Megan said as she poured milk into the bottom of her empty teacup in the English-Irish manner, before adding the tea she'd insisted on having triple-brewed. "Confession is good for the soul. Otherwise, all those daytime talk-show hosts would have to take themselves out into the world and try to find honest work for a change."

Katherine laughed. "Yes, and what would they possibly be qualified to do?"

"My job, probably."

"I doubt that."

Megan was one of the best child psychologists around. Her accomplishments were legendary at Arbor Hill Children's Center where she and Katherine had worked together for eight months now.

"We digress," Megan said with a twinkle in her brown eyes. "In case you might think I didn't notice."

"When can you ever recall there being anything you didn't notice?"

Megan feigned intense concentration for a moment.

"I know," she said. "I didn't notice that there were three billion calories on this silver whatsis here before I polished its cute little shelves clean."

She was talking about the three-tiered silver spindle laden with scones, Devonshire cream and tiny cakes that had accompanied tea. As usual, Katherine hadn't touched a thing. Appetite had been a problem for her ever since she left Chicago and even before.

"So talk to me, girlfriend."

Megan wasn't to be denied.

Katherine sighed. "I thought I was working my way out from under, and instead I find myself burrowing in."

"Out from under what and into what?" Megan licked the last bit of cream from her lacquered fingernails.

"I'd say *life,* but you'd laugh me out of here for being melodramatic."

"I'd be sorely tempted to do exactly that."

"Me too." Katherine toyed with her teacup. "It's just that I wanted to keep myself at a distance for a while."

"At a distance from what?" the relentless Megan chimed in when Katherine hesitated a moment too long after that last statement.

"Hurtful things. I wanted to keep myself at a distance from getting attached in the way that can lead to feeling hurtful things."

There. She'd said it, and she was only moderately tempted to dissolve into a puddle of tears.

"How successful have you been at that distance-keeping?"

Somebody else might cut Katherine some slack or commiserate with her, but not Megan.

"Apparently, not very successful at all. I seem to have taken on the hurtful-things department as my personal, professional territory these days. I'm getting attached to it, too."

"You could have said no."

Not a centimeter of slack, yet again.

"That would have been a violation of the pledge I made to myself when I came here, to start saying *yes* to things instead of worrying them to death first."

"Saying yes to life and hiding from it at the same time. You've got your work cut out for you."

Katherine laughed. "I was talking about saying yes to professional possibilities, whatever they might be. That's how I turned out to be an administrator of a public agency when everything I ever worked at up till then had been strictly about making money. But the first job that came up for a budget administrator after I came to town nine months ago happened to be at the Arbor Hill Center. The rest, as they say, is history."

"I wondered about that. We don't get too many job applications from MBAs."

"If you did wonder, I can't understand your not asking."

"I try to respect the privacy of my friends."

Katherine laughed fully out loud at that.

"I'm glad to hear you've got a laugh like that in you," Megan said.

"I guess I've been something of a sad sack since you met me."

"Not so much a sad sack as a workhorse."

Katherine nodded.

"And the children of Arbor Hill are duly grateful," Megan said. "That little place of ours has never run so efficiently. You know how to make a dollar do double duty, and that's just what we need over there."

"I wish that's what they'd kept me doing," Katherine said ruefully.

"You really don't like this Most Needy Cases Fund selection committee thing, do you?"

Katherine shrugged. The last thing she'd wanted when she took the job at the center was to be working up close and personal with the lives of the kids they served there—or their families, either. She'd signed on as a number-cruncher, no more, no less. The Most Needy Cases Fund was the center's annual drive to award cash grants to families at the holiday season. Unfortunately, there wasn't money enough to cover everybody who applied. A selection process was necessary, and that process had sometimes fallen short in the efficiency department in years past. As Megan said, Katherine had attracted a reputation for efficiency in her few months here. Consequently, when the fund-recipient selection committee was being formed for this year's campaign, the perfect choice to head up the effort was apparently obvious to everyone—everyone except

Katherine, that is. She'd tried to say no, but, with first-class persuaders like Megan lined up against her, Katherine's protests had barely been heard.

"It's important work," she said now. She'd had to resign herself to how true those words were and what that meant for her. "Somebody has to do it."

"But it's a bummer sometimes."

"Yes." Megan had a way of saying the right words when they were most needed. "A definite bummer."

Katherine would have sworn the Christmas lights strung across the tearoom window dimmed for an instant then, as if they agreed.

"Christmas is only a week away," Megan said. "After that, the fund campaign will be over till next year."

"You're right. I can stand almost anything for a week." *Including the Christmas season itself,* she thought, though she was well aware that seven days could feel like an eternity sometimes. "Just as long as they don't spring anything else on me."

"Here's to no more surprises."

Katherine and Megan clinked teacups. Katherine, while managing another smile for Megan's sake, noticed the holiday window lights blink and sputter and then click off altogether, as if something in the wiring had gone suddenly awry.

KATHERINE HADN'T TOLD Megan about going back to the office that evening. She'd have taken the opportunity to repeat her lecture on overwork for sure. Much as Megan was one of Katherine's favorite people in the world, she wasn't in the mood for being lectured tonight, or for going home to her empty apartment either. She drove from the teashop to Clinton Avenue instead, then the few blocks northeast to Arbor Drive. She parked her car and hurried

across the dark parking lot to the brown cement-block sin-
gle-story Arbor Hill Children's Center building at the edge
of a scruffy field. The baseball diamond and backstop fence
were in that field, mostly buried under sullied urban snow,
all made invisible by the evening's overcast sky. There was
a streetlight near the center's entranceway, but it was out
of order much of the time. Tonight was one of those times.
Vandals or municipal neglect. The light over the center's
entranceway was out, too, making it necessary for her to
watch carefully where she was stepping with the not-very-
practical high-heeled boots she wore to make herself appear
taller than her five foot five. That concentration on the
ground was the reason she didn't notice someone coming
up behind her till it was too late.

"It's not smart for a woman to be out here alone in this
neighborhood at night."

The edge of menace in that voice caused Katherine to
spin around too fast on her precarious footwear. She felt
her slide begin at the same instant she realized there was
nothing she could do to stop it. She also knew she wasn't
about to be a victim of this hulk of a man towering over
her now. These boots of hers were good for more than
falling down. This guy could expect a high heel in the groin
as soon as she was on her back and into kicking position.
She was already mentally prepared for that defensive move
when a startling steel grip halted her fall.

"I've seen those stupid boots you wear. It's a wonder
you haven't taken a header into the asphalt before this."

Katherine was bracing herself to rake her boot heel down
his shin when she recognized his voice, or thought she did.

"Maltese, from Recreation. Is that you?" she asked.

His short laugh was unmistakably derisive, and somewhat annoyed. She had heard from others at the center that
Vic Maltese had a way with kids. He respected them and

earned their respect in return. But, in her few encounters with him, she'd noticed that just beneath the surface he always seemed to be angry about something. Tonight was no exception.

"You got it right," he said. "Maltese from Recreation. That must be how you list me in those account books you keep."

"I'm not an accountant, and you can let me go now."

His grip was still on her arm.

"I think I'll hang on to you till you're safely at the door. We wouldn't want to lose our top-shelf bean counter to a patch of ice."

He'd started walking toward the building entrance with her arm clamped firmly in his big hand. She had little choice but to keep up, cursing with every skittering step the boots he had rightly called stupid. Meanwhile, she could feel her dignity about to slip away on a surface as glassy as this parking lot.

"I don't know where you came up with the idea that I'm an accountant," she said, doing her best to remain upright and sound like a serious professional at the same time. "My title is Administrative Budget and Program Coordinator."

Another derisive laugh. "Do you always talk like a corporate report?"

No, Buster, Katherine would have liked to say. *Lunkheads like you just bring that out in me.*

"Look, Mr. Maltese..."

"Victor. The name is Victor. Everybody calls me Vic. You should be calling me that, too. We're supposed to be colleagues. Right?"

He said the word *colleagues* as if it was a joke.

"Yes, we are colleagues." She deliberately didn't call him by name, either first or last. She had no intention of letting him take charge of what, for some reason, he insisted on making a debate between them. ''And that means your attitude right now is inappropriate. If you have some problem with me, you should come to my office during business hours and we'll discuss it.''

''Then who'd be here to keep you from tumbling onto your behind in the parking lot?''

Katherine didn't know what made her want to deck him more, his mocking tone or his mention of her behind.

''Will you let go of me now?'' she all but shouted, her irritation echoing across the empty parking lot.

They were at the gated door to the children's center building. High-quality security gates and window gratings were among the first additions Katherine had to find funds for when she came on staff here. A break-in shortly before she arrived had cost the center plenty. Otherwise, she might not have been able to convince the board of directors that such a large short-range expenditure would pay for itself in the long run. Not that they were stingy types. There was simply too much to be done and too little money to do it with. Right now, she could think of one cost-cutting measure that would definitely win her vote—elimination of the current Recreation Director.

''Consider yourself let go,'' he said, still unfortunately uneliminated, and dropped her arm.

''Thank you for your assistance,'' Katherine said, brushing away the creases his grip had made in her coat sleeve.

''There you go talking like a corporate report again. You really should try to do something about that.''

''I'll put it on my calendar.''

Katherine didn't want any conflicts with center staff, but if this guy insisted on being rude and sarcastic, he'd get the same from her in return.

''How about putting me on your calendar, too? Like for right now.''

Katherine fished her key ring out of her coat pocket where she kept it, along with a small money purse pinned to the pocket lining. She didn't carry a purse most of the time—one of the concessions she made to working on the poorer side of town—and her briefcase was inside her office.

"I told you, Mr. Maltese…"

"Vic."

"Whatever. The point is, I told you to make an appointment during business hours."

She turned the key in the lock and was about to push aside the accordion-style gate when Mr. Maltese's fist clamped around the metal with a belligerent clang.

"You're here to take care of business. Right? I don't imagine this is a social call."

He indicated the dark building and the fact that they were obviously alone. For the first time, it occurred to Katherine that maybe she should be concerned about more than just this guy's sarcastic mouth. He was a big man, after all, and obviously, from his present behavior at least, something of a brute. Her instincts told her sexual assault wouldn't be his thing, but she should be cautious anyway.

"Mr. Maltese," she said in her most authoritative tone. "I want you to leave now."

"I've wanted you to leave ever since they hired you."

That brought Katherine up short. She'd had no idea anyone felt so negatively about her.

"Why?" she couldn't help but ask.

"Don't take it personally. I feel the same way about all you ledger-heads."

"I told you. I'm not an accountant."

"Paper-pushers are all the same to me. You've got bottom lines where your hearts should be."

She couldn't see him sneer in the darkness, but she could

hear it in his words. He was standing very close to her, looming like a tall, broad wall between her and escape. She didn't really know him or what he was capable of. Most of what she'd heard about him had come from the center's female support staff, all of whom thought he was the hottest thing around. Katherine could hardly agree. She'd never been a devotee of the angry-young-man type. Beyond that, there was something of the wild, restless animal about Victor Maltese. She could feel it in him now. Maybe that turned some women on, but for Katherine it was something to be guarded against.

"Apparently, you have a problem with the way I do my job," she began, calm and impersonal to keep things cool.

"You're damned right I do. You're in charge of decisions here that can make or break people's lives, and I don't think you've got qualification number one for doing that."

"Are you referring to the Most Needy Cases Fund?"

"You guessed it. I've got a real problem with a bean counter running that committee. Who are you to be making the call about which families are in and which families are out when it comes to passing out money that's needed more than you ever needed anything in your life? What do you really know about these people and their lives? How close have you ever been to where they are? I'd lay down good money that says the only time you've ever spent in the street is at one of those cute little sidewalk cafés they opened up for all of you yuppies over in the Pastures."

Katherine had asked herself those same questions about her personal credentials for the job they'd given her, but she wasn't going to let this testosterone case know that.

"It's a bit cold for sidewalk cafés this time of year, Mr. Maltese," she said.

"Too cold for a lot of things," he shot back and shook the metal gate with another loud clang before letting go of it. "You'd better put me on that calendar of yours for first thing tomorrow, and the folks I bring with me, too."

He turned and walked away from her then with just enough arrogant street roll in his stride to make her want to scream, "Who do you think *you* are?" at his leather-clad back. But Katherine was a serious professional so she didn't.

COYOTE WATCHED them from the field where he was crouched down in the brush. He could tell they were arguing, but he couldn't make out the words except for Miss Fairchild yelling at Mr. Maltese to let her go. Coyote had been to this place a few times and knew the recreation-program guy. Last spring during baseball games, he had helped Coyote out with learning how to pitch straight and hard. Coyote had made a point of trying to steer clear of him, anyway. Mr. Maltese was the kind that wanted to be right up in a kid's business too much of the time. He did it because he thought he was helping out, but Coyote didn't need that attention. Well, maybe he did need it, but he didn't want it. Grown-ups who worked in places like this center had a way of getting in your life, messing around with it, then moving on while you were left with the mess. Coyote had seen it happen more than once, and he definitely didn't need that.

What he did need was this lady's help. He'd recognized her from the photograph in the newspaper, and he had to find a way to get to her.

After Mr. Maltese walked away and Katherine Fairchild let herself into the building, Coyote waited for a light to come on somewhere inside. Sure enough, a few minutes later, light appeared at the second set of windows from the end of the building. When Coyote got to those windows and peeked very carefully inside, he could see this was her office. But that wasn't what caught his attention and held it like a magnet to the spot.

At the top of a wire basket on the corner of her desk was a pile of unopened envelopes that must be her mail. About three pieces down in the pile, one stuck out from the others enough for Coyote to see it and recognize what was there— his handwriting, the thin envelope paper from Rite Aid, even a dirt smudge and some wrinkling where it would have gotten wet when he dropped it on the ground.

That was two nights ago. Ever since then, Coyote had been on the run, steering clear of Tooley's place for fear the large man from the long, black car would be watching there. In between concentrating on what it took to survive out here on his own, Coyote had thought about writing another letter, but he didn't have an address where some-body could contact him. He'd decided maybe coming in person to see this Katherine Fairchild was his only hope. He'd snuck over here tonight to case out the possibilities of that, thinking that he'd talk to her the next morning. All the time, though, he'd been wishing he'd put his letter into that mailbox in the first place. Now, here it was, on her desk like a miracle—or, like something else. Because if Coyote hadn't mailed the envelope, who did?

Chapter Three

Vic knew he'd been hard on Katherine Fairchild last night. He tried to tell himself she deserved to be put in her place, brought down a peg or two, but he knew that wasn't why he'd acted like such a creep. He'd been on his way to pick up some dinner and head home to his house on Livingston Avenue after work when he saw her pull into the parking lot of the center. Who could miss that big, expensive four-wheeler of hers? He'd decided to talk to her then, to tell her he was concerned about the way candidates for the holiday fund grant program were being picked. A reasonable discussion was what he had in mind, maybe even him volunteering to help her choose who would get the grant money. He would point out his background, tell her he came from the same kind of neighborhood as these families. At least, he had, before he'd left home at sixteen and started making it on his own. He'd planned to explain how that experience made him a natural to advise on this project. Then, last night when he was finally standing right next to her, all of his planning and reasonableness flew straight out the window.

Vic knew why that was, too. Something about her got to him, and he didn't like it. He didn't like it at all. She was just about the last woman he wanted to have pushing his buttons, but she pushed them, all the same. It wasn't the way she looked that got to him. He'd seen her enough times around the center to know she wasn't hard on the eyes. Still, she hadn't struck him as his type. She was too skinny, like she needed a few months of good meals to fill her out some. Her clothes tended to hang a little large on her, as if she might have lost a load of weight since she first tried them on.

There was also something a little comical about the way she tried to keep that wild hair of hers under control and neat, probably to go along with the strictly-business briefcase she always carried. Some days she'd have it slicked down. Other times she'd have it pulled back in a band or clasped into a big barrette, but none of that did any good. Puffs of the stuff would spring loose and be flying behind her as she dashed along. Still, endearing as that might be, it didn't turn Vic on. Then, tonight, he'd seen her teetering across the ice in those high-heeled boots of hers, and he was a goner. But the foolish footwear only made him surer than ever that she was a duck out of water in this part of town. What if some street tough came after her and she had to run? Those boots would do her in for sure.

That's what he'd had in his mind to tell her last night when he grabbed her arm to keep her from taking a nose-dive into the ice. She'd whipped around on him just before he grabbed her, and that's when it happened. The way she looked didn't have anything to do with it. The parking lot was too dark for him to see much in the way of details. He was feeling her more than seeing her, and what he felt took him totally by surprise. At that moment, she was no longer a skinny little bird of a thing who couldn't even make her hair behave. She was as fierce as a lioness, tensed to do him damage no matter what the odds might be against her. Vic had been in enough one-on-one tussles to know that

was where this particular opponent was coming from. She
was no helpless twit. She was scrappy as hell, and for some
reason that got under his skin, to a place Vic had no intention of letting this woman go.

Katherine Fairchild was about as far out of his ballpark
as she was from these rundown, mean streets she insisted
on walking in her uptown-lady boots and expensive clothes.
Even her name said, "Not your sort, Vic." It sounded like
one she'd picked up off a society page, but he'd heard it
was a hundred percent authentic. There'd been lots of talk
buzzing around the place when she first came on staff at
the center, when she'd breezed into town from Chicago
after she and her husband had split. She'd bought herself a
fancy apartment, and from the employee address list at the
center, Vic had seen she lived up on Washington Park
where lots of yuppie types were settling these days. Some
sad story went around too, about a sick kid or something
like that, but nobody had any details. Whatever the specifics
of her background might be, Vic knew she was definitely
out of the picture for a guy like him, who tended toward
good old girls from the neighborhood, even though he'd
never seemed to care about sticking with any of them for
very long.

All of that had set him off last night somehow, when she
spun on him and he felt the fire of her spirit flash hot in
his blood. He couldn't let her pick up on that, of course.
He didn't even want to admit it to himself. That's why he'd
acted like such a jerk, manhandling her the way he did,
practically dragging her across the parking lot and growling
at her instead of talking reasonably like he'd planned. He'd
even threatened to show up here this morning with his
troops in tow ready to do battle with all five feet plus a
few inches of her.

Fortunately, there'd been a long night between then and

now. Vic had used that time to pull himself and his head together. He'd reminded himself of what he was supposed to be doing here at the center—what he was all about. He wanted the best for these kids and their families. They needed desperately for somebody to cut them a break. The Most Needy Cases Fund was a chance for that to happen. Vic could make sure it did, but he'd have to work with Katherine Fairchild to do it. And, in order to work with her, he'd have to keep a tight lid on his nerve endings, and other parts of him too. He'd have to stay in control, stop reacting. Most of all, he'd have to keep his anger in check. That had never been an easy thing for him to do, not from the days of his adolescent brawls with his father till now. Vic paused for a moment outside Katherine Fairchild's office door and resolved to stay in control no matter what happened. No matter what!

CAROLS WERE PLAYING on the center's intercom. Katherine had always loved Christmas music until last year. Ever since then, it had reminded her of loss. She'd read about how the holidays were hard on people with problems. All those reminders of giddy shopping, families gathered together, wishes for peace on earth and well-being fell painfully on the ears of those for whom life was less than festive at the moment. Katherine had learned the truth of that first-hand last season. She'd wished she could shut it all out then, especially the carols. She'd done her best to plug her ears against the tinkling bells and swelling chords meant to make her feel that heavenly blessings were close at hand.

She was relieved to realize that she didn't feel quite so bleak about the holiday season this year. Sadness still plagued her, popping up when she was least prepared for its onslaught, but the sharpness had grown less keen and cutting over these twelve months and stabbed her less frequently now. She could actually hum snatches of "O, Little Town of Bethlehem" again, though she wasn't yet ready to sing along happily with the chorus of "Adeste Fideles" as she once would have done. She was congratulating herself on her progress toward leaving the doldrums behind, or at least beginning to shove them off to one side, when a knock came at her office door and she looked up to see who might be there.

She hadn't stayed long at the center the evening before. Her encounter with Victor Maltese had left her fuming and too worked up to accomplish much. Finally, she'd snapped off her computer in exasperation and slammed out of the place, cursing her sliding boots all the way to her car. She'd resolved there and then never to wear the ridiculous things again, though it irked her no end to appear to be taking that Neanderthal's advice. Now, here he was tapping at her office door, no doubt bent upon ruining her morning the way he'd ruined her evening.

Katherine took a breath and forced herself to smile before she said, "Come in."

"I wouldn't blame you if you told me to get lost after the way I acted last night," he said before he even had time to close the door behind him.

"I wouldn't blame me, either."

"What do you say we start over?"

He was smiling. Unlike last night in the dark, Katherine could see his features now. His eyes were dark and deep, the kind many women find mysterious and fall for without thinking what the nature of that mystery might be. The rest of him looked like he'd just hopped off a Harley-Davidson—black leather jacket over black turtleneck, blue jeans, engineer boots—just the sort of arrogant, aggressive macho style she'd always been careful to maintain a safe distance from.

"Start over in what way?" she asked.

Katherine told herself she should match his conciliatory tone, at least for the sake of the center.

"Invite me to sit down, and I'll tell you what I hope we can do together."

He smiled even wider with a flash of strong, white teeth. A dimple she'd never noticed before dented his left cheek.

"Sit down, then," she said, telling herself she needed to be reasonable here, despite the danger signals her instincts seemed intent upon telegraphing.

Vic Maltese lowered his tall frame into the vinyl-seated chair across from her desk. Blue denim stretched tight along his muscular thighs as he leaned back in the chair. Katherine turned her attention for the moment to straightening the file folders she'd been working on and setting them aside. She wanted to believe his thighs weren't the reason she was looking so deliberately away from him. Meanwhile, the instinct telegraph tapped out its message even more loudly than before.

"Are these the letters you've been getting for the Most Needy Cases Fund?" he asked, indicating the wire basket at the corner of her desk.

"That's the latest batch."

She couldn't figure out why he was asking that. The basket was labelled "Most Needy Cases Fund Correspondence," and Mr. Maltese didn't strike her as the obvious-question type. Maybe this was his attempt at small talk.

"There's lots of people writing in, I see," he commented.

"We've had a big response to the publicity in the newspapers."

"You mean that interview you did a few days ago in the *Chronicle*. The one by Mariette Dugan. I saw that. You have to watch out for her, from what I hear. She's supposed to be a real shark.''

"I've heard that too, but she did well by the center this time.''

Small talk, all right. Katherine had a feeling Mr. Maltese couldn't have cared less about the state of journalistic ethics in the Capitol District. She was sure he was working up to something, but she couldn't imagine what that might be. She was trying to decide whether or not to ask him right out what he was after when he reached into the wire basket and scooped up the top half of the Most Needy Cases Fund letter pile in his large hand.

"I'd like to help you out with these," he said.

"That really isn't necessary," she began.

He was out of his chair and leaning over her desk so abruptly that she was almost frightened by the move.

"I know you don't have reason number one to believe this, but all I want to do is what's best for the kids we work with here. And for other kids and families just like them.''

His dark eyes had turned very intense as they honed in on her. She had to will herself not to back away from their impact.

"I have no doubt your intentions are most admirable,'' she began again, trying to impose some formality on what appeared to be in danger of turning into an emotional exchange.

"Then let me work with you on this.''

He held up the fistful of letters.

"I appreciate your offer, Mr. Maltese, but we already have a committee in place.''

"I know you have a committee, but none of them have the neighborhood experience I do.''

So, that was it. He didn't think the rest of them were

equal to the job, probably especially not her. He'd said just about the same thing last night in the parking lot.

"I believe we are capable of handling the project on our own," she said, her tone more formal than ever and turning frostier by the second.

"I'm not suggesting that you aren't capable." He leaned closer still. "I'm only saying we could do an even better job together."

His face was inches from hers, well into what Katherine pretty much unconsciously took for granted as her intimate space. She was entirely conscious of it now.

"Mr. Maltese..."

Whatever she had been about to say—and the exact words hadn't yet quite formed themselves in her mind—was interrupted by a sharp knock on her door, which opened before she could respond.

"Katherine..."

Megan Moran stood in the doorway. Her mouth was open but silenced in midsentence as her stare moved from Katherine to Vic Maltese looming so closely over her. She recognized instantly what Megan had to be thinking. Maltese straightened to his usual towering height. If he felt any of Katherine's sudden awkwardness, he certainly wasn't letting it show.

"Megan," he said. "How's everybody's favorite head-shrinker this morning?"

"Like I always tell you, Vic, I may be good but I'm not ready to take on a cranium as thick as yours."

He laughed. Their easy camaraderie surprised Katherine. She hadn't realized that Megan and Vic Maltese were friends. Katherine found herself wondering if they'd ever been more than that.

"Actually, Vic, you're the one I barged in here looking for," Megan said. "The boy who takes care of your equipment came to my office a few minutes ago. There's a kid asleep in your equipment room. He may have been there all night.''

THE MINUTE Coyote woke up he knew he'd made a terrible mistake, and not by falling asleep in a strange place so he couldn't remember quite where he was this morning. He'd been doing exactly that for three nights now. His terrible mistake was back before that. He'd taken a step that put him on the path toward trouble, and he hadn't been able to get his feet off that road ever since. Except he still couldn't figure out what that wrong step had been, unless it was asking for help in the first place. He'd written that letter he thought would save Sprite and him, but all it had done so far was put him in the way of danger. He had to get that letter back.

As he peered up at the faces circling him above the pile of tumbling mats where he'd fallen asleep, he could hardly believe what he saw. There the letter was again, sticking out of the gym teacher's hand. He was holding a bunch of other letters, too, but Coyote had no problem spotting his own. He'd come to see that blotched, crumpled envelope even in his dreams last night. He couldn't quite remember why, but the letter had been chasing him up and down North Pearl Street. Now, here he was, waking up to find it had caught him.

Chapter Four

The boy appeared to be about eleven, maybe a little older, though with the way he was rubbing his eyes and yawning at the moment, he might also have passed for nine. A dusting of freckles crossed his cheeks. His hair was dark, and there was no telling whether straight or curly because he'd cut it short in what used to be called a brush cut and was now known as a buzz. He was a good-looking boy, wiry but not overly thin. Except for some wrinkles in his jeans and T-shirt, he looked clean enough too.

"I know this kid," Vic said, staring down at the sleepy-eyed boy on the pile of mats in the gymnasium equipment room. "His name is Coyote Bellaway."

"I've heard that name before," Katherine said. "I think I may have read it somewhere. Megan, could that have been in one of your reports?"

"I've never seen the little guy. I'm sure I'd remember a name like Coyote."

The gentleness of Megan's tone made Vic aware that they were gaping at the boy as if he were a bug in a jar.

"Let's give him a chance to wake up before we start grilling him," Vic said, backing off a little so the others would follow. "In fact, why don't I handle this?"

An instant of relief flashed in Coyote's eyes, then disappeared. Vic couldn't remember when he'd ever seen a kid who more obviously wanted to get up and run away.

"Okay, everybody. It's time for you to get back to business," Vic said. "Coyote and I need to have a talk, just the two of us."

"I think you're right about that," Megan agreed. "Come on, Katherine. Let's go."

Katherine hesitated. Vic recognized concern in her eyes. For the first time, he wondered if he could have been wrong about her having an account book where her heart ought to be. She turned to follow Megan out of the equipment room.

"Let me know what you find out," she said before shutting the door behind her.

"Well, sport, do you want to talk here or in my office?" Vic asked Coyote once Megan and Katherine were gone.

"I don't care."

Vic could tell from the belligerence with which those words were spoken that this wasn't going to be an easy interview. He knew everything there was to know about belligerence. He'd carried around a snootful of it himself since he was not much older than this kid here. One thing Vic was certain of, applying pressure wouldn't get him anywhere in this situation.

"I'll tell you what. I didn't have time for breakfast this morning," he said. "How's about we go to the kitchen and see what we can scrounge up to eat."

Another flash of relief relaxed the set of Coyote's jaw for a moment before he clamped it down tight again.

"I don't care," he repeated.

Vic didn't believe that for an instant. He had a suspicion food was one thing this boy really did care about. From the look of him, he might have missed a few meals lately. Unfortunately, Vic had seen that look before.

"Well, I care," Vic said, taking Coyote's arm and helping him up off the matting. "Pretty soon my stomach's going to be rumbling so loud I won't be able to hear myself think. We can't have that happening, can we?"

Vic didn't expect an answer. He'd had enough experience with kids who'd shut themselves down like this one to know this was going to be a one-sided conversation for a while. With that in mind, Vic kept up a casual line of gab all the way to the center's kitchen. He also kept his hand on Coyote's shoulder in case he should try to bolt like he so obviously wanted to do. This was just as obviously a boy in some kind of trouble, and Vic was determined to discover what that trouble might be.

The center ran a breakfast program for neighborhood children. Those kids had already eaten and left for school. Sandra Thomas, who ran the breakfast program, was finishing the morning cleanup. She waved Vic toward the oversized refrigerator when he told her what he was there for.

"You'll find whatever you need in there," she said, "or in the pantry. But you'll have to fix it for yourself, and you'll have to wash up after, too. I'm way past the end of my shift, and I have to be moving on out of here right this minute."

"We can take care of ourselves, Sandra. Thanks," Vic said.

"You're very welcome," she said.

Her legendary dictatorial tone warmed as she glanced at Coyote. She might run this kitchen like a captain runs a ship, but Vic knew her to have a heart as big as the ocean. She even smiled at the boy as she pulled off her apron and dropped it into a hamper under the long, stainless-steel counter.

"You help yourselves to whatever you can find in here,"

she said. "And don't forget to leave my kitchen just exactly the way you found it, spotless as an angel's wing."

"We'll be sure to do that, won't we, sport?"

Vic was only slightly surprised to hear the previously close-mouthed Coyote answer, "Yes, ma'am." Sandra Thomas was hard to resist and almost impossible to defy. She smiled one more time before pushing through the double, swinging doors from the kitchen into the multipurpose room.

"Come on, Coyote. Let's see what we can scare up in the way of breakfast. I'm about to starve," Vic said, though he knew he wasn't truly the hungry one.

Their encounter with Sandra had taken some of the edge off Coyote's belligerence. He actually helped Vic pour cereal into two bowls and slice bananas on top while whole wheat bread heated to golden crispness in the industrial-sized toaster. They sat down together on stools at the long counter after that, where Vic watched Coyote dig into his raisin bran with undisguised eagerness. However closed off he might be capable of making himself appear, he was still only a boy who couldn't hide the fact that he was very hungry. Vic saved his questions till Coyote had eaten his fill.

"Did you sleep here all night?" Vic asked then.

"Nah," Coyote denied. "I came in early this morning."

Vic was pretty sure that was a lie, but he went along with it for now.

"What were you doing here so early? Did you come for breakfast?"

"Yeah. That's right. Breakfast."

"Then why'd you go into the gym instead of coming in here where breakfast is served?"

Vic could see the curtain of caution and distrust lower

over Coyote's eyes. He didn't respond for a moment, probably while he came up with an answer.

"I was looking for you," he said at last.

For some reason, Vic had the feeling that might be the truth.

"What did you want to see me about?"

Coyote hesitated again, a little longer this time.

"I wanted to ask you about signing up for basketball."

Vic had an even stronger feeling that this was *not* the truth. He was considering what might be most productive to ask next when one of the swinging doors pushed open and Katherine Fairchild leaned her head through the opening. Her hair had already begun to escape the band she'd had it pulled back into when he first saw her earlier in her office.

"Vic, could I speak to you out here for a minute, please?" she said.

She'd called him by his first name at last. He could hardly believe how much like a breakthrough that felt or how good it sounded to him.

"I'll be right back," he said to Coyote. "Why don't you take these dishes to the sink and get started washing them like Mrs. Thomas said?"

Coyote nodded, and Vic headed for the door.

The ceiling of the multipurpose room was draped with handmade paper chains. They reminded Vic that, sometimes in some places, simple, real holiday things still happened. Life for children wasn't all problems, even though that too often seemed to be the case here at the center. He'd walked through this room the day the kids were making these chains, connecting red and green construction paper in circle after circle till they heaped on the floor around the metal legs of the folding chairs. The kids were laughing and chattering. Occasionally, they pretended to menace one another with the staplers they were using to fasten the circles.

Vic remembered when he had made chains in elementary school back in Troy, New York. They'd used paste for the fastening then, the kind that tasted pretty good but didn't keep things stuck together for very long. The paper colors were brighter now. The construction paper he remembered always looked like it had been left out in the sun to fade before they used it. Other than those couple of changes, however, the process looked about the same, even after the quarter of a century or so that had passed since he was ten. Noticing that had made Vic smile.

Vic tended not to get into the jolly part of the holiday season, at least not as much as some people might think he should in his position here at the center. In fact, he sometimes felt his usual undercurrent of anger move even closer to the surface. It had something to do with the way so many kids in the world didn't have a good sock to put on their feet much less one for Santa to fill up with presents. That wasn't all of it, though.

He hadn't been so fresh out of the Christmas spirit when he was a kid. The difference was that, in those days, he didn't have a clue as to what was really what where some of the members of his own family, the Malteses and their numerous kin, were concerned. He'd actually believed that the houseful of boisterous relatives, the mountains of food and the piles of presents were all about love and celebrating a holy occasion. He'd jumped wholeheartedly into that celebration with the rest of them until he found out the truth that lurked underneath the hugging and backslapping and claims of deep affection. After that, remembering the hypocrisy of those scenes made him almost physically sick.

Vic turned away from the paper chains. ''What's up?'' he asked Katherine.

They had pushed through the heavy door and were out of earshot of the kitchen now.

"I remembered where I saw the name Coyote Bellaway before this morning. It was in the return address on one of the letters that came in for the Fund yesterday. I looked through them, like I always do, when they first arrived. I remember his letter in particular because it was pretty banged up. In fact, it looked like it had been run over by a truck."

"Where's the letter now?"

"It wasn't on my desk, so it must be one of the ones you took with you."

Vic had all but forgotten the pile of mail he'd stuffed in his jacket pocket earlier when he first started talking to Coyote.

"Then it has to be in the kitchen."

Vic had taken off his jacket and left it on the counter while he and Coyote made breakfast. Something told Vic he'd better get back in there and retrieve it straight off. He turned and shoved through the door without saying another word. Katherine was right behind him, but they were both too late. Coyote was gone. The breakfast dishes were still on the counter, but Vic's jacket was on the floor with the Most Needy Cases Fund letters scattered around it. Coyote's letter wasn't among them, and the fire exit door, which Vic hadn't taken into consideration when he left the boy alone here, was ajar.

"Damn."

Vic poured all of his frustration into that one word. Once again, he'd misjudged the true motives of the person he was dealing with, just like he used to do with his family when he was a kid. Only he wasn't a kid anymore. Now, he could make up for his mistake, and that was just what he intended to do.

"I WANT TO COME along," Katherine had said when Vic announced he was going to the neighborhood elementary school where he seemed certain Coyote had to be enrolled.

"Maybe this is something I should do on my own. Dealing with more than one person at a time seems to spook him."

"Please." She put her hand on his arm to emphasize what she was saying. "This means a lot to me."

Vic looked down at her hand gripping his leather sleeve. She pulled away. Some people didn't like to be touched without permission. Maybe he was one of those.

"Sorry. I didn't mean to presume."

"That's okay," he said. "You surprised me is all. You can touch me any time you want."

He looked into her eyes when he said that. The words alone would have made her uneasy or worse. The intensity of his gaze set her nerves jangling as well till she was afraid her teeth might start chattering even though they hadn't yet stepped out into the cold.

"It really does mean a lot to me to tag along on this one," she repeated hastily to fill the sudden silence that she had begun to imagine vibrating around her.

"Why is this boy so important?" Vic asked.

She'd caught up with him at the main door out of the center, the same entranceway where they'd had their misunderstanding last night. Katherine wished they could go to a more neutral and private place if she was going to discuss this subject, which was so difficult for her.

"Coyote reminds me of someone," she said sounding almost as unsettled as she felt.

Vic continued to watch her, probably expecting more in the way of an explanation. He was right. This kind of hands-on case work was not her designated territory. Her job here at the center was strictly administrative. Yet, ever since the moment she saw that little boy sleeping on those mats, she'd wanted to be more than what Vic called a paper-pusher, at least in this one instance. She'd have to justify such out-of-the-ordinary involvement, of course. She was about to ask him to come into her office for a moment. This was too sensitive for her to go into out here in the hallway. Before she could make that suggestion, however, Vic reached out and touched her arm this time. She'd had her hand on leather with no real physical contact made. She was wearing a sweater over a long, gray wool skirt which she'd put on today, for some reason, instead of her usual suit. She could feel the pressure of his fingers through the pale gray cashmere. She was surprised, maybe even thrown off balance, by how natural it seemed to have him touch her.

"We'll talk about it in my car," he said almost gently. "Get your coat, and I'll meet you out there. It's the black Trans Am."

He was out the door then, and whatever sensation she'd been obsessing about just a moment ago was gone. As she hurried to her office for her coat, she told herself that Coyote and the connection with difficult memories he caused in her must have sent her emotions haywire for a while. Still, she was glad to swathe herself in a heavy navy camel-hair coat and a scarf wound twice around her neck. If Vic Maltese should touch her again, she wouldn't feel his hand any more than he could have been aware of hers through his leather. She resecured the covered elastic band at the nape of her neck then pulled her knit hat down over her still rambunctious hair. Unless Vic decided to touch the tip of her nose, she'd be safe from inappropriate responses now. Or would she? Katherine was on her way back to the building exit, chiding herself that this should even be a question, when Megan popped out into the hallway from her office.

"Where are you off to in such a hurry?" she asked.

"We're going to Arbor Hill School to check on Coyote Bellaway," Katherine answered without slowing her pace.

"Who's we?"

"Myself and Victor Maltese."

"I approve."

Megan had been bustling along to keep up with Katherine's dash toward the door. Katherine stopped abruptly now while Megan's momentum carried her on a few more steps.

"What do you mean by that?" Katherine asked rather sharply of Megan's still advancing back.

Megan stopped and turned around. Katherine expected to see a mischievous twinkle in Megan's eyes, but her expression was quite serious.

"I'm glad to see you out of your office for a change and actually spending some time with an attractive man."

"This is business," Katherine protested.

"It's a start."

"Oh, Megan," Katherine said as she resumed her hurried trek to the door. "Psychologists aren't supposed to be romantics."

"Who says?" Megan called after her.

When Katherine looked back she saw that a wide grin had replaced the somber look on her friend's face. She shook her head and waved in response before pushing through the door. Vic had pulled up to the edge of the parking lot just outside. Exhaust billowed from the rear of his rumbling vehicle in white clouds even thicker than those created by Katherine's breath. Vic reached across the seat and pushed open the passenger door of the low vehicle.

Katherine hesitated a moment. She'd always associated cars like this one with street punks.

"Get in," he said. "I want to get there before early lunch hour. The place is a zoo then."

She smiled and crouched down to keep from banging her head as she climbed into the low-slung car.

"Buckle up," he added as she slammed the door. "The roads may be icy, and this thing fishtails sometimes."

She pulled the belt across her body and fastened it into the latch at the side of the bucket seat as he'd suggested.

"Maybe you should try driving more slowly," she said.

"I drive slow enough."

Vic hit the gas pedal as if in deliberate contradiction of his words, and they were across the parking lot in what felt like an instant. Katherine gasped.

Vic laughed. "Don't be scared," he said. "I'm just teasing you. Trust me. I don't take any chances on slippery pavement. You're safe with me at the wheel."

He did take it easy then as they drove out of the parking lot and up the first rise of the slope that was called Arbor Hill. Fortunately, road crews had been out that morning and the incline was well coated with salt and sand. The sun was out and sparkling on the otherwise dingy snow on either side of the street. Maybe it would warm up enough later in the day to melt some of this packed stuff from the roadbed. Katherine hoped, probably in vain, that would happen before they drove back down this way. She still hadn't quite shaken the street punk association and half expected Vic to take off with a squeal of his mag-wheeled tires at any moment.

"If you feel like talking," he began instead, "I'm a good listener."

"Talking about what?"

"That thing you said back at the center. About Coyote reminding you of somebody."

Katherine glanced at Vic. He'd put on black leather gloves, which held the steering wheel now in an easy grip. His eyes were on the road ahead, his expression neutral. She didn't get the impression he was pumping her out of idle curiosity. Something in his manner made her believe he was offering just what he claimed, a listening ear.

Katherine sighed. "Yes. That," she said.

She'd known she would have to talk about this eventually. She'd never guessed till this very minute that she would ever dream of doing so with Victor Maltese in his hot-rod car.

"Coyote reminds me of a boy named Daniel," she said. She was surprised by how steadily she could speak the words and by the relief she felt at having them spoken. "He was my stepson. He died."

Chapter Five

Vic felt rather than heard the grief beneath her attempt at a matter-of-fact tone. His first instinct was to pull the car over to the side of the road and take her in his arms. He kept on driving. He sensed that she needed him to maintain an even keel here and not do anything while she got out what she had to say.

"I'm sorry for your loss," he said.

Out of the corner of his eye, he saw her nod once.

"Daniel was nine-and-a-half," she said. "He had leukemia. They couldn't find a blood match for a bone marrow transplant. Eventually, his body just gave out."

"You said he was your stepson. Were the two of you close?"

"Yes. I loved him very much."

She turned to look out the window on her side of the car. Vic let the silence between them play out as long as she needed it to. He could feel her sadness as if it was his own, but she didn't cry, at least not so he could notice. Several moments passed before she turned back from the window again.

"This is the first time I've told anyone here in Albany about Daniel," she said. She'd managed to put her matter-of-fact tone back together again. "I haven't even talked to

Megan about him. I hope you don't mind my dumping such a heavy load on you when we hardly know each other.''

''I don't mind at all. Sometimes it's easier to say hard things to somebody you don't know so well.''

''Hard, hurtful things.''

Vic nodded but didn't reply. There was no answer to real sadness, especially the sadness of losing a child. He would have liked to ask about Daniel's father. He knew he probably should be talking to her about something else—the fact that she was identifying too personally with the Coyote Bellaway case. But Vic generally let the shrinks and social workers worry about things like that. He saw even less reason than usual for changing that policy now. They drove in silence the rest of the way to the school.

''Coyote Bellaway has been absent for the past three days.''

Vic had suspected something like that even before he and Katherine were escorted to the vice principal's office.

''Ordinarily, we wouldn't pay much attention to that short an absence,'' Stefan Piatka was saying. ''But Coyote has had perfect attendance up till now, and his grades have been exemplary.''

Vic had worked with Stefan consulting about other students who hung out at the center. Not very often were their school records anywhere near as favorable as what Stefan was describing now.

''Are you saying Coyote's a good student and he's never been in trouble before this that you know of?'' Vic asked.

''Not that I know of.''

To Vic, that meant, if Coyote was taking a wrong direction for some reason, he was definitely worth turning around.

''Of course, his sister is another story,'' Stefan went on.

"Coyote has a sister?" Katherine asked.

"Yes, he does," Stefan said. "She's two grades behind him. They call her Sprite."

"Has she been out of school for the past three days, too?" Katherine asked.

"No, she hasn't. That's another reason we've been concerned about Coyote. He and his sister are usually inseparable. They come to school together. They go home together. Coyote even asked to have the same lunch hour as his sister so he could keep an eye on her. Unfortunately, she does need that kind of extra supervision."

"The sister's a behavior problem?" Vic asked.

"She has been this semester."

"Have you asked Sprite why her brother has been out of school?" Katherine asked.

"She says she doesn't know, but Sprite tends to be uncooperative."

"Do you think we might ask her again?"

"Maybe we're jumping the gun here," Vic broke in. He had the feeling that Katherine was running away with this interview and he shouldn't be letting that happen.

"I agree with Ms. Fairchild," Stefan said. "I sense something wrong here. Maybe Sprite can help us find out what that is. I'm going to bring her here to my office. She might have an easier time talking in a neutral space out of sight of the classroom."

"Thank you, Mr. Piatka," Katherine said.

Her smile couldn't help but light up Vic's heart. The rest of her did the same in a curious way he didn't quite understand. When she'd pulled her winter cap off earlier, her hair had sprung free into tendrils around her face. A spot of rosy color bloomed at the center of each of her cheeks, maybe from the school's overheated rooms, maybe from the high tension of this visit. One thing Vic knew with absolute certainty—right at this minute, she was the most beautiful woman he'd ever seen. As the principal left the office, Katherine turned to face Vic, and that beauty hit him full force, straight out of the brightness in her blue-gray eyes.

"What I'm going to tell you may seem odd," she said, "but ever since Daniel was so sick and died, I seem to have tuned in to danger where children are concerned. And I feel that Coyote Bellaway's in serious trouble."

Her eyes weren't only bright. They were glittering. Vic's captivation with her beauty gave way to something closer to uneasiness.

"Are you telling me that you think you have a sense the rest of us don't have?" he asked.

"It's a kind of psychic sense. But I think anyone who has gone through what I went through with Daniel could have the same strong intuitiveness."

Vic only nodded. He was suddenly very aware of how little he knew about Katherine Fairchild. She'd been a real whiz at organizing the Arbor Hill Children's Center, but those were administrative issues. They didn't have anything to do with the kids at the center and their problems in real life. Now that Katherine was entering that much more emotional territory, she was acting like she might be out of control. She'd already told him about the death of her stepson. Vic could tell how deeply she'd been affected by that tragedy. Maybe she'd been more than just affected. Maybe she wasn't quite right mentally as a result. He'd known people who were derailed by less powerful losses than the one Katherine had obviously experienced.

"Why don't you let me take the lead when Stefan brings the little girl back here?" Vic suggested. He was careful to speak gently.

"Don't worry," Katherine said. "I *do* know what I'm

doing. I've taken courses in social work. I'm thinking about going back to get my master's degree.''

Vic nodded again but didn't say anything. He'd always believed that the kind of work he and others at the center did, and especially the knack for that work, had to be learned somewhere other than in the classroom. He stared out the window, which was all but covered by paper cutout decorations for Christmas, Hanukkah and Kwanza. Vic couldn't help but wonder if he might have made a big mistake by bringing Katherine here.

KATHERINE COULD TELL that Vic thought she might be a little bit out of her mind. She probably shouldn't have mentioned the psychic connection with children she'd found herself experiencing for more than the last two years, ever since the doctors told them how sick Daniel really was. Psychic connection wasn't the correct thing to call it, anyway. That sounded a little too loony even to her. She'd simply attuned herself so closely to Daniel in those long months of his steady decline that she could almost feel his pain and anticipate his needs. That attunement extended beyond Daniel eventually, till she could look at a child and tell almost immediately if that child was in distress. That was what had actually drawn her to the job at the children's center, more than what she had told Megan about saying yes to new opportunities. Katherine had wanted to be of help.

Still, what she'd said to Megan about keeping at arm's length, at least from the hurtful things, was true. That had been Katherine's most deliberate intention up to and including most of yesterday. Now, here she was, about to wade knee-deep into the trauma of two children's lives. Katherine was not a person to let such uncharacteristic behavior on her part go unexamined. Oddly enough, she couldn't get over the feeling that all of this had a lot to do with Victor Maltese. It was as if last night when he grabbed her arm in the icy parking lot at the center, he had jolted her back to life somehow.

Starting with the anger his arrogance had stirred in her then, she had experienced more emotion in the past several hours than she'd allowed herself to feel in all the months since the day of Daniel's death. She'd deadened herself along with him, in a way, in order to be able to stand the pain of his loss. That shadow was lifting now. She could almost feel the weight of it rising from her shoulders. For reasons she couldn't yet entirely explain, she had Vic to thank for that—or, perhaps, to blame.

As the office door opened and Stefan Piatka led Sprite Bellaway by the hand into the room, Katherine could hardly have been more aware of her own newly opened heart. The little girl's eyes were large and blue. Her hair was curly and almost blonde, much like Katherine's, though Sprite's curls were more relaxed. With her fair skin and small bones, the child could have been Katherine's own. Maybe that was part of the reason she found herself responding so strongly. She had to ball her hands into fists and press them against her sides. Otherwise, she would have wrapped her arms around the little girl and rocked her gently till the worried expression left those wide, blue eyes and they shone clear again. But that might startle the child, and it would certainly shock Vic Maltese.

Meanwhile, Sprite was obviously doing her best to look belligerent. Her lips pouted and her chin thrust out, but all Katherine saw was the worry in Sprite's eyes. Katherine could tell that much of what should be carefree about childhood had already been stolen from this child. She was thinner than she should be, and Katherine guessed that wasn't from neglect. Sprite's clothes were simple and not new, but they were clean, as was the rest of her. Her thinness had to be yet another sign of the burden she carried. That burden was obviously far heavier than her child's shoulders were meant to bear, no matter how tightly she shrugged them together beneath the faded cotton of her T-shirt.

Vic stepped forward at almost the same moment the little girl shrank away. He would want to comfort Sprite just as Katherine did. She'd heard how much he cared for the children at the center. That morning, she'd seen proof of that caring in his gentle firmness with Coyote and had heard it in the voice Vic used then. But his size could be imposing. She had felt that herself last night in the parking lot. His impact would be all the more intimidating for a little girl as fragile as Sprite. *Fragile but fierce,* was the thought that flashed in Katherine's mind. Like herself again. She was also too thin from tension and worrying. She also, once in a while, felt like a heavily burdened little girl.

Katherine touched Vic's arm gently and without making any quick movements. When he halted, she lowered herself, just as slowly and carefully, till her eyes were level with Sprite's. The little girl's hand had travelled to her mouth. She pressed her thumb knuckle there, maybe in memory of the comfort that thumb had once given her. Her eyes were wide open above her fist, and Katherine could hear breathing that had speeded up from fear.

"Hello, Sprite," Katherine said in an even voice. She spoke almost as slowly as she had moved. "My name is Katherine. I've been wanting to meet you."

The little girl had tensed visibly, ready to pull her small chest back even more tightly between her rigid shoulders. She didn't exactly relax at the sound of Katherine's soothing words, but she did stop shrinking away long enough for Katherine to sense the change and recognize it as a signal to proceed, though very cautiously, still.

"I met your brother this morning. You look a lot like him," Katherine continued at the same slow, calming pace.

"He's taller than me," Sprite said from behind her fist.

"Yes, but you'll catch up before long."

"I don't want to catch up. I want to stay small."

Sprite's quick comeback was as belligerent as the set of her chin, but Katherine could hear the tremble in her voice. She avoided the temptation to press for a reason for Sprite's statement. The little girl needed relief now, not close questioning. She needed to be put at ease.

"I used to feel like that," Katherine said.

"When?"

Skepticism way beyond her years added even more of an edge to Sprite's belligerence, but Katherine's voice and manner remained unaltered in their placidity.

"It was the year I got my first two-wheel bicycle. I didn't want to grow too big to ride it. I was seven years old then."

"That's how old I am."

"When's your birthday?" Katherine asked.

"June 14th."

"Flag Day," Katherine said. "Your birthday's the same time as the Flag Day Parade."

"I never saw a parade on my birthday."

The skepticism was still there, but it came in a somewhat lighter tone, as if she thought Katherine might be making a joke and Sprite was acknowledging she knew that.

"I swear," Katherine said, putting her hand over her heart. "June 14th is Flag Day, and I'll bet if we looked around we could find a parade. Right on your birthday. Would you like to do that?"

Sprite didn't say anything right away. She studied Katherine, who understood that seeking a response so soon after they'd met could be tricky. If Sprite chose to answer, that would mean she'd chosen to participate in a conversation with Katherine which would, in turn, be a major step toward the beginnings of trust.

"Can Coyote come?" Sprite asked at last.

"Sure."

Katherine was careful to keep her voice from showing her excitement at Sprite's response. Keeping the emotional level of their exchange on an even keel was crucial, especially for what Katherine was going to ask next.

"Would you like to go and tell Coyote about it, you and me?"

Sprite tensed a little, and Katherine hoped she hadn't moved too fast. Then Sprite sighed, and her shoulders dropped some of their hunch.

"I don't really know where he is," she said. "I asked him, but he said he couldn't tell me."

Katherine almost sighed herself, from grateful relief at hearing Sprite's confession. The code had been broken. A small door had opened in the wall that was Sprite Bellaway's defense against the world that made her at least as frightened as she'd just revealed her brother to be. There would be more revelations now, until she had told whatever she happened to know.

"Is he playing hide-and-seek?" Katherine asked.

"He's not playing. He's scared."

Katherine remained crouched on the floor of the vice principal's office, probing gently for the information she and Vic needed. For the moment, she tried not to think about Coyote and where he might be right now, out there in the world that frightened his little sister so much.

Chapter Six

Katherine did have the knack, after all. She was wonderful with kids. Vic felt his heart swell with pride for her, and he didn't like that. He'd better not let himself get hung up on her. He didn't need another dead-end relationship. He'd been through too many of those already, scenes that went nowhere from the start, and he hated the whole messy business. Relationships like that just about always ended up not worth the hassle and hard feelings. Still, as she knelt beside the chair talking softly and smiling so he could almost see her heart shining through, all for the sake of an unhappy little girl, Vic wondered if Katherine Fairchild might be worth just about anything. When Stefan Piatka leaned forward to speak quietly to Katherine, Vic realized he'd almost forgotten the vice principal was in the room.

"Maybe Sprite could tell us what she thinks Coyote is afraid of," Stefan suggested.

Sprite lowered her brows and pouted. She couldn't have made it more clear how little she wanted to talk directly to Stefan if she'd shouted the words out loud.

"I'd like to know what Coyote's afraid of," Katherine said gently. "Would you mind telling me about that, Sprite?"

"The man in the car," Sprite said at once. "He's afraid of the big man in the black car."

"What car would that be?" Katherine asked.

"I saw it by our house the day after Coyote went away, and yesterday too. The man didn't get out. He sat inside the car and looked over at Tooley's place. He did that for a long time."

Sprite heaved a sigh as if the long speech had ended up to be more than she started out to say and she was glad to have it over. Katherine patted the child's arm approvingly while Vic and Stefan exchanged worried glances. Men in parked cars watching children were a concern of everybody who worked with kids.

"Did you get a look at the man?" Vic asked.

Sprite drew back a little, and her small hand darted to her mouth again.

"This is Mr. Maltese," Katherine said in the mesmerizing tone that already had Vic as well as Sprite, and maybe even Stefan, under its spell. "He's a good friend of mine."

Vic felt a ridiculously irrational surge of warmth to hear himself described that way by her. Sprite's fist unclenched and moved slowly away from her mouth as she looked at Vic with a nervous gaze that went straight to his heart. No child this young should have to be so suspicious and scared. Vic saw way too much of that in his line of work, and he never stopped being upset by it.

"Vic—Mr. Maltese—wants to know if you saw what the man in the car looked like," Katherine said. She caught Sprite's self-protecting hand where it wavered between her mouth and her lap and held it gently. "You can talk to Mr. Maltese. He knows Coyote. And he's a good man."

She said those last words so sincerely that Vic's heart couldn't help but swell once more.

"I just saw the top of his face," Sprite said. "The car

had windows you can't see through, but his window was rolled down a little.''

Vic was careful to speak in a non-startling way, as Katherine had been doing. "Do you remember what the part of him you could see looked like?"

Sprite put her other hand on top of Katherine's. The little girl looked as if she was hanging on for dear life, as fear opened her wide eyes ever wider. Vic wished he could be asking her to forget, rather than to remember.

"He had shiny black hair," she said in little more than a whisper.

"What made his hair shiny?" Katherine asked.

Sprite thought for a minute. "He looked like he just came out of a swimming pool. Like his hair was wet."

"You mean it was slicked back?" Vic asked.

Sprite nodded. Vic didn't want to press her further, but he had to.

"Did you see anything else about the man in the black car?" he asked.

The knuckles of Sprite's small hand were white from clutching on to Katherine's.

"His eyes," Sprite said barely loud enough to be heard. "He had very scary eyes."

TEN BROECK STREET, where Tooley Pennebaker and the Bellaway children lived, had known better days. In the midnineteenth century wealthy families of powerful men had made their homes here. Back then, the street was referred to as Millionaires' Row. Vic enjoyed reading the history of this town he'd grown to care about. He didn't enjoy looking at how far some parts of that town had fallen. Here on Ten Broeck Street, the facade of beautiful old St. Joseph's Church was off-limits now behind scaffolding that warned of falling debris. The row houses in this last block before

Clinton Avenue were too sad and dingy these days to be called anything like Millionaire's Row. *Just Barely Making It Row is more like it,* was the thought that crossed Vic's mind as he looked around.

Vic hadn't wanted to bring Katherine along on this chase after a scary-looking man in a black car. All of that might be more the creation of a little girl's imagination, or the waking memory of a nightmare, than anything having to do with real life. Still, there was the possibility of danger. And definitely there was a boy in some kind of trouble. Katherine's confession in the car earlier told him she'd already had trouble enough in her life, and Vic didn't want to expose her to more of the same. Unfortunately, when he tried to drop her off at the center, she'd refused to get out of the car. So here they were.

"What we're suspecting is a child molester," she was saying. "Isn't that right?"

"It's one of the possibilities," he answered in a grim tone.

There was nothing he hated more than the kind of animal who preys on children. Vic could feel his rage heat up just thinking about it.

"But, if that's the case, why would Coyote run off? Why wouldn't he just tell somebody at the center? We make a big point of letting kids know they can do that and that they should. I'm sure they do the same thing at the school. Why wouldn't he just talk to someone, you for example?"

"Unless the creep is a member of Coyote's family. Kids are more reluctant to talk when that's the case."

Katherine shook her head, and coils of fair hair tumbled around her face from beneath her knit cap. Vic did his best to concentrate on what she was saying instead of on how the chill of the afternoon had brought a bloom to her cheeks, or the way the car heater was now turning her skin dewy.

"I don't think it's a family member," she said. "Otherwise, Sprite would probably have recognized him or at least made an association with the car."

Vic would have liked to ask her how anybody could be so smart and so beautiful at the same time, but the still-sensible part of his mind told him how corny that would sound. He nodded instead and turned the car heater down a little. Maybe the rising temperature was starting to addle his brain and that was why all he could think about was the way Katherine's mouth naturally curved up slightly at the corners. When he started wondering what it would be like to place the tip of his tongue there, he knew he had to say something to distract himself.

"Maybe the kid was too afraid or too ashamed to tell someone," Vic said off the top of his head.

Katherine shook her head again. "That doesn't sound right to me either. If the man in the black car was a child molester, that would make him a threat to Sprite, too. From what Stefan Piatka said, Coyote is very protective of his little sister. I believe that if he thought she was in danger he'd go to somebody for help, no matter how frightened or embarrassed he might be. I have a feeling we've got something other than the usual garden-variety child predator here."

"Do you have any ideas about specifically what that other something might be?"

The reminder of the reality of how much danger Coyote could be in was bringing Vic's head out of its fog of lust or infatuation—or whatever—fast.

Katherine sighed. "I don't have a clue, really. Except that I don't like the sound of a shiny new car in a neighborhood this marginal."

"I agree with you there," Vic said. "Those kind of characters usually come into a neighborhood like this because they're up to no good."

"I'd like to take a closer look."

Her hand was on the door handle and pulling it backward before he could react. She had the door open and was about to get out of the car by the time he could grab her arm.

"I'm not sure you should do that," he said.

She turned slowly to look down at his grip on her arm.

"You have a habit of latching on to women, don't you," she said in a tone that made him let go of her immediately.

"Sorry," he said. "But I thought we already decided that with Sprite back at the school and Coyote on the run and Tooley Pennebaker at work this time of day, according to the school records, their apartment must be deserted."

"I want to take a look at it anyway."

She put one foot out of the car, and Vic had to restrain himself from grabbing her again. That was obviously a no-no with her, especially after the way he'd behaved last night.

"What if the bogeyman in the big car is around?" he said.

"Don't you think he'd have figured out the same things we did about the place being deserted this time of day? If he really is watching for Coyote, then we can assume he wouldn't waste his time here right now."

She slid the rest of the way out of the car then and shut the door behind her with a resolute slam. Vic had no choice but to follow.

KATHERINE HAD MORE than one reason for getting out of the car. The rising tension in there was about to make her jump in her skin. It wasn't just Vic's blasting car heater that warmed her face to the flush she could feel creeping downward to other parts of her. As she sat there talking to him, she'd been unable to ignore the charges of challenge leaping back and forth between them, and that challenge had everything to do with the fact that he was a very sexy man. She'd known many men she thought of as attractive, but very few struck her as sexy. Maybe none had ever struck her this hard. Certainly, something had changed between them in the time they'd spent together. Something had altered the way she viewed Vic Maltese. She could actually feel her temperature mount when she was around him no matter how cold the weather might be. She stepped onto the frigid sidewalk and could see her breath steam in front of her. Still, her cheeks and the back of her neck flamed.

He'd wanted to leave her behind earlier. Now she wished she could do the same with him. These new feelings about Vic came to her entirely unbidden and weren't particularly welcome. She'd been a long time without a man in her life, even longer without a man in her bed. She'd been taken entirely by surprise when she turned toward him just moments ago in the car, and experienced the unmistakable impact of a spark darting straight from his eyes into hers and, from there, along her nerve endings and through her blood. She knew instantly, of course, what it was. She simply hadn't known it was going to happen. Meanwhile, he was at the moment following her out of the car, and there was nothing she could do to stop him.

Katherine hurried into the crunch of snow just off the curb. She started to congratulate herself for wearing more sensible boots today. Then she remembered Vic practically carrying her across the parking lot last night and how that had embarrassed her into wearing the flat, rubber-soled footwear she had on today. Which in turn reminded her that she had been on close terms, if you could call it that, with Vic for less than twenty-four hours now. He shouldn't be igniting passions in her, or whatever it was he did, anywhere near so soon. As a matter of fact, she didn't want him, or anyone else, igniting anything in her at all. She had her share of burn scars already.

"Do you know which apartment is theirs?" Vic asked from the other side of the car.

He seemed to want to keep his distance from her as well. She hoped that was what he would do.

"The file at the center listed the apartment only as B," she said, ducking her head against a sharp blast of cold she couldn't help but feel even in her present, rather overwrought state.

Katherine continued across the two-lane road. There wasn't much in the way of traffic. The workday activity of State Street and Capitol Hill was many long blocks from here. The house where the Bellaway children lived with their aunt was no worse for wear than the rest of the block but no better off either.

There was a stoop outside the house. Katherine climbed the seven cement steps to the door and checked out the smudged nameplates beneath the doorbells. The Pennebaker plate had "1F" in parentheses after the B.

"According to this, I'd guess they're on the first floor in the front, but I can't tell which side of the building that is," she said.

Vic had stopped at the foot of the steps to the stoop. He didn't look like he was about to move closer. Katherine suspected he might have felt the electrical thing between them as well. Maybe he didn't care to be zapped by it again any more than she did. He only nodded in response to her comment.

"I'm going to ring the bell," she added.

She pressed the flat button that appeared as if it might

once have had the luster of mother-of-pearl. Nothing happened. She pressed the bell once more, harder this time, and a sharp buzz was audible then from what sounded like the right side of the first floor. Katherine waited a long moment but heard nothing more from inside the building. She buzzed again and listened again.

"Like I told you before," Vic said. "I don't think anybody's at home this time of day, unless Coyote came back here and he's hiding inside."

"And, if he's hiding, he won't answer the bell."

"That would be my guess."

From the stoop, Katherine tried the handle of the door to the entryway of the building, but the door was locked. She cupped her hands around her face and peered through the glass in the door. She couldn't see much of anything through the curtain that covered the pane.

"I think I'll take a peek through those windows," she said, indicating the pair that abutted the edge of the stoop.

"Be careful," Vic said. "You don't want anybody to see you."

He was right. Anyone inside observing her surveillance could be alerted in time to run off, if they hadn't been so alerted already. Or, a neighbor might notice Katherine snooping around and call the police. She gazed up and down the street but saw no one, not even a face behind a frosty window. She proceeded cautiously to the edge of the stoop and leaned just far enough over the rail to peek around the frame of the first window. What she saw made her pull back and flatten her body against the wall.

"Vic," she said in the loudest whisper she could manage without guaranteeing she'd be heard by anyone who happened to be inside. "Come here."

She made a quick, beckoning arm motion she hoped would communicate her urgency.

"What?" he asked.

She pressed her gloved finger to her lips. "Shh."

He apparently took her seriously because he said no more and stepped as noiselessly as was probably possible for a man his size onto the steps.

"What's wrong?" he whispered when he got to her side.

"It looks like the place has been trashed."

Chapter Seven

Once they had called the police, Katherine retreated across Ten Broeck Street to lean against Vic's car. Her coat was smudged with winter road soot from its dusty metal surface, but she didn't care. She breathed deep and drew in air as needle-sharp as Chicago's notorious frigid wind had ever been. She wished she could will her heart to freeze as solid as the ice at the corner of Vic's windshield. In the instant it took for that thought to form and fade away, Katherine understood she should will her heart to freeze against him as well.

Her gaze darted to Tooley Pennebaker's stoop, where Vic stood on the sidewalk with one booted foot on the bottom step as he leaned to listen to the much shorter policeman at his side. A dark lock of Vic's hair fell forward as he leaned down. He shoved the lock back with an impatient swipe of his hand, and she felt the movement like a touch.

She turned quickly away. No matter how confused she might have been emotionally during these past difficult months, there was one thing of which she was absolutely sure. She must not set herself up for loss and devastation again. She was still too vulnerable to risk that.

After Daniel's death, she'd pushed her feelings as far

down beneath the surface of herself as she could get them to go. She'd run away and ended up here in Albany, where she'd kept herself furiously busy with work ever since. That combination of running, hiding and hard work had assured her safety, at least from additional heartache—till today.

Despite the progress she had made on her emotional front, still sometimes she could be assaulted by an almost overwhelming sense of loss. When that happened, she'd become acquainted yet again with what she thought of as her soft center, a place like a pool filled with sadness. She never knew in advance which experiences or associations might send her plummeting back to the sorrow of Daniel's death. Otherwise, she would have avoided those circumstances as surely as a gun-shy soldier avoids battle. Otherwise, she would have run from Ten Broeck Street and never set foot on Tooley Pennebaker's stoop that afternoon.

If forced to guess at the cause of her sadness today, she'd have to choose one of two things. The sight of the police car was one possibility. A police car with its dome light flashing an eerie, rotating glow, first red then white, had accompanied her last ambulance ride with Daniel to the hospital. He was beyond the help of hospitals by then, or sirens or flashing lights.

Another possible trigger for today's flashback to devastation could be the similar devastation she'd seen through Tooley Pennebaker's window. The living room and its contents had obviously been threadbare even before someone went in there and started tossing furniture around. Many of those poor pieces were broken now, and Katherine couldn't help but imagine what hardship that might cause for Coyote, Sprite and their aunt. Katherine had never known much material want in her life, but she was no stranger to bleakness. What she'd glimpsed through that window this afternoon was bleak almost beyond her capacity to bear.

Katherine shook her head and sighed. A couple of kids with pleading eyes living one rundown tenement apartment away from homelessness, and a man who drove hot cars and wore black leather. She couldn't have come up with three people more likely to put her already wrung-out heart through a wringer again if she'd ordered them from central casting.

Katherine pulled herself out of the hunch she'd slid into against the dusty car. She adjusted her scarf and pushed the escaped bits of hair back under her cap. She resolved that from now on she'd be wise as well as smart and keep her heart to herself, where it belonged. The husky voice at her elbow interrupted her second repetition of that resolution.

"What's going on over there? Do you know?"

The woman at Katherine's side was only about five feet tall, but she was very solidly built. She was scowling as if she wanted to punch somebody. Katherine hoped that somebody wouldn't be her.

"You with them?" the woman asked, gesturing toward Vic and the policeman on the opposite side of the street.

"Yes."

Katherine resisted the impulse to clarify that she was with the Arbor Hill Center contingent of the official gathering across the way, not the police. She understood that the police weren't likely to be very popular in this neighborhood.

"What's your business here?" the woman asked.

"I'd have to know who you are before I answer that."

The woman looked Katherine up and down. She wished she couldn't feel against her cheek the corkscrews of hair that had popped out yet again from beneath her cap in a way that she knew made her look about fourteen years old.

"Who are you to be asking who I am?" was the woman's response.

"My name is Katherine Fairchild. I'm from the Arbor Hill Children's Center."

Katherine wished she could back away. Though she was several inches taller, she couldn't help feeling that the force of this woman's personality towered over her. Until, suddenly, her entire demeanor appeared to change. A wide smile broke across her face, and the angry flatness in her eyes came suddenly alive.

"That's the place my Coyote hangs out in sometimes," she said. "He's told me there's good people works over there."

"You're talking about Coyote Bellaway?"

"Could there be more than one kid with a name like Coyote?"

Katherine was bewildered. "Are you Tooley Pennebaker?" she blurted.

"That's my name. Call me Tooley." She extended a mittened hand toward Katherine's gloved one.

Katherine accepted the handshake and found herself caught in a grip as commanding as she might have known it would be.

"You're Coyote and Sprite's aunt? Their mother's sister?"

The woman hesitated, then finally admitted, "Not so's you could tell it by looking at me." Her skin was the color of deep, rich chocolate, as dark as Coyote and Sprite were pale. She sighed. "I expect Coyote's been telling that one about me being his blood kin."

"That's exactly the one he's been telling," she said.

Tooley gave Katherine a penetrating look. "I care about those poor children as strong as if they were my blood, that's for sure. And their ailing mama, too. She and me go way back."

She shook her head. The expression on her broad face

made clear how sad she considered the story of the Bellaway children and their mother.

"Are you going to let him keep on telling it?" she asked.

"Do you mean, am I going to report that you're not a
blood relative of Coyote and Sprite?"

"Mmm-hmm. That's just what I mean."

Katherine hesitated.

"You know what the welfare will do when they find out,
don't you?" Ms. Pennebaker asked. "They'll clamp those
two sweet children into foster care faster than you can say
Jackie Robinson. They most likely won't keep them together, either. Coyote could handle that okay. He probably
could handle about anything. How Sprite would take it
though, I don't know, and that precious girl's already missing her mama so bad it ought to make you cry your heart
out."

Katherine would have preferred another answer to the
one she must eventually and inevitably give.

"I won't be the only one making that decision," she
said.

"That's what they call passing the buck, honey."

Katherine didn't deny that. She didn't say anything. Instead, she started across the street with Tooley Pennebaker
bustling right behind her.

VIC SAW the two women approaching and swore silently.
Under most circumstances, he'd have been pleased by the
prospect of Katherine Fairchild joining him, standing by
his side, maybe gazing up at him with those eyes that reminded him of a blue-gray mist just before sunrise. Even
now, he felt a rumble in his chest at the sight of her. He
hadn't experienced that particular sensation, at least not so
he remembered it, since high school. He wished that real-

ization came happily to him. Instead, he found himself suddenly more disgruntled than ever.

"I still want to know what you've really got to do with
this scene," the young cop was saying.

Vic's sigh stretched out long enough to make his exasperation unmistakable.

"I've been through that with you twice already," he
said. "How many times do you have to hear it?"

"Till my gut stops warning me you're not telling everything you know."

I couldn't give a damn less about your gut, Vic would
have liked to shout. He could feel his face redden from the
strain of repressing that outburst. The kid flatfoot was right,
of course, but he'd have been guessing all the same. He
looked as if he might have been on the force about a week
and a half, or not anywhere near long enough anyway to
have acquired the instincts he was crediting himself with.
He'd heard Vic's name before around the station house, his
last name in particular. That was the only special insight
this rookie had going for him. Anybody on the local force,
or in the police departments from any number of area towns
and counties for that matter, could have come to the same
conclusion just by hearing Maltese. What Vic had happening to him here was a roust, plain and simple. He'd been
through this same routine, or some variation of it, so many
times he scarcely paid attention anymore. Except that, on
those other occasions when one of Albany's finest—or
Schenectady's or Troy's or whoever's—decided to get his
jollies from giving Vic a hard time, Katherine hadn't been
on hand to witness it.

"Why don't you just come clean, Maltese?" the cop was
asking.

"Why don't you just cut me some slack?" Vic hissed
back at him from between gritted teeth, once again restrain-

ing himself from adding "jerk" or "squirt" or any of the many slurs he would have thought suited this rookie to a T.

"Vic, is something wrong here?"

Katherine was at his elbow now, and she sounded sincerely concerned.

He turned quickly toward her. "Nothing," he said, more sharply than he'd meant to do.

She backed off a step. He could tell from the way she was studying his face that it must still wear the scowl he'd intended for the pain-in-the-neck policeman. Vic did his best to relax.

"Everything's under control here," he lied. "Why don't you go back to the car and wait for me?"

The breath from those words was still white on the frigid air when he realized he shouldn't have said them.

"I don't think so," she answered in a tone that rivalled the weather for coldness.

"I just meant that you'd be warmer in the car, and nothing much is going on here."

So much for Vic's lame attempt to cover the mistake of suggesting that Katherine, a professional at least as fully accredited as himself, shouldn't be as much involved in this case as he was. Arrogance might have seemed like the right attitude to use with her last night, but he'd changed his mind—or maybe some other part of himself—about her since then.

"There's someone you need to meet," she said, still with enough chill in her voice to frost his heart.

Vic glanced at the short, hefty black woman at Katherine's side. He thought about mentioning that this might not be the best time for introductions. He decided it had to be an even worse time to question Katherine's judgment. Her facial expression was now about as dark as he'd imagined his own to be a couple of minutes ago.

"This is Tooley Pennebaker," she said indicating the woman next to her.

Vic understood that Katherine had his mind running haywire at the moment. Plus, he was rattled by the very upsetting fact of how strong an effect she had on him. Still, something even beyond that confusion made him aware that her last statement wasn't right somehow.

"You know," Katherine went on. "The Bellamy children's aunt."

The still-wet-behind-the-ears police officer had been watching this exchange with obvious interest.

"What children would those be, miss?" he chimed in now.

"A boy and girl we work with at the Arbor Hill Children's Center, Officer," Katherine said, and favored him with a smile so dazzling and sweet that Vic could see the rookie blush straight through the peach fuzz he probably called five-o'clock shadow.

"Do either of those kids have a record of vandalism?" the rookie managed to ask without his voice cracking as Vic half expected it to do.

"Oh, no," Katherine said, even more sweetly. "These are very young children." She held out her gloved hand to illustrate a height much shorter than Coyote's, or Sprite's either, for that matter. "Way too young to be involved in anything like that."

Vic had to bite back a smile of his own, though not quite what you'd call a sweet one. The woman was smooth as silk. She could lie like a trooper and get away with it, too. That angel face of hers, complete with a halo of blond mist around it, did the trick for her. He couldn't help wondering if he'd be as susceptible himself as the rookie was sure to be.

"Good. Then they probably had nothing to do with tossing the apartment in this building," the young policeman said in a tone as cooperative as it had been the opposite when he was talking to Vic.

Katherine had charmed the rookie into submission just the way Vic had figured she would. In the meantime, Tooley Pennebaker didn't look to Vic like she was in the least bit charmed.

"What're you talkin' about?" she cried out, grabbing a hunk of the rookie's coat sleeve. "Which apartment you sayin' got tossed around here?"

"That one on the front right, ma'am." The rookie pointed.

"*No!*" Tooley wailed. "That's my place."

This woman, who up till now had appeared to be very substantial, even formidable, all but crumpled on the spot. Katherine wrapped her arm around the much broader woman.

"It's not so bad," Katherine said. "Just things tossed around, as far as I could see."

"You saw this happen?" the police officer asked.

"No, no. Nothing like that," Katherine assured him. "I'll explain in a minute."

The cop would never have taken that kind of delaying tactic from Vic. Katherine was apparently a different story as far as this officer was concerned. The rookie nodded and waited, just as she'd requested him to do. Meanwhile, her companion was pulling away in the direction of the apartment she'd said was hers. Katherine held fast to the larger woman's waist and moved along with her up onto the stoop.

Tooley fumbled in her coat pocket and pulled out a set

of keys. She rattled through them a couple of times, visibly confused and shaken, then finally selected one and opened the front door to the building. Vic watched as Katherine followed Ms. Pennebaker into the entryway hall.

"Is it really that woman's place that got ransacked?" the rookie asked. A shriek from inside the building answered the young cop's question for him.

"Yeah," Vic replied anyway. "I'd say it's her place, all right."

"The kids she was talking about, they live here too?"

"The kids live here too," Vic affirmed.

He knew, for Coyote and Sprite's sake, he had to keep this cop from nosing too deep into what was going on here.

"Where are those kids?" the rookie asked.

Vic was listening to the cop with new attentiveness now. Vic took note especially of how curiously the rookie was watching the door to Tooley Pennebaker's building. The less he figured out about what was actually happening to the Bellaway family, whatever that might be, the better the children were likely to end up. That's how Vic saw it, anyway. He'd learned a long time ago, when he was still not much more than a child himself, that it paid to keep family business in the family.

"They're over at the center working on setting up for the Christmas pageant," Vic said, lying yet again and taking a chance that the rookie wouldn't check the story. "They didn't have anything to do with this."

"Who do you think did have something to do with this?"

The rookie sounded like he was thinking Vic was mixed up in the break-in somehow.

Vic shrugged. "A street punk looking for goods to sell would be my guess."

"In this dump?"

Vic shrugged again to hide how much he agreed with the cop's assessment. The likelihood of this rundown building, or the even more rundown Pennebaker apartment, holding anything very salable was slim to none.

"Desperate people don't always think too clearly," Vic said.

The rookie nodded. "I'll write up an incident report."

"You do that," Vic said.

He knew how little official action would actually be taken as a result of this guy's investigation and report. Vic might be disgusted by that, but he was also relieved. He didn't want this cop or any of his buddies in blue poking around any further. Vic especially didn't want them nosing into the relationship between Tooley Pennebaker and the two children who were supposed to be her niece and nephew.

Vic had already figured out that Katherine had been trying to get a message across to him before about the racial improbability of that aunt-offspring pairing. Of course, there were a number of possible explanations, intermarriage or adoption to name two. Katherine's raised eyebrows when she mentioned Tooley and the kids suggested to Vic that the story might be different than either of those. He also had the feeling that this issue, as well as a couple of others, made it all the more crucial that they find Coyote Bellaway, and find him fast.

COYOTE WATCHED the whole scene from the top of the building across the street from Tooley's apartment. He'd even been up there, crouched down behind the short wall that bordered the roof, long enough to see the big man from the alleyway the other night—the one who'd chased Coyote with a gun—drive up in a black car and go inside Tooley's building. A half hour or so later, the man came out and drove away. Coyote snuck down to the street after that, crept across Ten Broeck and let himself into the apartment. He'd had his own key ever since he and Sprite started calling the place home almost a year ago. It looked more like a junk heap than anybody's home now. Coyote tried to keep the tears from sliding down his face. They slid down anyway. This was all his fault. All Tooley's stuff had been tossed around because of him.

Coyote was sniffling so loud by then that he nearly didn't hear Miss Fairchild and Mr. Maltese outside in time to make it out of the room before she was at the window looking in. Luckily, he'd locked the door behind him after he came in. Coyote knew that they couldn't get into Tooley's place without forcing the lock, which gave him the few minutes he needed to run out the back way and sneak over to his rooftop watching post without being seen. He watched as the policeman came, then as Tooley showed up a little later on and started into the building. After that, he couldn't get himself to watch anymore.

Instead, he busied himself gathering up the things he'd collected in his makeshift lean-to of double-layered cardboard shipping cartons. Some boosted blankets and a stack of newspapers from the recycle pile outside one of the stores on North Pearl Street had kept him pretty warm these past nights. He couldn't drag those boxes and papers away with him now. He'd attract too much attention if he tried to do that. But he did have to get out of here. The police showing up let Coyote know that was how things had to be, no question about it. He'd need to come up with some other way of keeping warm tonight. At the moment, he didn't have a clue what that way would be.

Chapter Eight

On their way back to the center in Vic's car, Katherine shook her head and chuckled at herself. She often felt like shaking him in exasperation when they were alone together. Yet, as soon as she sensed that he was under attack from the police officer, she'd leapt to champion him like a she-bear at a threat to her clan.

"What's so funny?" Vic asked in response to her chuckle.

"Oh, nothing," she replied.

She was correct about that, of course. There wasn't anything the least bit funny about withholding information from the police or about what could happen to her, and maybe to the center as well, if she were to be caught in the act of doing so. Equally lacking in humor was the question that had been niggling at the corner of her brain ever since she'd started across Ten Broeck Street toward Vic with Tooley Pennebaker at her side. Why had that young policeman been treating Vic so rudely?

The officer had been sneering at Vic in the most disrespectful manner she could imagine. She'd been on the defensive on Vic's behalf from the instant she saw the expression on the young policeman's face as he and Vic talked together, or snarled at each other, to be more exact.

The officer behaved quite politely to Katherine once she'd introduced herself. He'd been gracious, even gentle, with Tooley, doing his best to comfort her in her distress over what had happened to her home and belongings. He'd even assured her that the police department would do its level best to find the person who committed the break-in. Katherine suspected that was an empty promise on the policeman's part. Vandalism cases like this one more often than not remain unsolved, but he was trying to make Tooley feel better, anyway. Still, when he turned to talk to Vic, the sneer reappeared on the officer's face, and the challenge was back in his voice. Katherine had to assume some previous history there. So, what was Vic's relationship with the police? And, how did it come to be so antagonistic? She might have put it down to something personal between him and this particular officer if it hadn't been for what happened as she and Vic were walking back to his car.

"Cops," he growled. "They're all alike. I can't stand any of them."

She might have asked her questions about Vic and the police right then, except that a dark frown had descended across his brow. She couldn't remember ever having seen a person look quite so fierce before. She'd decided that wasn't the moment to begin an interrogation, or to talk to him at all for that matter. They drove the few blocks from Tooley Pennebaker's place to the center in silence, other than for that brief exchange over Katherine's chuckle.

She was back in her office pondering the possible reasons for that silence when a knock sounded at her door. For an instant, she thought it might be Vic. Her heart made a little flip, as disconcerting as it was unexpected. Just as unsettling was the stab of disappointment when she glanced up to discover someone definitely not Vic outside her office waiting to be invited in.

The woman at the door was tall, what one might refer to as statuesque. She was also beautiful. She was, at first sight at least, all but perfect, the kind of woman other women look at and say, "Why can't I put myself together like that?"

Katherine realized she was staring and hurried out from behind her desk to open the door.

"May I help you?" she asked.

"I do hope so," the woman replied, in the closest thing to a purr Katherine could ever recall hearing in real life.

"Please, come in and sit down."

Katherine stepped aside and motioned toward the chair facing her desk.

"I'm Lacey Harbison."

"Katherine Fairchild." She extended her hand. Ms. Harbison took hold of only Katherine's fingers and gave them a restrained, ladylike shake.

"I know," she said. "I've been following the accounts of your good work in the *Chronicle*. I am most favorably impressed."

"Thank you."

Katherine had the definite impression she was being charmed, and wondered why.

"It's that work I've come to talk to you about," Ms. Harbison said.

"What aspect of what we do interests you in particular?"

Katherine wished she could stop sounding like an oral report.

"Your Most Needy Cases Fund has struck my husband's fancy, and mine also. We would both like to become involved with the program."

"We welcome community support," Katherine said.

Maybe the Harbisons wanted to make a contribution. Katherine estimated that Mrs. Harbison was wearing the equivalent of several holiday dinners with all the trimmings and some presents besides, and that was without counting the fur coat she had draped over her arm. Katherine widened her own smile to match her visitor's.

"We would like to take two children into our home for the Christmas holiday," Mrs. Harbison said.

Katherine hesitated a moment. "That's a rather unusual request," she said.

"It's for my husband more than myself." Lacey Harbison's voice had gone even softer, as if she were sharing an intimate secret straight from her heart. "He was raised in an orphanage without a true family of his own. Now, as it turns out, I can't have children."

She cast her gaze downward. Her posture, suddenly not so statuesque, suggested the grief caused by her childless state. Katherine wanted to sympathize, but she held back.

"What, specifically, did you have in mind?" she asked.

"We would love to have a boy and girl with us for the holidays, the boy about ten, the girl about eight. Those are the ages the two babies I lost would be if they had lived."

She looked up again, and Katherine could see the pleading in the woman's face. Still, Katherine's heart didn't respond. She was surprised by that. When she heard the sad stories of the families applying for Most Needy Cases Fund grants, she'd been close to tears with each one. Maybe she was prejudiced against Mrs. Harbison because of her expensive clothes. Katherine hoped that wasn't true. She knew from her own experience that material comforts were no protection against pain. Yet she continued to watch Mrs. Harbison from a cool distance.

"Do you have two children who fit that description? A brother and sister would be perfect, if that's possible."

"Tell me again exactly what you and your husband are proposing."

"Well, we have a large home, which we plan to fill with gifts and decorations and maybe even a party for your other children."

As Mrs. Harbison went on, Katherine nodded, but she was only partly listening. Her instincts kept telling her not to believe a word this woman said.

"This is a very interesting idea," she responded finally, just as Mrs. Harbison was launching into a description of the party she and her wealthy husband would throw for their holiday charges and their friends. "Let me go and get the files for our program applicants and see if we have two children who match what you're looking for."

Lacey Harbison paused, her deep red, only slightly glossed lips parted. She was putting together some pieces of her own. Katherine could almost hear her doing it.

"I'll only be a moment," Katherine said.

She was out from behind her desk and through the office door in seconds, smiling widely all the way. She waited till she was just out of sight before she began sprinting down the hallway toward the gym. Vic had changed into gray athletic shorts, a T-shirt and sneakers. She registered the tense, long muscles of his upper thighs and the round curve of his biceps somewhere in her consciousness, but she didn't let herself think about them. Instead, she grabbed his arm and was towing him back toward her office before she could even begin her breathless explanation.

He followed her more readily than she would have thought. They hurried along so fast she barely had time to blurt out her suspicions regarding the too-coincidental similarity between Coyote and Sprite Bellaway and the plan that had been described to her by the woman sitting beside Katherine's desk. Unfortunately, when Katherine and Vic got to her office, it was as empty as she had feared it would be. They made a quick search of the rooms at that end of the building and a dash to the parking lot. But the woman was gone, along with any trace of who she was or why she might be trying to get to the Bellaway children.

"SHE KNOWS who you are and that you're connected with the Bellaway kids."

Vic had been trying to make a point to Katherine for nearly half an hour, but she'd made it clear she wasn't paying much attention.

"I think you should listen to him, Katherine," Megan Moran said.

Vic didn't usually look for support from anyone. Still, he was glad to have it now, especially since he could feel the leash he tried to keep on his temper wearing thinner by the second. Obviously, Katherine Fairchild possessed the ability to aggravate him as much as she did the ability to attract him.

"I've listened to both of you," Katherine said, "and I don't agree. I'm not the target, the children are. Not even both of them, either, just Coyote."

"I've got a bad feeling about this whole deal," Vic said. "Tooley seemed to think Coyote could handle himself out on the street, even though she had no idea where he might be. But I think there's a lot more to what's going on than any of us can even guess at. We could be up against some very bad people here."

"What makes you think so, Vic?" Megan asked.

He shrugged. He didn't like to be an alarmist. He especially didn't like to be seen as one. He knew his statements were reinforcing that image, but Katherine's safety was more important than what anybody might think about him right now.

"Call it a sixth sense," he said, and he could tell Katherine picked up on his reference to their earlier conversation. "I've been out here long enough to sense dangerous situations, too."

"I didn't claim to have a monopoly on the ability."

Katherine sounded pretty aggravated herself.

"Something besides just instinct is bothering me here," he went on. "I got a closer look at Tooley's place than you did, Katherine, and I didn't like it."

"What exactly did you see?" Megan asked.

He searched for the right word. The one that came to mind struck him as too far out, but he decided to pass it on anyway.

"Rage," he said, "and I didn't only see it. I felt it. Whoever tore that place up was angry enough to…"

He hesitated. Once again, he didn't want to cause alarm, except what he was thinking had him most alarmed of all.

"Angry enough to do what, Vic?" Megan pressed.

"Angry enough to kill."

The word echoed in the silence that followed his saying it, as if that one syllable had the power to strike everybody dumb.

"Well, nobody's going to kill me," Katherine said finally, breaking the spell. "In fact, if you want to know what I think, we're all more likely to drown in this flood of melodrama that you've both got gushing over us than at the hand of some evil villain."

Vic opened his mouth to fire back an answer in a tone at least as sarcastic as hers. He clamped his lips together instead. Nothing he really wanted to say to her was either sharp or sarcastic. Only tender words of concern and protection came to mind when he thought about Katherine. He knew she wouldn't care to hear those things from him now, maybe not ever. So he said nothing at all.

KATHERINE COULD HAVE kicked herself for the ludicrous statement she'd thrown at Vic in her office. She disliked deceit above all things, but she'd had a good reason for violating that rule. If he had found out about the arrangement she'd made with Tooley Pennebaker—that she was going to pick Sprite up at school and take her home with her—he'd have tried to stop her. Katherine was certain of that. Yet, her apartment was a much safer place than Tooley's for the little girl right now. Besides, the vandals, whoever they might be, had broken Sprite's bed and sliced her mattress open. Tooley, who had her hands full just figuring out what to do about the mess that had been made of her life, was very happy to have Katherine take over where Sprite was concerned.

Katherine tried not to think about how the stuffing from the child's mattress had been ripped out in huge chunks or about the amount of physical force and determination it must have taken to do that. Most of all, she didn't think about those chunks of stuffing as possible confirmation of Vic's theory of an enraged and lethal, maybe desperate, attacker. Yet, it was precisely that scenario which made Katherine so intent upon acting as Sprite's protector. Katherine had been compelled to watch helplessly while Daniel suffered and struggled and was eventually taken away from her. There'd been nothing at all she could do to stop that. "Make him as comfortable as you can" was all the doctors could say. She'd never felt so totally without personal power in her life.

She wasn't going to let that happen again. She wasn't going to sit idly by while another innocent child suffered. Instead, she had offered her apartment as refuge for Sprite instead of a public facility. Tooley was offered the same alternative for herself but chose to stay at her home and keep watch over the few belongings the intruder had left intact.

Sprite and Katherine would be on their own for the night. Katherine had been on her way to Arbor Hill School to meet Sprite when Vic burst in with Megan in tow, both of them insisting that she should stay at Megan's for a few days, or however long it would take to find out who was after the Bellaway children. If she went along with that arrangement, she'd have to tell them she had volunteered to take Sprite home for the night. Katherine was fairly certain Vic would object to that, and insist on the children's shelter alternative, and that Megan would agree with him. They would have the law on their side as well.

Social Services Department statutes and child-custody codes were clear. Sprite's natural mother was incapacitated. Tooley had no legal guardianship status and, therefore, no legal authority to assign Katherine to take care of the child. Sprite would be considered a temporary ward of the state until a judge could rule on the case. Katherine could petition for guardianship and, with Mrs. Bellaway's approval, might even be awarded custody, at least for a while. Unfortunately, that was a time-consuming process. Katherine wasn't about to wait for the wheels of family-court justice to grind slowly toward a conclusion. She'd done enough waiting with Daniel. Now, she intended to act.

Consequently, she had extricated herself from Vic and Megan's overprotective clutches as soon as that was possible and headed for the Arbor Hill School. Tooley had called to inform the school that Katherine would meet Sprite at the end of the day. The little girl waited in the vice principal's office, her eyes wide and fearful above the small fist with its thumb shoved into her mouth. Katherine understood immediately that being abandoned had to be one of this child's greatest fears. Abandonment had been a recurring experience of her young life. First her father had left, then her mother, now Coyote. Whatever their reasons for going, they had all deserted little Sprite at one time or another. Katherine didn't want her to feel that Tooley was abandoning her as well. Katherine dropped to her knees next to the couch where Sprite was huddled, her frail body almost hidden among the cushions.

"Hello, Sprite. Do you remember me?"

She spoke slowly and kept her voice soft as she smiled with what she hoped the child would recognize as reassurance. Sprite sucked audibly at her thumb, her eyes more round and huge than ever.

"I came here this morning to talk to you and you told me all about your brother, Coyote," Katherine went on.

Sprite stopped sucking and pulled her thumb partway out of her mouth.

"Did Coyote come home yet?" she asked.

"He'll be back soon," Katherine said, not exactly answering.

The thumb shoved in again, and the sucking sound resumed as Sprite heaved a small but deep sigh.

"I have a surprise for you," Katherine said gently. She had to steer the conversation away from Coyote and the other distressing elements of Sprite's situation. "Do you like surprises?"

Sprite hesitated a moment before nodding her head once only.

"I was thinking we could go to my house and have a party, just the two of us. Do you like parties?"

The nod came a little more readily this time.

"What do you like best for a party? Cake or ice cream?"

The thumb came out almost all the way.

"Cake *and* ice cream," Sprite said.

"Cake and ice cream it will be."

Katherine held out her hand. Sprite stared at it for a

moment without moving, but the sucking had been suspended, at least temporarily.

"We'd better hurry up before the cake-and-ice-cream store closes," Katherine said.

Sprite pulled her thumb all the way out of her mouth and slid to the edge of the couch cushion.

"You have a cake-and-ice-cream store?" she asked, sounding a little incredulous and almost happy.

"Yes, I do."

Their conversation continued out of the schoolyard, up and down the aisles of Price Chopper Supermarket, and all the way to Katherine's apartment building on State Street across from Washington Park.

"You've got a snowman place right in front of your house," Sprite exclaimed, indicating the expanse of snow-covered park on the opposite side of State Street from Katherine's wrought-iron railed stoop. "Can we make a snowman tomorrow?"

"After school, we could do just that," Katherine said smiling.

Sprite had already wheedled one agreement out of Katherine to return to Price Chopper, for apple pie this time. Tomorrow was going to be a busy day. Katherine felt her heart bubble with laughter at the thought, in the special way her heart hadn't done since before Daniel got sick. She reminded herself that somewhere between those excursions tomorrow she would have to fit in some shopping for Christmas decorations. She was entertaining herself with the fantasy of teaching Sprite to frost windows with finger paint and spray-on sparkles when Katherine opened her apartment door and snapped on the light.

The scene in her living room was nowhere near as blatant in its carnage as what had been done to Tooley's house. There were no broken furniture pieces or jagged windows, no pile of ravaged belongings on the floor. Yet, what Katherine saw now was as devastating to her as if the entire building had been set on fire and burned to the ground. The damage was slight and subtle, but she noticed it immediately, probably because it had been done to the object her eyes automatically sought out whenever she entered this room.

A small portrait of Daniel, painted in the days before they'd learned of his illness, sat on Katherine's mantelpiece in a stand that matched the portrait frame. The portrait had been slashed, just once diagonally, from corner to corner. Katherine hurried to the fireplace with tears already in her eyes. She loved this portrait. How could anyone have known how much she loved this portrait? She picked up the ruined likeness and pressed it to her heart. She felt the urge to rock and keen just as she had done so many times in the months after Daniel's death.

''What's wrong?'' the small voice asked from the doorway. ''Did you break your picture?''

Katherine turned quickly. She'd forgotten Sprite for a moment. She hung back now from entering the room, her large eyes frightened again. If her thumb hadn't been encased in a mitten, it without doubt would have been in her mouth.

''Nothing's wrong, Sprite,'' Katherine said forcing cheer and her former reassurance back into her voice.

She laid the small portrait facedown on the mantelpiece. That was when she saw the note that had been left there. It was typewritten and read:

We know you are holding out on us about the boy. We will find him anyway. If you want to keep the little girl alive, you'd better not try to stop us.

Katherine grabbed the note and crumpled it in her fist.

"Nothing's wrong at all, Sprite," Katherine fibbed yet again. "But I almost forgot that Mr. Maltese likes cake and ice cream, too. Let's have our party at his house."

Katherine was careful not to latch onto Sprite's hand too hard or too quickly while hustling her back out the door as fast as was possible without startling her.

"Does he have a Christmas tree?" Sprite asked as Katherine glanced furtively up and down State Street before hurrying them down her front steps to the sidewalk.

"What was that, Sprite?"

"Does Mr. Mowtese have a Christmas tree?"

"I don't know," Katherine said, her mind far away from thoughts of the holiday decorations. She was too concerned with keeping Sprite safe.

Chapter Nine

Vic was startled by the flurry of knocks at the door of his restored, nineteenth-century row house on Livingston Avenue. Several sharp, persistent raps in quick succession were followed by just as insistent pressure on the doorbell. Someone really wanted to get in. His immediate impression was of a person in trouble, maybe a kid from the center. This wouldn't be the only time one of them had shown up here with a crisis on his hands. That thought set Vic moving fast into the front entryway. His next thought stopped him in his tracks. Most of all, this assault on his door sounded desperate, and desperate people can be dangerous. Vic had learned that lesson long ago.

He hurried to the small, three-drawer stand in the hallway. He pulled out the bottom drawer and snapped open a compartment at the back. No one but Vic knew it was there. This hidden niche, a practical departure from the original design, was an example of his talent with tools and wood.

The object he pulled out of that secret space cast off a reflection of the light from the living room. He moved cautiously along his entryway wall, carrying the cold gleam of steel in his hand. A gun was a necessity for someone with his history. Still, he had never liked guns and couldn't imagine that he ever would.

He thought he could hear his name being called from the other side of the door, but he couldn't be sure. He'd bought that sturdy door at the demolition sale of an eighteenth-century farmhouse near Coeymans, and had planed it down to fit his doorjamb like a hand in a glove. Not much seeped through that tight framing. Besides, a storm had blown up in the past hour, gusting snow in front of a howling wind. He usually liked that sound. Right now, though, he would have liked this storm to quiet down enough to let him listen for clues to the identity of his visitor—or visitors.

Vic settled the grip of the gun firmly into the palm of his hand. The barrage at his door began again. He reached for the doorknob. On a silent count of three, he took a deep breath, tripped the latch on the door and pulled it open. He kept the door in front of him like a shield and his pistol poised. Still, he was all but knocked over as the door was shoved open and someone—or some*thing*—rushed through into the hallway with a gust of wind-swirled snow in its wake.

"Stop where you are," Vic commanded. "Put your hands above your head right now, or I'll shoot."

Everything in him prayed shooting wouldn't be necessary. Everything in him had also been expecting for years that a moment like this would come someday. Then he heard what sounded like a child's small whimper.

"Please, mister, don't shoot us," it said.

"Vic, it's Katherine."

Her voice was so shaky he barely recognized it. His left hand had been halfway to the light switch when she spoke. He flipped that switch now. The soft light from an overhead globe fell on the snow-covered bulk of Katherine in her long, dark coat. A small child peered out from behind her. The large, terrified eyes told him at once that the child was Sprite Bellaway. Those eyes were staring straight at the firearm Vic still held suspended in midair. He dropped the gun instantly to his side, snapping the safety on as he did.

"Katherine, what are you doing here?" was all he could think of to say.

"Sprite and I thought we'd come over and see if you've put up your Christmas tree yet."

She followed that bewildering statement by glancing pointedly down at the little girl then back toward Vic. It was then that he realized Katherine's eyes were almost as big as the child's and that they were filled with the same fear. That realization brought his fuzzy thoughts into perfect focus in a flash, and he recognized the Christmas-tree story as a cover-up to keep Sprite from guessing what was really going on. Vic wanted more than anything in the world to find that out himself, but he knew he had to go along with the cover story, at least for now.

"I put it up last weekend," he said.

If it hadn't been for the fact that he was pretty sure something very unfunny was happening here, he would have laughed at the expression on Katherine's face, momentarily changing from terror to amazement. Obviously, she hadn't expected to hear he had a Christmas tree. Her look told him she wouldn't have been any more amazed if he'd said this was the three bears' cottage and they were all eating oatmeal in the kitchen.

"Let's go in the living room and take a look," he said, stepping toward the woman and child.

"Don't kill us," Sprite wailed and ducked behind Katherine.

"I wouldn't hurt you. I promise."

Vic took a step forward, but Sprite did not emerge. Katherine nodded in the direction of Vic's right hand. He was still holding the gun.

"This old thing?" he said, making his voice sound light

and cheerful even though he was feeling like the biggest jerk in the universe. "I was just playing a joke with Katherine. This old thing couldn't hurt a fly."

Vic hated lying to kids, especially since that was what had been done to him the whole time he was growing up. He'd kissed his family goodbye because of it, and other things. Consequently, there was hardly anything he disliked doing more. Katherine's disapproving expression gave him no other choice right now. There was little he wouldn't do to erase that veil of disapproval from her usually bright, blue-gray eyes.

Vic moved toward the hallway stand where he kept the gun. He was vaguely aware that his own face must be wearing a fairly goofy expression as he tried to portray himself as harmless to Sprite, who was now peeking out with one eye from behind Katherine. He was reaching for the drawer with the hidden niche when he hesitated. Nobody in the world other than himself knew about that compartment. He kept it secret for safety reasons, other people's safety and his own. He glanced at Katherine, whose eyes held questions now as well as disapproval. He told himself he'd be a fool not to trust those eyes, that hid so little of what she was thinking and feeling. Still…

"Let's go into the living room and see that Christmas tree," he said.

Vic slipped the gun into the back waistband of his jeans and pulled his sweater down to cover the weapon. He knew Katherine was watching his movements with suspicion, but the caution he'd learned from years of being a Maltese told him he had to remain secretive. Meanwhile, Katherine and Sprite had begun to look overly warm in their snow-soggy clothes.

"Let me help you," he said and stepped toward the two of them where they still stood in his hallway.

Katherine backed hastily away, and the obvious rejection of that stung his heart as surely as if she had struck him across the face.

"I don't think she's ready for that," Katherine said, looking down at Sprite.

Vic had a feeling Katherine was also talking about herself.

"Okay," he said. "Let's go into the living room, then. The two of you should get out of those wet things."

That apparently grabbed Katherine's attention because she began walking toward the archway into Vic's living room. She moved awkwardly with Sprite still attached to her coattail, but Vic didn't try to help this time. The memory of Katherine's rejection kept him at a distance as much as any practical consideration of encouraging Sprite's cooperation could ever have done.

"You do have a Christmas tree!" Sprite exclaimed. An instant later, she was darting toward the tall, green hemlock in the bay window of Vic's living room.

"She seems to have gotten over her fear," he said.

He always marvelled at the way kids could jump from one moment to the next sometimes, as if what came before had never happened at all.

"Yes, she's apparently forgotten all about it."

Katherine's tone made it clear that she hadn't done the same. She stared at him as if she might be able to see straight through his body to the gun in his waistband. He guessed she might have more questions about that gun than he cared to answer.

"I'll take your coat and hang it up to dry," he said, reaching out a hand without stepping any closer to her. He didn't want to cause her to back off from him again. "Give me Sprite's coat, too."

Katherine hesitated a moment before unbuttoning her

coat and handing it over to him, all without coming any closer to him. Instead, she went to Sprite, who was touching one of the metallic glass balls Vic had hung on the tree and staring at the distorted image of herself in its shiny gold surface with obvious delight.

"I'm going to take your coat off now," Katherine said in a calm, careful voice as if she might be afraid of startling Sprite with anything more loud or sudden.

"Okay," Sprite answered and unzipped her jacket without taking her eyes off the ornament.

"I think she likes the tree," Vic said.

Katherine turned and handed him the damp garment. "Children react so strongly to new experiences."

She didn't have to speak sharply for Vic to hear the pointedness of her comment. He decided not to respond. He was in a no-win position here and he knew it. Anything he said was just as likely to dig him deeper in as it was to help him out. He draped Sprite's jacket over his arm on top of Katherine's coat and turned to leave the room.

"Are you going away?" Sprite asked, diverting her attention from the tree.

A little of the whine that he'd heard before had crept back into her voice and some of the fear was returning to her eyes. She might have forgotten the gun he'd held a few moments ago, but Vic would guess she hadn't forgotten how scared she was in general, scared enough to want as many protective adults around her at all times as she could get.

"I'll be right back, sweetheart," he said. "I'm just going to hang your coats up where they can dry."

"Good," Sprite said, apparently reassured, and returned her attention to the tree.

The gentleness of his words to the child had inspired a similar softening in the way Katherine was looking at him.

His heart lightened at the sight. He hurried out of the room before she could pick up on the relief he was feeling. His reactions to her were way too extreme, considering the brief time they'd known each other. He knew, from long-ago sad experience, that wearing your heart on your sleeve is a good way to get shot down.

He took the coats to the small first-floor bathroom, picking up two hangers from the hall closet on the way. He hung the coats on the shower bar and smoothed out the damp material of both. Sprite's jacket was too lightweight for winter wear. Vic remembered noticing the same thing about Coyote's clothing that morning. Now, he was out in the storm somewhere. Vic would have liked to quiz Sprite for any information she might have on her brother's whereabouts, but she probably didn't trust Vic enough for that kind of questioning just yet. The incident with the gun had set him back several paces in the trustworthiness department, which reminded him of his intention to get that particular item back into its hiding place ASAP. He was on his way to the hallway stand when Katherine stepped through the archway from the living room.

"Did you find a warm place to hang our things?" she asked.

"Yes, I did." He examined her face and saw the flicker of fear that remained in her eyes. He lowered his voice and asked, "What's going on? What brought you and Sprite here at this time of night?"

From what he had figured out about Katherine so far, she didn't come across as the kind of person who would show up at somebody's door like this without calling first. What *was* going on with her? That question resonated in Vic's mind as she glanced furtively back toward Sprite before answering.

"Somebody broke into my apartment," she said in a near whisper.

"Broke in?"

Katherine raised her finger quickly to her lips and shushed him. She glanced back again at Sprite who had sat herself down in front of the tree and was playing with Vic's miniature train set, one of the few mementos he'd been able to bear to keep from his childhood.

"She's not paying any attention to us," he said. His own voice dropped to a whisper now. "Tell me what happened at your apartment."

"I don't know," she said, just a little tremulously. She'd managed to get rid of that tremor by the time she spoke again. "All I know is that somebody came into my home and damaged something I value very much."

"What was that?"

Vic longed to cross the space between them in a single, eager stride and take her in his arms, but he needed to know what she was talking about even more.

"They slashed a small portrait I keep on my mantelpiece."

She paused. Vic could see on her face the effort she was making to calm and control herself. He almost did take her in his arms then.

"It was a portrait of Daniel," she whispered before he could move toward her.

Vic stayed where he was. The slope of her shoulders and the angle of her neck as she clutched her hands in front of her and stared down at them told him she didn't want to be touched right now. She needed to be self-contained, at least for the moment, inside the grief he could feel emanating from her. He respected that need while his own heart ached for her pain. He waited for her to lift her head slowly to look at him again before he spoke.

"Do you have any idea who might have done such a thing?"

Vic asked that so gently he wondered, when she didn't respond right away, if maybe she hadn't heard him. Then, she reached into the pocket of the skirt he recognized to be the same one she'd had on all day.

"They left this."

She handed him a piece of paper that had been crumpled into a ball. He smoothed it out and read the typewritten warning.

"This is about the kids," he said. "Coyote and Sprite."

They both glanced over at Sprite this time. She was lifting the toy-train cars one by one from the red felt skirt beneath Vic's tree and setting them up again, one after the other, in a line on the carpet. She was obviously way too engrossed to have noticed the mention of her name or her brother's.

"I think it has something to do with the woman who came to my office today," Katherine whispered after she'd turned her attention back to Vic. "Lacey Harbison."

Vic nodded agreement. "So, you're finally tying her into the melodrama."

To his surprise, Katherine flushed at this reminder of the statement she'd made in her office.

"Well," he continued, "I agree with you. I think she and whoever she's mixed up with are after Coyote and Sprite for some reason. We have to find out what that reason is."

Vic stepped forward, but Katherine took his arm.

"What we have to do first is get some food into Sprite," Katherine said. "She hasn't eaten since lunchtime at school. She needs nourishment."

Vic looked at the small, pale child in his living room and then back at Katherine, who was almost as thin.

"I'd guess you could use a good meal yourself."

Katherine shrugged. "Maybe we could send out for pizza or Chinese food."

Vic raised his hand in protest. "We don't do takeout in this house," he said.

He took Katherine by the arm before she could answer and led her back into the living room.

"Come with me, ladies," he said, extending his free hand to Sprite. "You have a very special treat in store."

Chapter Ten

This had been a day of shocks and bewilderment for Katherine. She might have thought there was nothing left in the world to surprise her at the moment. At least, she might have considered herself way too exhausted by it all to master so much as a show of mild curiosity. Yet, when she burst through Vic Maltese's front door and then had a moment to calm down a bit, what she found there could hardly have been less expected.

She'd seen Vic's hot car and his wardrobe. She'd listened to his wisecracks and observed his edge of street savvy and impatience. None of that had prepared her for the hearth crackling in his living room or the Middle Eastern wool-weave carpets on polished fir flooring as warm in its luster as the milk-glass sconces on his walls. Cut-velvet drapes in pale olive were tied back by braided cords to reveal a veil of snow outside as it swirled in the illumination of the two carriage lamps on wrought-iron posts, one at each side of the half dozen steps leading up to Vic's door.

She hadn't really registered those lamps on her way up the steps except to say a quick prayer of thanks for the light that made his house number visible through the storm and darkness. She'd been in a state of barely controlled panic at the time, unable to shake the fear that whoever had invaded her apartment might have been lying in wait for her outside and could have followed her here. She'd had to force her foot to lighten on the gas pedal, no matter how much she wanted to propel her Cherokee across town like a rocket to what she hoped would be safe refuge with Vic. Even four-wheel drive might not have been equal to avoiding a disastrous skid if she accelerated too fast in this weather.

So, she had endured the cautious but maddeningly slow journey from State Street to Livingston Avenue. About halfway between the two, it occurred to her that he might not be at home. Consequently, his carriage lamps had shone like rays of hope for her. Then she'd knocked on the door— and knocked and knocked and knocked. She told herself he had to be inside, because she had no idea what to do if he wasn't. So she'd knocked until the door flew open at last.

Now here she was in the most unanticipated circumstances she could imagine. Vic had sat her down in a cushioned spindle rocker with an afghan tucked under her chin. They were in his kitchen on the basement level of his house. A green-painted cast-iron woodstove gave off a cozy heat. Vic had settled Sprite beneath a quilt among the pillows of a window seat with heavy hemp-cloth curtains drawn behind her to shut out even the hint of a draft. The child's eyelids were already almost closed despite her obvious struggles to keep them open. With a pang of too-sharp memory, Katherine could see Daniel doing the same thing, fighting against sleep for fear of missing so much as five minutes of whatever might happen next.

"Are you all right?" Vic asked.

He'd stopped stirring the pot on the restaurant-sized range.

"I'm fine," she said, but she could tell by the look on

his face that he didn't believe her. She needed to throw him off this track before he asked her more questions she couldn't bear to answer right now. "I'm just feeling a little overwhelmed by..."

"By what?"

There was his impatience again. She lifted her arm from the folds of the afghan and made a sweeping gesture to indicate the room.

"All of this," she said, amazed by how light her hand felt at the end of her arm, as if it might fly straight off if she were to swing it too hard.

Vic laughed and turned back to his stirring.

"What did you think? That I'd live in a flophouse?"

Katherine didn't answer. She couldn't tell him she'd been thinking something very much along those lines.

"I didn't expect you to have a Christmas tree."

"Oh, that." He chuckled. "I have an open house for the kids from the center a couple of days before Christmas. I put up the tree for that."

"You wouldn't do it otherwise?" Something in his tone made her ask that.

"Probably not."

"I see." This time something in his tone made her say no more, at least not on that subject. "What are you cooking?"

"Sauce and pasta," he said and chuckled again. "I know what a cliché that is. The guy whose one dish is spaghetti."

"Some clichés are nice."

Katherine heard the wooziness in her voice. She was beginning to feel like Sprite, as if she had to struggle to stay awake.

"For your information, I cook lots of things," Vic said.

Katherine managed a sleepy smile. "For your information, I'll bet you do,'' she whispered before her voice trailed off.

The comfort of the rocker and the warmth of the wood-stove had already transported her too far down the road toward dreams for her to be surprised by much of anything any longer.

VIC CARRIED SPRITE upstairs first. He'd turned the burner off under the sauce pot and set the drained pasta aside before making the climb. He settled Sprite on the bed in the guest room on his second floor and covered her carefully. She hardly stirred through all of that, or when he tucked his long-saved teddy bear into the curve of her arm. He left the door ajar and a light on in the hallway outside the guest room. He was a veteran of enough haunted nights to be aware of the need to keep the darkness at bay.

He went back down the two flights of stairs at the rear of the house to the kitchen. What he saw there caused him to come to a dead stop, and not just because he didn't want to disturb Katherine's sleep.

Light from the fading flames of the woodstove threw shadows across her face, across the pale skin of her brow and the long lashes against her cheek. Her full lips were parted just slightly. The urge to kiss them thrilled through Vic like an earthquake tremoring straight to his loins. God, she was beautiful. And so still that, before he could think how nonsensical it was, he leaned closer to hear above the anxious beating of his own heart if she might have stopped breathing. He noticed the flush of her cheeks then, too high, too red even for her.

This had been the kind of overwrought day that might put anybody under the weather. Speaking of weather, she'd been out running around in a snowstorm, too. Working at a place like the center meant being exposed to the virus germs kids carry with them, especially during the winter, as readily as they carry a basketball. Being adolescents and resilient, they most likely wouldn't come down with anything more serious than a twenty-four-hour bug. An adult, on the other hand, could be more susceptible, particularly one who pushed herself as hard as Katherine did and looked so much like she needed a good, hearty meal.

He touched her forehead with the back of his hand. Her skin was moist and warm but not hot enough to be feverish. Vic sighed with relief. He didn't want her to be sick. He was amazed at how strongly he didn't want anything bad, or even a little uncomfortable, to happen to her. He was resisting the temptation, which felt more like a deep need than an impulse, to caress her cheek, when her hand crept out from beneath the afghan and she clasped his wrist. The movement was unhurried and delicate, like the flicker of firelight on her cheek. Still, he couldn't have been more startled if she'd struck him in the face.

Her lips moved. Vic couldn't understand her murmur.

He leaned closer. "What did you say?" he asked.

This time, when she spoke, he could make out the words but couldn't believe what he heard.

"Take me to bed," she whispered.

Her voice was dreamy, and her face remained soft with slumber. Her eyes didn't open, and her lips had barely moved. Surely she was talking in her sleep, maybe referring to an almost subconscious desire to rest somewhere more comfortable than a rocking chair. Nonetheless, her words seared Vic's nerves all the way to the white-hot center of himself that had lain all but dormant for quite some time. In fact, at the moment, he wouldn't have been able to remember when he was last stirred so powerfully if his life depended on it. All he knew was that taking her to bed was exactly what he longed to do.

Vic bent down and slipped his arms beneath Katherine's body, one arm under the crook of her knees, the other across her back just below her shoulders. He lifted her out of the chair with the afghan still tucked around her. She was as light as he'd expected her to be. The scent of her hair and skin, heightened by the warmth of the fire, filled his head with such sweetness that for a moment he thought he would have to sit down himself until the intensity of that first wave of fragrance had passed.

"Get a grip on yourself," Vic told himself forcefully.

He stiffened his spine along with his resolve and concentrated on taking even, gradual steps toward the front of the house. With what was left of his sensible mind, he figured he'd carry Katherine up the front stairs. This way, he could avoid passing Sprite's room and maybe waking her. He didn't like to think that he had ulterior motives for not wanting a conscious child in the vicinity. Still, he was a man, and the most male parts of him were very aware of that right now.

His bedroom was the only other one on this floor. Vic carried Katherine through the doorway he'd ripped off and replaced again with his own hands. This was his place, and he'd imagined more than once what it would be like to bring a woman here who was equally his. That wasn't the case now, and he knew it. He had no claims on Katherine Fairchild. She was only here because she'd been scared out of her wits by what she found in her apartment.

The memory of that ruthless vandalism and the heartbreak over it he'd seen in Katherine's eyes brought Vic at least partway back to himself and what was really going on here tonight. He carried Katherine to the bed and put her down there gently, just as he'd done with Sprite in the room down the hall at the other side of the master bathroom. He pulled his arms free from beneath Katherine's body and straightened up to reach for the extra blanket folded across the foot of the bed. He draped the blanket over Katherine and was tucking the satin-trimmed edge under her chin when she took him by surprise yet again, as she'd done downstairs in the kitchen.

Now, her arms were suddenly around his neck, disengaged from the blanket and the afghan before his disbelieving mind could grasp what was happening. She pulled him toward her, and it never occurred to him to resist. She lifted her face toward his with her eyes still closed. Their mouths found each other instinctively, even in the dim light.

Her lips were soft and warm and still gently parted, as they had been in sleep downstairs by the stove. Was she sleeping now? Vic couldn't think clearly enough to figure that out, and he didn't really care. He wrapped his arms around the bundle of her, blankets and all, and lowered himself over her. She clung to him, and they pressed as closely together as the layers of wool between them would allow.

He could taste her lips and feel them, full and willing, beneath his, but he hesitated. He didn't crush her mouth as his most basic urges were commanding him to do. He didn't thrust his tongue between her lips though he ached to take possession of first her mouth then all of her. Something held him back, like a No Trespassing sign or an invisible bar at the door. Then, she parted her lips and tightened her arms around his neck.

Vic's senses received her message even before his mind could register its meaning. He groaned deep in his throat and let his tongue be welcomed by hers. They tasted each other and breathed each other in. Her hunger was as great as his. He could feel it. He wanted to cry out with a bellow from the bottom of his lungs. Instead, he covered Katherine's mouth ever more devouringly with his and marvelled at how she responded with an eagerness as primal as his own. She was definitely awake now.

Vic tore at the tangle of blanket and afghan between them. He felt her hand grappling as well, helping him clear away the barriers separating them from each other. The blanket fell to the floor, but the afghan was more difficult to unwind from her body. Still, he had just begun to allow himself the fantasy of her silken skin beneath his fingers when a scream split the night and sliced through their passion with as brutal a cut as any cleaver could have made.

KATHERINE RUSHED down the hall behind Vic. The aura of what had just happened between them back there on the bed clung to her as tenaciously as the afghan, which had trailed with her all the way to the door till she kicked it aside before dashing into the hall. She pushed away the image of herself in Vic's arms as well. She'd have to deal with that later. Sprite was screaming. For the moment, nothing else could matter more than getting to her side. Katherine squeezed past Vic through the doorway at the end of the hall. The room was suddenly flooded with light. Vic had flipped the wall switch. Sprite's scream rose to a thin, high shriek in response to the startling brightness.

"Turn that off," Katherine snapped.

She'd have to apologize for her tone later on. The light dimmed again, but Sprite's screams didn't diminish either in pitch or intensity. Katherine had reached the bedside, but she didn't take hold of Sprite right away. Instead, she began making soft sounds of comfort and reassurance.

"We're here, Sprite. Everything will be all right now."

Katherine repeated variations on that theme in a cooing monotone she hoped wouldn't surprise or frighten the obviously terrified little girl. She understood that the words were less important than the calming tone in which they were spoken. She sat down slowly and carefully on the edge of the bed. Sprite was lying in a tumble of the same quilt she'd been covered by downstairs. Her face was shadowed in the dimly lit room. She sucked in gasps of air between screams as her small hands flailed in front of her face. Katherine made the first physical contact by touching those hands gently. She continued her murmur of reassurance and hushing sounds.

Sprite kept on flailing but just enough less vehemently for Katherine to detect the change. She let her own hands move with Sprite's while, at the same time, encouraging them toward quiet. The child's screams had begun to subside. Katherine thought about turning on the bedside lamp but decided against it. Any sudden change wouldn't be wise just yet. Meanwhile, Sprite's screaming had started to shape itself into words. Katherine strained to understand, but the child was still too tightly in the grip of hysteria to do anything other than gasp out incomprehensible syllables. Katherine continued her gentle monologue a few moments longer before pressing for more.

"Try to take a deep breath, Sprite," she said, just above a whisper. "Breathe with me. Then we'll talk."

Katherine took slow, deliberate, exaggerated breaths and moved one hand to Sprite's back and stroked up and down there. Katherine kept those strokes even and circling in a hypnotic rhythm. Sprite responded slowly, but her sobs were quieter now. They grew more so by the minute under Katherine's patient ministrations. At last she thought it might be all right to attempt a more complicated communication.

"You can tell me whatever you want to," she said.

Sprite sniffled and shuddered. Her large eyes were wide open, catching the faint glimmer of light from the hallway.

She said something but shoved her thumb into her mouth at the same time so the words were lost. Katherine took hold of Sprite's hand and eased it away from her mouth.

"I couldn't understand you," Katherine said. "Could you please tell me that again?"

The shadow deepened across Sprite's face so her eyes were no longer visible. Katherine realized that Vic had stepped closer, into the path of light from the door. He was probably trying to hear what Sprite had to say. Katherine thought about asking him to back off in case the child might be intimidated by his size. She would have done just that if Sprite hadn't breathed a small sigh right then and started to talk.

"My brother," she said.

"What about Coyote?" Katherine asked, being very careful not to let her eagerness to know the answer creep into her soothing voice.

"He's up on his roof," Sprite said. As her gasping slowed, her words took on a plaintive, pleading tone.

"He's on a roof?" Katherine encouraged. "What's he doing there?"

Sprite shuddered. "He's freezed into a snowman. I have to help him get down."

She collapsed against Katherine and began to sob. Katherine embraced the little girl's thin shoulders. They swayed together in a rocking motion. Katherine could feel Vic hovering nearby. She could almost hear the questions he must be dying to ask, and Vic wasn't known to be a patient man. However, he would have to be patient now, for as long as it took this precious, frightened child to feel safe enough to speak again.

Chapter Eleven

Vic still had the gun tucked in the back of his waistband. Ordinarily, he would have hated walking heavy, like the tough kids at the center called it, but not tonight. Tonight the pressure of metal against the small of his back felt as if he'd brought a friend along. Vic was grateful for the presence of that friend, because this wasn't a night to be out on your own, even for him, especially not where he was going.

The snow danced and blew, fine snow that silted into his face like wet sand and made him blink his eyes to see. He'd parked the Trans Am near Clinton Avenue at what he hoped would be an inconspicuous end of the block. This weather would probably keep the car heisters at bay, and he did have a steering-wheel bar lock and a guard on the column. Still, it would be just his luck to end up on the victim list of the one really dedicated auto thief in the neighborhood.

He was back on Tooley Pennebaker's street again, across from her building where Sprite's terrified revelations had sent him. She claimed that her brother, Coyote, had a hiding place on the roof of one of the buildings on the other side of the street from Tooley's. Sprite had described where it was, but in a blizzard at night with only streetlamp light to go by, Vic wasn't exactly sure which building was which.

One positive thing could be said about this weather. It made Ten Broeck Street, this block anyway, look better than its usual shabby self. The pale snow brushed everything clean, like a cityscape Christmas card, with pools of soft light here and there from the pole lamps that were still in working order. The blowing snow played other tricks on the eyes, too, creating the illusion of dark, moving shapes, almost visible in the whirling cloud of flakes. He skirted around those shapes more than once before telling himself they were about as real as the phantoms in Sprite's nightmares.

That thought didn't play well with his more sensible side. Even as he walked toward the alley of what he figured had to be the right building, Vic considered exactly what he was doing. He'd come out here to wander through what was basically a very dangerous part of town, even for him, in the middle of a snowstorm. He'd done that on the strength of the word of a sleepy little girl who suffered from night terrors. This could be the wildest of all wild-goose chases, and Vic had begun to feel like the goose.

Sprite said Coyote told her he got into the building through an unlocked window off the alleyway. Front doors would be kept bolted tight at night in this neighborhood if anybody in the building had any sense. A kid who'd clocked as many hours of street time as Coyote would know that. He probably managed to sneak in that front way once during the daytime then rigged the basement window so nobody could tell it was no longer locked. Vic understood about such tactics. He'd used them more than once himself when he was younger. He hadn't been as young as Coyote then, but still too much of a kid to be on his own.

One of the things Vic had learned back in those days

was to keep his behind out of alleyways after sundown. He peered down this one now. All he could see was a dark tunnel between two dark buildings. Every breath of city smarts Vic had in him said he shouldn't go in there. But— what if Sprite knew what she was talking about? What if Coyote was huddled up on top of one of these roofs? He could be frozen by now, even in the makeshift shelter she seemed to think he'd put up for himself. Vic pulled the yellow, hard-rubber flashlight from his jacket pocket and stepped into the alley.

The flashlight was even less use than he'd expected, hitting the snow that fell from the space of sky between the buildings and turning it to gray fog. He aimed the beam at the ground ahead of him in the hope he would be lucky enough to pick out any obstacles before he tripped over them. He switched the light toward the building wall on his right every now and then to check the location of the windows. He tried each one as he came to it, rattling the frame and checking the ledge for shims Coyote might have stuck in to keep the bottom of the window ajar.

Vic kept an eye on the alleyway in both directions, too. He didn't care to be snuck up on, and this flashlight he was holding made him more visible than he was comfortable with. His rattling had produced no movement at all from the first three windows. He was beginning to think his doubts about Sprite's claims were right. Why would a boy Coyote's age tell his kid sister about his secret hiding place, anyway? This was a jerk's journey Vic was on, and he knew it. He flicked off the flashlight. He'd pretty much decided to get out of here before trouble found him. He gave the next to the last window a halfhearted shove all the same, and nearly fell over when it angled inward a few inches. A harder push and the opening was wide enough for a skinny kid to get through. Vic wasn't quite so neat a fit. He had to crouch down and go in feetfirst, which put him in a much more vulnerable position than he liked. He had to ease his shoulders through one at a time. He told himself that when he left this place he was going out the front door.

A short drop and he was on the basement floor with the flashlight snapped instantly on and beaming around into every nook and cranny among the boxes and other odd stuff that gets left in the cellar of an apartment building. Vic was fully aware that somebody besides Sprite could know about the open window and be using this place to flop in. Folks that desperate tended not to like being stumbled upon and generally carried some kind of weapon to use against intruders. Vic reached behind him for the handle of his own weapon as the light beam made its sweep. Fortunately, he didn't see anybody. He was alone down here.

He exhaled harshly. He didn't mind admitting that this scene had his nerves on the edge for sure. The light found the exit door, and he hurried toward it. He was going to get this over with and be on his way back home as fast as he could manage it. The thought of home reminded him of Katherine waiting there, and little Sprite with her eyes huge and round from fear for her brother. Vic pushed the exit door open onto the stairwell from the basement. Nothing on the stairs but a couple of crumpled candy wrappers. This was the kind of private corner kids sought out as an escape from apartments crowded with family, but there was nobody here now. Vic pressed on. The image in his head of Sprite's eyes gave him no other choice.

He climbed all five flights of stairs from the basement to the top floor without incident. If anybody in any of the apartments along the way heard him passing or saw the flicker of his flashlight in the dim halls, they gave no sign. A stealthy presence outside the door late at night in a neighborhood like this one wasn't likely to invite open curiosity. More often than not, anyone who knew Vic was out here would keep quiet till he passed by, then slip another chain or bolt or police lock into place with a prayer that, like the dark angel, he'd just keep on moving. Nobody'd call the cops, either. That kind of thing could bring reprisals, and all most people in this neighborhood wanted was to be left alone.

Vic was wishing for the same thing, and wasn't disappointed all the way up those five flights of stairs and through the heavy fire door at the top of the additional flight to the roof. He found a brick in the corner just inside that door and propped it open. He figured somebody had left the brick for just that purpose. This could be Coyote's secret place after all. He could be up here right now. Vic hurried out onto the roof, almost forgetting to flash the light in front of him before he did.

The cold was much more biting up here than it had been at ground level. The wind was stronger, too, whipping wet snow into his eyes and down his collar. The flashlight beam was all but useless against this wall of snow. Vic kept it trained downward anyway. The last thing he needed was to come upon the edge of the roof by surprise. The walls atop these buildings tended to be short enough to fall over, especially for a guy his height on a night like this.

Vic kept as close as he could to what he guessed was the center of the roof, but he knew how easy it could be to get disoriented and miscalculate his location under these conditions. He swept the light beam back and forth across what he could make out of the roof floor, which wasn't much. He might have missed the white-covered topple of cardboard slabs altogether if his boot hadn't hit the slick surface of one of them beneath the snow and almost sent him sprawling. He trained the light more closely on the

mound of cardboard pieces. It was high enough for someone to be hiding under, especially a pint-sized kid.

"Coyote, are you in there?" Vic called out.

The sound of his voice was carried away so quickly by
the wind that he barely heard his own words. He dropped
to one knee and began scraping snow away, pulling lengths
of cardboard clear and tossing them aside. All the while he
searched, he was praying silently. Much as he wanted to
find Coyote, he didn't care to have that discovery happen
here and now. This rooftop was way too cold for a kid in
a flimsy jacket, even under all this cardboard. Vic flashed
the light over each layer as he uncovered it, all the way
down to the floor of the roof, which had been kept sur-
prisingly dry by the heap of dismantled cartons on top of
it.

Coyote wasn't here. Vic searched on all the same, scanning the floor and the crevices between the remaining
pieces of cardboard for any evidence that Coyote had in
fact been here at all. Vic found what he was looking for in
a corner of the tumbled structure, not far from the roof wall.
The envelope was crumpled and much the worse for wear,
and the paper inside was too. Still, Vic knew right off that
it was Coyote's letter to Katherine and the Most Needy
Cases Fund. Coyote had been here, all right. Now he was
gone, God only knew where. As Vic made his way cautiously back across the rooftop in the wild winter night, he
was saying yet another small prayer and speaking it aloud
this time.

KATHERINE WOKE UP, as always, at quarter to six. She
could feel in every muscle of her body how much she
needed to rest longer. She'd never been able to lie around
in bed in the morning, except once in a while on Saturday.
She was fairly sure this wasn't Saturday, so she threw off

the covers and sat up. She hadn't fully opened her eyes till her fingers touched the satin hem of the blanket. Her duvet cover was made of cotton, not satin. She stared down at the fabric in her hand by the light of the small lamp on the bedside table. Instead of blue flowers on an off-white background, the blanket she held was a deep-burgundy-colored wool. She gripped the satin trim for an instant then let it go. Where was she?

In an uncomfortable moment of confusion she looked around at a room she'd never seen before—a tall cherry-wood dresser, the wall behind it papered in wide vertical stripes of yellow with white bands edged in burgundy-red between the yellow panels. A pleasant room—a man's room! A flat brush on top of the dresser. A pair of black boots under the stool next to the dresser. The boots brought it all back to her. Vic. Vic Maltese. She was in his house. She'd run here last night, after...

Memory of the ruined painting of Daniel stabbed Katherine's heart with a slash as sharp as the one that had slit the canvas. It felt like having that sweet little boy cut out of her life all over again. How could they do that? she asked herself, just as she had last night. No answer came this morning either, only the thought of yet another child. Sprite Bellaway. Sprite had been with her last night. Sprite was the reason Katherine ran here for safety and protection. Otherwise, she would have stood her ground, dared the intruder to come at her one more time, the way she would have liked to dare Daniel's disease to try taking her on instead of a frail boy. But she had to get little Sprite out of there, so they ran.

Katherine recalled the screams that had woken her the night before. She had spent a long time with Sprite in an attempt to settle her down. Finally, the child had fallen asleep again. Exhausted, Katherine had stumbled back to

Vic's bedroom and the warmth of his double bed. Vaguely, she recalled an image of Vic in that bed with her, but she shoved the thought away. It must have been a dream.

Katherine stood up. She had on the same sweater and long skirt she'd worn all day yesterday. The skirt was a mass of creases. She'd have to go home and change. Sprite would need a change of clothes, too. It was a school day. Katherine had reoriented herself enough to the waking world to be certain of that. She headed for the bedroom door. She and Sprite had never made it to the apartment on Ten Broeck Street the evening before as Katherine had planned. She'd have to take the little girl to Tooley Pennebaker's for some clean clothes. An image of the chaos of Tooley's ransacked living room flashed across Katherine's mind. She hoped she'd be able to find what was needed in that mess. She'd have to speak to Tooley about finding another place for Sprite to stay. Obviously, after the destruction of Daniel's photo and the note that had been left beside it, Katherine's apartment was no longer safe for the little girl.

She located Sprite just down the hall in the room past the bathroom. A low-wattage lamp had been left on there as well, and Sprite was sleeping peacefully under a patchwork quilt with a teddy bear clasped in her arms. Katherine was sure they hadn't brought the bear here with them. She eased the toy from Sprite's grip. The small, brown animal had definitely seen years of wear. One black button eye was missing, and the belly stuffing had been pressed flat by what Katherine guessed to be lots of hugging. Suddenly, she knew this was Vic's bear. The thought of tall, tough, leather-clad Vic as a child young and vulnerable enough to cuddle a bear washed over her in a wave so tender she had to hug the stuffed animal to herself for a moment before resting it gently on the pillow next to Sprite's tousled head.

"Come on, sweetheart," Katherine said softly. "Time to get up."

She found their coats and boots in the hallway closet downstairs. Their scarves, hats and mittens had been draped to dry along the banister. Vic must have done that. She'd done almost nothing last night after arriving here except fall asleep. She retrieved their outdoor things from the bathroom and put a hand on Sprite's shoulder to move her into the quiet hallway. Vic must be sleeping in some other room Katherine hadn't yet come upon. Something made her want to get out of here without waking him up, some uneasiness she couldn't quite explain—until she saw him.

They had paused in the hallway to don their coats, and there he was. He'd fallen asleep half sitting, half lying on the couch next to his Christmas tree, which was still lit up with steadily glowing colored bulbs and slow, white flashers that flickered off and on across his face. Katherine remembered that same face very close to hers. The image brought with it a flash of feeling so startling she almost dropped Sprite's hand. Had it not been a dream, as she'd told herself? Had the kiss really happened? Katherine couldn't lie to herself. The memory of Vic's arms around her and how much she'd loved having them there was too intense to be a fantasy. And, with a tiny pang of guilt, she acknowledged that she had initiated the kiss.

Had anything more than that happened between them last night? She couldn't remember, and she was suddenly confused again, just as she'd been when she woke up this morning. This time the feeling frightened her. She recalled Sprite's scream, their mad dash to the bedroom, and what it had interrupted. If the sensation of Vic's kiss came back to her this powerfully, then surely anything beyond that would be even more indelibly imprinted on her senses. Still, she couldn't be absolutely positive. Her clothes had all been on when she woke up, but they were in total disarray. Had Vic used the kiss as an invitation to take things further? He didn't strike her as the type of man who would take advantage of a half-conscious woman. On the other hand, what did she actually know about what type of man he was? Katherine was tempted to dash into his living room, shake him awake and conduct a thorough interrogation on that subject right here and now.

"Are we going to get breakfast?"

Katherine had almost forgotten the child at her side till she heard Sprite's voice, still misty with sleep. She knelt next to Sprite and began buttoning her coat.

"Yes, Sprite, we're going to get breakfast."

The mention of food made Katherine remember dropping the plastic grocery bag on the floor of her living room when she first spotted Daniel's ravaged portrait. She could imagine the mess of melted ice cream there still. There was so much mess around her to clean up now, and melted iced cream was the least of it.

As she adjusted Sprite's scarf more closely around her face, Katherine sighed. She'd figure out something. She always had, except for Daniel. She hadn't been able to figure out a way to make things right for Daniel. She was determined to do better by this child next to her now. Katherine hugged Sprite as tenderly as she'd hugged the teddy bear upstairs. That brought Vic back to mind, and Katherine's questions about what might have happened last night. Just because a guy had a teddy bear in his house, that didn't mean he couldn't be a brute when the opportunity arose. She had no doubt how much she must have looked like an opportunity last night. Had he given her anything to drink? Could she have been drugged as well as sleepy? That kind of thing happened these days.

Katherine helped Sprite with her mittens, knowing she

wasn't helping herself by letting her imagination run away with her. She couldn't help it. She was out of her depth here, far away from the safe, familiar, passionless territory she'd inhabited with Daniel's father. She wasn't accustomed to running off to men's houses in the middle of the night, much less to sleeping there. In fact, running off was what she needed to do right now. She gripped Sprite's hand and was about to make a beeline for the door. She glanced one last time at Vic on the couch to be sure he was still asleep and she would actually be making a clean escape.

That was when she noticed the crumpled sheet of paper on the floor. It lay near the curled fingers of Vic's hand where his arm hung off the couch onto the richly patterned carpet. A moment ago, her eyes hadn't yet adjusted themselves to the dim light from the hall sconces and the flickering bulbs on the tree. She hadn't seen the paper then, or felt the probably nonsensical urge to know what it was. Nothing made sense about this morning, anyway.

"Wait here a minute, Sprite," Katherine whispered. She really didn't want to wake Vic up now. "I'll be right back."

She tiptoed carefully across the carpet to just within reach of the piece of paper. She bent down slowly, without a sound, and picked it up, all the time expecting Vic's eyes to pop open and catch her sneaking around his living room. Fortunately, he kept right on sleeping, his breathing soft and even and unnervingly near as Katherine squinted to examine the paper in her hand. The signature at the bottom of the page had been printed out larger and more boldly than the rest. *Coyote Bellaway.*

Katherine took Coyote's letter with her as she tiptoed out of Vic Maltese's house with Sprite at her side.

Chapter Twelve

"Dressing down and it isn't even Friday?"

Megan looked Katherine over with a wide smile.

"Right," Katherine said.

Down was certainly the word to describe this morning for Katherine. She didn't know whether she was angry or depressed. She did know she was nearly miserable. She couldn't keep Vic Maltese and their kiss—and whatever else they might or might not have shared—from her thoughts.

"I'd like to think this new look means you're lightening up on that serious side of yours."

Megan was talking about the jeans and dark green chenille turtleneck sweater Katherine had on with her rugged-soled hiking boots.

"I was in a hurry this morning. This was the fastest thing I could find to put on."

Katherine was speaking the truth about the hurrying. Rushing Sprite to Tooley's for fresh clothes, making alternate arrangements for Sprite for that evening, then racing to the school in time for the first bell had been a challenge and a half. Still, that wasn't the whole reason Katherine didn't bother putting together her usual professional look for work today. She simply hadn't cared enough to make the effort.

"Did you oversleep?"

Katherine saw that Megan was watching her carefully.

"Not exactly."

"Don't mind me. I'm only prying."

Megan sat down in the chair opposite Katherine's desk.

"Don't mind me. I'm only clamming up."

Katherine was surprised at herself for managing even that much wit. She definitely didn't feel either amused or amusing right now.

"Listen, Katherine." Megan leaned forward and rested her elbows on the desktop. The customary twinkle in her brown eyes had turned almost solemn. "I know you've been through a lot this past year, and the holidays don't make that any easier. Maybe you ought to try to talk about what you're feeling."

"Are you trying to say I need a therapist?"

Megan's face showed no reaction to the sharpness of that question.

"I'm trying to say you might need a friend," she said.

Katherine sighed. "I'm sorry. I must have gotten up on the wrong side of the bed this morning, and I seem to be taking it out on you."

"Maybe you might try getting up on the right, or even the wrong side, of a different bed for a change."

Katherine nearly smiled. Megan teased her about her solitary life-style sometimes. It was a continuing theme of their friendly banter.

"How do you know I didn't?" was not Katherine's usual answer.

Megan drew back into her chair again and stared at her.

"Maybe I should keep on prying, after all."

Katherine shrugged. "It's not that interesting really." She hoped that was true.

"Let me be the judge."

Katherine wanted to talk to somebody. She just wasn't sure what she would say.

"Maybe later," she said. "Right now I'd like you to take a look at this."

She opened the top drawer of her desk and pulled out Coyote Bellaway's rumpled, smeared letter to the Most Needy Cases Fund. She handed it across the desk to Megan.

"This was written by the boy we found sleeping in the mat room yesterday. Now he's missing," Katherine said.

Megan looked the battered letter over, front and back.

"I hope he hasn't been going through whatever happened to this piece of paper," she said.

"I think he could be in some serious trouble. This letter is the only clue we have to his possible whereabouts."

"Where did you get this, anyway? Weren't you looking for it yesterday after Coyote took off?"

Katherine hesitated. She didn't actually know the details of how the letter had resurfaced. She'd have to talk to Vic to find that out, and she wasn't ready to do that just yet.

"I got it from Vic Maltese" was all she said.

"When did he give it to you?"

"This morning."

If Megan had taken that in as ammunition for her natural tendency toward matchmaking, she didn't let it show. She was dealing with the case of a little boy in trouble now. Megan always turned very focused, all teasing and jokes set aside, when a serious situation like this one came up.

The door behind Megan opened and Vic stepped through it. The sight of him took her so much by surprise that her knees felt weak, and she was grateful that she was sitting in her office chair. That kept her from making a fool of herself, and the wide desk before her helped her to maintain a professional attitude.

"I was just showing this to Megan," she said, gesturing to Coyote's letter. "I'm hoping there's a clue in there somewhere." She turned to Megan. "Do you see anything?"

"Well, he's obviously a bright boy. He's pretty articulate for—how old does he say he is?" She scanned the page, then looked from Vic to Katherine, who could see her friend's sharp, brown eyes taking in everything. Megan wouldn't be likely to miss the atmosphere of tension that had invaded the tiny office all of a sudden.

"Eleven," Vic said.

Katherine kept her gaze on Megan to avoid looking into his eyes. "He claims to be eleven, but I'm not sure we can trust the details of what he says."

"Why do you think that?"

"He's straining to be the perfect candidate for fund money in there. I can almost feel him trying as hard as he can to say just the right thing."

"Don't all the applicants do that?" Vic asked.

She was forced to drag her gaze to his. "Not quite as smoothly as Coyote does it."

"Hmm," Megan said. "Now that I read this through again, I see what you mean. So, we're dealing with a boy with what we call in my profession, well-developed manipulative skills."

"Exactly."

That meant he'd be harder to second-guess and harder to find before he got into deeper trouble, or before someone made that trouble for him. She thought about Lacey Harbison and what she was more certain than ever could have been a thinly veiled maneuver to get at the Bellaway children. She was also thinking about whoever had been in her apartment last night and the sinister tone of the note they left there. She shuddered.

"We have to figure out where Coyote might be," she said, feeling even more strongly how critical that was. "He's out in the street on his own, and there was a blizzard last night."

"I don't know where he was last night, but I found where he'd been holing up," Vic said. He described Coyote's rooftop hideaway.

Megan tapped the letter in her hand. "This tells us he has good survival instincts. He's smart enough to know he has to plan a strategy in order to get what he needs. That's a positive. I think we may be safe in assuming that this boy didn't sleep in a drift somewhere," Megan said. "My guess is that he worked out something more practical than that."

"But we have no way of knowing what he worked out or where he is." Katherine didn't even try to hide her frustration.

"He may be smooth and good at saying the right thing, but he's still a kid," Megan said. "He may have left some tracks here to follow, after all. We just have to get close enough to find them."

Katherine sighed again. That sounded like wishful thinking.

"Look at this," Megan said, her red curls bouncing as she sprang forward in her chair again, more enthusiastically this time, and stabbed her finger at the paper. "It could be a clue."

"What is it?" Vic asked.

"'Me and my little sister, Sprite, are real close,'" Megan read. "'I do my best to take good care of her. I keep an eye on her all the time.'"

"What clue do you get from that?"

Vic sounded skeptical, and Katherine had to admit she felt the same.

"He probably wrote that partly to show what a great kid he is so we'd think he deserved the grant money. But," Megan added, "I think he could be telling us the truth about himself, too."

"What truth is that?"

Katherine didn't quite grasp what Megan was getting at.

"I think he may still be watching his younger sister. If he can manage it, anyway. Where is she now?"

"At Arbor Hill School. I dropped her off there myself this morning."

"I'm going to call Stefan Piatka and tell him to be on the alert about this. Coyote may come lurking around there to make sure Sprite's all right." Megan got up from the chair. "I'll make a couple of photocopies of this letter, too. I assume we're going to give one to the police."

"We're keeping the police out of this for the time being," Vic said.

"You haven't notified the authorities that this boy is missing?"

"The children's guardian has asked us to handle this privately for now," Vic said. "There are special circumstances."

He was speaking to Megan but staring at Katherine as he said that. Megan continued to watch them both with obvious curiosity.

"What circumstances?" she asked.

"Why don't you go make those copies, Megan," Katherine cut in. "And call Stefan Piatka. Mr. Maltese and I need to talk privately for a moment."

"Yes, we do," Vic said in a tone that made Katherine's knees threaten to buckle again.

She told herself she had to stay strong and resolved.

Megan, meanwhile, glanced from Katherine to Vic once more, then walked out the door. She'd be back, of course, with lots more questions to ask. Katherine was sure of that.

"I SEE YOU were the one who took Coyote's letter from my place this morning," Vic said.

All Vic had found when he finally came to earlier in his living room was the envelope crushed underneath him where he'd collapsed on the couch in the middle of the night.

"I woke up and you were gone. I had no idea what might have happened to you, or to Sprite either. Whoever got into your apartment yesterday could have come after you again at my house."

"Well, they didn't."

She sounded almost belligerent, probably because he was putting her on the defensive, but he didn't care. She'd given him a scare, and he wanted her to know that.

"I went over to your place, and nobody was there either. I stopped by Tooley's. She was the one who told me you and Sprite were okay." He looked steadily at her and tried to keep his voice just as steady. "You could at least have left me a note."

"I probably should have done that."

She sounded less belligerent and more apologetic. She was looking down at the desk, so he couldn't see her face to read her expression. Still, he wasn't quite ready to let her off the hook.

"After I'd gone out looking for Coyote, I came back to my place and fell asleep. I'd been on my way upstairs to check on you, but I sat down on the couch and—"

Katherine's head shot up. "Check on me?" Her eyes were smoky with anger. "Was that all you were going to do when you came upstairs?"

Vic could feel the heat of her indignation steaming across the desk at him. He would never have guessed that someone who was usually so cool and reserved could also be this angry.

"I don't know what you mean," he said.

"I mean that you shouldn't have been on your way up there at all. I came to your house last night because I thought Sprite might be in danger, not because I wanted you wandering in and out of my bedroom all night."

That had Vic more confused than ever. What the hell was going on here? He didn't like being yelled at like this, especially when he didn't understand the reason for it.

"First of all, that's my bedroom you were in," he began.

"Then you should have had me sleep on the couch. Either way, I was practically unconscious, and you had no right to take liberties."

Vic stared at her for an instant while what she'd said sank in. When it did, his temper raged at least as hot as hers appeared to be.

"Take liberties?" he demanded. "What are you talking about?"

"Lower your voice," she said.

Her own volume was suddenly under control. He hated it when a woman turned the tables on a guy so fast his head felt like it was spinning off. He especially hated that she was right about not shouting here at the center, where anybody who happened to be passing by might hear.

"What are you talking about?" he repeated in a quieter voice. The effort made him seethe inside. He told himself he had to calm down. "What's this bull about taking liberties?"

"I remember—" she hesitated, looking flustered all of a sudden "—things. I just don't remember how far it went between us."

Vic stared into her blue-gray eyes. He could hardly believe what he was hearing. He could feel the leash he tried to keep on his temper running out to its end.

"You think I..." He searched for less corny words but couldn't think of any, so he spluttered out the corny ones. "You think I took advantage of you?"

"Did you?"

At the moment, he couldn't remember when or why he'd seen softness and warmth in her eyes. They were as cold and hard as flint now. Vic heaved a sigh so explosive he half expected the file folders to fly off her desk in the blast. He told himself to turn and march out of there without favoring her insult with the answer it didn't deserve, but he was too angry to listen to what was probably very good advice.

"Let me tell you something, lady. *You* asked *me* for that kiss—not that I wasn't happy to oblige. I don't know what you've dreamed up about what supposedly happened between you and me in my bedroom after that, but I'll tell you something else, and you can take it to the bank." He put his hands flat on her desk, crushing a couple of those file folders he'd been thinking about a moment ago. He leaned forward, looking straight into her face. "You've got me a thousand percent wrong."

He turned abruptly and stormed out of Katherine's office. Too bad having the last word didn't feel anywhere near as satisfying as he'd hoped it would.

KATHERINE WAS STILL staring at the door when Megan appeared on the other side of it. Vic hadn't actually slammed the door behind him, but he hadn't exactly shut it gently, either. Besides, they'd both been talking loudly in here before that, and it was well past midmorning so the full center staff would be on board. Katherine could guess what the gossip around the coffee machine would be about for the rest of the day. Thank heaven the kids were in school. She wouldn't have wanted them to hear her and Vic carrying on like a couple of hotheads instead of two professionals who should know better. She motioned for Megan to come in.

"Let the interrogation begin," Katherine said with what she wished sounded more like good humor. She tried to forget the niggling sense of guilt she felt about Vic. Had she completely misjudged him?

Megan flopped down into the chair in front of Katherine's desk.

"Why do you think I would want to interrogate you?" she asked.

"Because that's what you head-shrinkers do."

"I'm not a psychiatrist. I'm a psychologist. Nor am I a member of a remote Amazonian tribe that specializes in skulls. Therefore, I don't think the head-shrinker label really fits."

Katherine sighed. "Don't mind me. I'm a little off my stride this morning."

"Good. You're properly humbled. Now the interrogation can begin."

Katherine laughed.

"So, did you get what you wanted out of him?" Megan asked.

"What do you mean?"

"You had to be pushing his buttons like mad to inspire that kind of reaction, even out of Mr. Maltese. When we push somebody's buttons it's usually because we're looking for something in particular."

"Good old Megan. Straight for the jugular."

Megan didn't answer.

Katherine sighed again. "I suppose there's not going to

be any more work done by either of us till I satisfy your not entirely professional curiosity.''

"You could be right about that."

Katherine settled back in her desk chair. Megan was doing some button-pushing herself right now, and Katherine knew it. She also knew she needed to talk about the confusing things that were going on in her life.

"I had to find out something from Vic about last night," she said.

"Does this have anything to do with your earlier remark about getting up on the wrong side of the bed?"

Katherine nodded. Megan had a therapist's memory. She almost never forgot what was said to her.

"Did he tell you what you had to know?" she asked.

Katherine thought about that for a moment.

"Yes, I suppose he did," she said.

"Was it what you wanted to hear?"

Katherine thought again. Unbelievably, she felt both happy and upset about her confrontation with Vic. Happy, because he had not taken advantage of her. Upset, because that fact made her wonder whether he found himself at all attracted to her. She decided to give Megan an honest answer instead of a cautious, non-revealing one.

"Was it what I wanted to hear?" she repeated. "Yes and no."

"Ah, ambivalence," Megan said with a twinkle in her eye. "One of my personal favorite emotions."

"Not one of mine."

"Sometimes life is more interesting when one's ducks aren't entirely in a row."

Katherine knew that sounded right. She wasn't so sure it felt right, at least not for her. She'd always preferred to keep her ducks, and her life, pretty much in line.

"I'll have to think about that," she said. "For now, let's change the subject."

"Balmy weather we're having," Megan quipped with a glance toward the frost-edged window.

The sun might be out, but the temperatures were still frigid enough to keep frost from melting.

"Did you call Stefan Piatka about keeping an eye out for Coyote in case he should show up to check on Sprite?" Katherine asked.

"Not yet. I'll get on that right now." Megan was half-way out of the chair when she plopped back down again. "I have an idea."

"What could that be?"

Katherine wasn't sure she was up to one of Megan's brainstorms right now.

"Why don't we try to smoke Coyote out from wherever he's hiding?"

"How do we manage that?"

"Give him what he's after, and see if he comes to get it."

Megan's voice had lost its mischievous tone. Whatever she had in mind, she was totally serious about it.

"What are you suggesting?" Katherine asked, though she was beginning to recognize the track Megan was on.

"The grant. Give him a Most Needy Cases Fund grant. Announce it in the paper and say he has to come and collect it. Then, all we have to do is wait and see if he does."

Katherine didn't say anything. She was thinking.

"The Bellaway children certainly fit the requirements for the program," Megan went on. "Their situation is pretty desperate."

"That's true," Katherine said slowly.

"And, there's that reporter over at the *Chronicle*. What's her name?"

"Mariette Dugan."

Katherine's mind was on the same track as Megan's now.

"Right. Mariette Dugan," Megan said. "She'd be happy to drag this series out one more day, especially if there's a sob-sister angle to it. I'm sure we could come up with one of those. A real three-hanky story."

Katherine didn't answer. She was already reaching for the phone.

Chapter Thirteen

Vic was more angry with himself than he was with Katherine. He should have known better than to get tied up with her from the start. He'd told himself he was going to steer clear of her. He should have listened to that advice. They were from opposite ends of the universe. She'd made it crystal clear she saw that, too. After what had happened in her office this morning, there was no longer a doubt in his mind on the subject of how she felt about him. As far as she was concerned, Vic Maltese was some kind of scum, a lowlife who would put moves on a woman when she was passed out and even do it in his own house, where she'd gone to stay safe.

Vic could feel the bitterness of his thoughts like a harsh echo inside his head. He didn't like the feeling, especially because he understood all too well where the bitterness came from. He was no dummy, after all. Katherine Fairchild might have him pegged as a bottom-feeder, but—

Vic chopped that thought off at the knees. He was doing it again, popping off into the ozone as if somebody had pushed his hot button.

That was just what Katherine had done, and he knew it. She'd pushed his hot button, the one he'd been carrying around since he was fifteen years old, when he'd found out who he really was, what he'd really come from. Ever since, down deep inside he'd known that at least part of him was just what Katherine's accusation this morning made him out to be. Part of him was something a straight-arrow person like Katherine ought to scrape right off her shoe.

That was his hot button, no doubt about it. He hadn't spent all those hours in staff consultation meetings with psychologists for nothing. The Bellaway boy hadn't come up in any of those discussions because, till now, he'd never appeared to have any special problems. Just being poor wasn't special all by itself around here. Being poor was the usual thing. Plenty of other kids had problems though, and listening to what the professionals had to say had taught Vic probably as much as a degree at the university could have done. Everything came out of the family. What happened to a kid growing up had an effect on all the years of his life from then on.

So, he'd worked on himself and his temper. He'd been proud of his progress, too. Too bad he'd let that temper get the best of him in Katherine's office this morning. He understood why, too. He'd let himself care too much what she thought about him.

Vic had kept himself very busy since this morning, and he had also kept himself away from Katherine's end of the building. He'd even gone out through the rear fire exit off the gym to grab some lunch at the diner instead of making himself something in the center's kitchen like he usually did. Too much chance of running into Katherine there. Unfortunately, he couldn't reenter the building through the fire exit, as it automatically locked behind him.

He hadn't seen Katherine on his return, but he did spot Megan as he was hustling toward his office. She had a look on her face as if she wanted to talk about something. He had the definite feeling that something might be Katherine.

She and Megan were pretty close friends. His guess was that Megan had matchmaking, or maybe match-mending, on her mind.

Vic, on the other hand, could hardly have been less in the mood to be either matched or mended right then. He'd headed, like a hunted man searching for refuge, straight to his office and locked the door behind him. He'd spent the rest of the time since then catching up on the part of his job he enjoyed the least—paperwork. Eventually, he'd had about all he could take of shuffling reports and filling out insurance forms. Still, the kids wouldn't be out of school and pouring in here for another hour or so. He suddenly found himself feeling so restless he had to get out of his office, whether he ran into Katherine or Megan or not.

Vic was on his way down the hall to the vending machine when he heard a woman's voice calling his name. He considered the possibility of making a run for it, but that was too undignified. He blew out a heavy sigh as he stopped in his tracks and steeled himself for whatever would come next. Mariette Dugan, that pesky reporter from the *Chronicle,* was in his face almost the second he turned around. He took a step backward, but he'd seen enough of her before this afternoon not to be surprised. She was the in-your-face type.

"So, what's the story on this kid you guys want me to headline?" she asked.

She was like that, too. She didn't lead into a thing. She just blasted it right at you without a greeting in front of it.

"What kid would that be?"

"This kid with the sister and a mother in the hospital. What's his name?"

Mariette thumbed through the small pad she'd pulled out of the pocket of her down coat. He could feel a sneaking suspicion coming on that he wasn't at all happy with the subject she had on her nosey reporter's mind.

"Here it is," she said. "Coyote Bellaway, and his sister's name is Sprite. Didn't they tell you about this? Giving this kid one of your Most Needy Cases Grants, then making a big deal out of it with a spotlight article in the paper and all? Why him, anyway?"

Vic didn't like what he was hearing, but the last thing he should do was let Ms. Dugan know that. She was a reporter, and she'd like nothing better than to catch a whiff of conflict. If that happened, she'd be back over at the *Chronicle* before you could say Lois Lane, cranking out a story about all kinds of controversy over here at the center. Some folks might think any publicity was good publicity, but Vic definitely wasn't one of those folks.

If there was going to be public attention focused on the center, he wanted it to be all about what they did here and how much it meant to the community. Stories of squabbles or even features about individual personalities weren't his idea of what needed to be said about this place. He and a lot of other people put their heart and soul into it every day. All the same, he knew he'd better not get all heated up over protecting it, at least not so this press person with her notepad could see it. She was staring at him a little too closely for comfort already.

"Coyote and Sprite are very deserving of one of our grants," he said.

"More deserving than any of the other people you're giving the money to?"

"No, not more deserving. Just appropriate to benefit from the program."

A knot of tension made Vic's teeth grind together. In a second or two, his cheek would start twitching. He had to get away from her before she noticed he was ready to explode. She wasn't the one he wanted to pop off at, anyway. Whoever had this harebrained idea about putting the Bellaway kids in the paper, that was the one Vic had the itch to get his hands on.

"Who told you about Coyote and Sprite?" he asked, trying to sound casual.

"That new gal you've got here. The one from Chicago."

"Katherine Fairchild?"

"Right. I did an interview with her a week or so ago. She called up the office this morning, with this thing about wanting me to do a feature on these two kids. I've got a small piece going in tonight's edition. I'm over here now to see if there's enough to it to do a follow-up. Fairchild seems to think there is. What do you think?"

Mariette Dugan had her pen poised over her pad. She was looking at Vic so hard she almost could have bored a hole through his head with her eyes. He had to give her some kind of answer and stay cool about it. The trouble was that she'd asked him what he thought about putting the Bellaway kids in the paper. What he really thought was that this was the most stupid idea he'd heard in he didn't know how long. Coyote was trying to lie low right now, and that was the best thing for him to do. If Vic didn't agree with that and if he wasn't sure Coyote knew how to take care of himself out there and keep out of sight, Vic would have called the cops into it by now himself, much as he didn't like cops. A low profile was what Coyote needed now, not headlines. How could Katherine not know that? Meanwhile, Dugan was still staring.

"I think that any publicity that helps the Most Needy Cases Program is good," Vic said, picking his words like he was tiptoeing through a minefield. "There are lots of families to write an article on if that's what you want to do."

"Fairchild thinks these Bellaway kids are special. Do you agree with her?"

"All the kids who come here to the center are special."

Vic knew that wasn't what she wanted to hear and that she wasn't likely to let it go at that. He turned away from her all the same and started walking down the hall again toward the administrative area of the building.

"Why don't we go over to Fairchild's office and talk about this some more," Dugan was saying as she hurried to keep up with him. "I'd like to hear that dialogue between you two."

I bet you would, Vic thought.

"I need an angle for the story if I'm going to do a focus piece like this," she went on. "The two of you kicking this back and forth could be the hook I'm looking for."

That's not all I'd like to kick back and forth, was what popped into Vic's head.

He didn't say anything and he didn't look down at Dugan, though he could feel her still scurrying along next to him. He didn't dare look at her. What felt like a fireball of anger was building up inside him the way a head of steam does in a boiler. He had to get out of this situation or there was going to be the devil to pay. He was trying to make himself scarce, but the reporter wouldn't stop dogging him.

"This is Katherine Fairchild's department," he managed to say more calmly than he would have thought himself capable of at the moment. "I don't think it would be appropriate for me to horn in."

"That's kind of a new tack for you, isn't it?" Dugan asked. "Every other time I've talked to you, I could hardly write fast enough to get all your opinions down on paper."

That was true, all right. He'd spent time shooting his mouth off. Now, that fact was back here to haunt him. He could hear the curiosity in Dugan's voice. She'd caught a whiff of something going on. He had to get her off the trail somehow. He was racking his brain to figure out how to do that when Megan Moran dashed out of the main reception office and nearly knocked him down. Vic grabbed her by the shoulders to keep her from toppling over him, and maybe also to give himself something to do till he came up with an answer for Dugan.

"You'll never guess in a million years what's happened," Megan gushed. "Or maybe I should say half a million."

She giggled then. Her brown eyes were uncommonly bright, and her red curls corkscrewed up from her head as if she'd been running her fingers through them over and over again.

"What's this all about?" Dugan asked as she flipped her notebook to a fresh page.

"Yeah, Megan. What's going on?"

Vic let go of Megan's shoulders even though he felt like hugging her for getting Dugan off his back, at least for now.

"I guess this is for publication," Megan said. "There hasn't been any official word on that yet, but I can't see that it would do anything but good for the center. I'll tell you, but we'll have to get an okay from the director before you can print it. Otherwise, I can't tell you."

"Okay, okay," Dugan said. "I'll wait for authorization before I take it to press, if it's even a story, that is."

"It's a story all right," Megan said. She was gushing again. "The biggest one that's ever happened around here."

"What gives?" Vic asked.

"What gives is absolutely right, or maybe 'what's been given,' would be more to the point," Megan said. "Who's giving it's another story. We don't know that yet. Maybe we never will."

She had to be really excited. Megan usually made more sense than this.

"What are you talking about?" Vic asked.

She turned the full beam of her smile on him. "I'm talking about the answer to all of our holiday prayers. I'm talking about being able to help out just about everybody who wrote in to the Most Needy Cases Fund."

"How're we going to manage that?"

He knew that the money they had for grants was nowhere near enough to do what Megan was saying. Meanwhile, Mariette Dugan was scribbling like mad on her notepad.

"We're going to manage that," Megan said, "because some wonderfully generous soul has donated half a million dollars to make it happen."

Vic was glad Dugan hadn't brought a photographer along. One of the last things Vic Maltese wanted to see in this world was a picture of himself on the front page of the *Chronicle* with his mouth hanging open.

Chapter Fourteen

Katherine couldn't understand what had Megan so excited. She had rushed into the office, grabbed her by the arms and pulled her out from behind the desk.

"What are you doing?" Katherine asked.

She was already feeling as tired as if it were nine o'clock at night rather than four in the afternoon. A dose of Megan's exuberance might be more than she could handle just now.

"I'm telling you that our wishes have come true, our prayers have been answered," Megan gushed. "Now, there's only one thing left to do. We have to jump up and down."

Megan began doing precisely that, springing straight up from the gray tile floor in front of the desk. Katherine made an awkward half hop and thumped back down in response to being dragged along by Megan. But she resisted the next leap, anchoring both of them to the ground.

"Have you taken complete leave of your senses?" she asked. "What are you jumping about?"

"Didn't they call you from the office? They were supposed to give you the message. I can't believe you're the only one who doesn't know. You of all people should have been told before anybody else."

Megan was gushing again, even more effervescently, and Katherine was beginning to experience some excitement of her own despite the downbeat tone of the day so far.

"Tell me what's happening," she said.

"Half a million bucks, that's what's happening," Megan chirped. "Half a million smackeroos. Somebody's donated half a million to your project. Somebody's giving the center a half a million dollars to use for holiday grants."

"I don't believe it," Katherine said. That was the truth, but the wonder of Megan's words was beginning to dawn.

"Believe it. I saw the bank-draft check myself."

"For a half million dollars?"

Megan nodded vigorously. "A half million dollars."

"Five hundred thousand?" Katherine was so dazed she'd barely been able to make that calculation.

"The same."

Katherine was about to repeat that she didn't believe it when another question occurred to her.

"Who's the contributor?"

Megan shook her head. "Nobody has a clue. The donation was anonymous."

"Somebody gave us that much money and doesn't want credit for it?" This was becoming more fantastic by the second. "And you're sure it's real? This couldn't be some kind of joke?" Katherine heard how bizarre that possibility sounded, too, but she'd witnessed some bizarre things lately.

"They already called the bank from the office. The check is real and negotiable. All we have to do is deposit it in the Most Needy Cases Fund account and we can start writing grant awards against it immediately."

Katherine shook her head slowly. "This is a miracle," she said, even though her mind hadn't yet entirely come to understand that what Megan was saying was true.

"We'll call him the Secret Santa," a new voice chimed in from the doorway to Katherine's office.

She looked up to see Mariette Dugan, holding the notepad she carried around with her so perpetually it might have been growing out of the ends of her fingers. She looked very pleased.

"The guy who sent the check," she was saying in response to what Katherine had no doubt was the dazed expression on her face. "I'm going to call him Secret Santa. For the article I'm writing."

"Wait a minute. I'm not sure we want this in the paper just yet," Katherine said. She was trying to think what the best approach would be, but her thoughts were still moving at bewildered post-shock speed.

"Sorry about that, honey," Mariette said. "You can't sit on this one. It's front-page stuff, and I've got the exclusive."

She looked around at the small crowd gathered outside the office door, as if spying out any other reporters who might have shown up in the past few minutes. Katherine followed that gaze. Vic was standing at the back of the gathering and a couple of feet away from it. Unlike the rest of the ecstatic crowd, Vic looked anything but elated. In fact, she couldn't imagine him looking more displeased. Before she had time to form an opinion about why he might be playing the killjoy at such a moment, Megan tightened her grip on Katherine's arms again.

"As I said, there's only one thing to do," Megan chirped in a happy singsong.

Katherine tore her gaze away from Vic's face. "You're absolutely right," she said. "Only one thing left to do."

"Jump up and down," she and Megan chimed together.

They resumed their leaps into the air. The crowd at the doorway followed suit almost instantly, jumping up and

down and hugging one another to the accompaniment of
such glee as only a pealing chorus of holiday bells might
have matched for merriment.

Only Vic Maltese did not join in.

VIC HAD BEEN what his mother used to call "stewing in his
own juice" ever since this afternoon. He winced at the
thought of his mother now. She was the only thing that
ever bothered him much about having walked away from
his family and his past.

She used to make a big deal out of Christmas when he
was a kid back home. He'd put serious money on a bet that
she still did that. She was probably over there in that big
tomb of a house right now, engineering a yuletide extrav-
aganza with mountains of food and presents and the place
decorated beautifully as always.

Vic knew that, however many times he might do his bah-
humbug number on the outside, in his heart he missed his
mother's version of the holiday season. The truth was, back
in those days, he'd loved every bit of it. He still remembered, sharp as yesterday, the smell of pine boughs and
baking. Most of all, he missed his mother. He'd thrown out
the baby with the bathwater, as they say, tossed out the best
part of his life in order to get rid of the worst, and she was
the best part. Even so, that wasn't what bothered him most
about the damned holidays. He knew how sad it must make
her not to have him around anymore, and that sadness
would be sadder still at Christmas. No length of time would
dull the pain of this particular loss for her. She was that
kind of mother, and he would feel guilty forever because
his decision hurt her.

A second truth was that Vic also thought about his
mother when his present life was giving him a hard time
for one reason or another. He could have used her advice

in times like those. He could use her advice tonight. She'd know how to untangle this mess real fast. She'd see straight through to the heart of the situation, no matter how messed up and confusing things appeared on the surface. She wouldn't walk away from her emotions, either, the way he had a talent for doing. He could almost hear her telling him not to do that now. This was the down side of advice. As many times as not, it turned out to be exactly what he didn't feel like being told.

He had managed to avoid listening to his mother's imagined words, right up till the end of this long workday. Even after that, he almost convinced himself the only thing he cared about was getting to the diner to pick up a burger for the supper he wasn't really interested in eating, much less cooking. There was a pot of pasta sauce in his refrigerator, but even thinking about that reminded him of last night. Reminders of last night made his mother's voice echo louder than ever, letting him know that he had to face up to what was happening inside him. He made it all the way to the diner parking lot before he gave in and turned around with a spin of wheels that fishtailed the Trans Am dangerously close to a telephone pole.

It was a safe guess that Katherine would still be in her office. She worked late most nights. He pulled into the center's parking lot and spotted the light from her window. He angled his car in next to her four-wheeler and killed the engine. Wind buffeted the car windows in the silence that followed. On his way here, he'd seen shoppers hurrying along the streets, juggling packages. Three days till Christmas. He wished he didn't want so much for that to mean more to him than it did. Instead, he felt as desolate right now as the film of dry snow skittering along the asphalt pavement. There might be lots of holiday activity not very far away, but this place was deserted.

Vic registered the significance of that. Katherine was alone here. She might have worked late at her office many other nights, but this night felt different to him, more dangerous. He'd been experiencing an annoying itch of his instincts ever since that anonymous donation had come in that afternoon. Something about it didn't set right with him.

Vic knew he was the suspicious type. He had to keep that from coloring the way he saw things until he'd come up with strong proof that his suspicions could be real. He had no such proof now. Still, he couldn't help wondering about a possible connection between what was going on with Coyote and this out-of-the-blue answer to everybody's prayers for the holiday grant program, the same program Coyote was applying for when this whole mess got started. Sure, there were folks who got so turned on with holiday spirit now and then that they'd fork over half a mil to help out other folks. What bothered Vic was that this particular burst of goodwill happened to occur at the same time Coyote was missing and maybe on the run from a bad guy in a black car. This guy, and whatever cronies he might have, were obviously hot to track Coyote down.

Besides Coyote himself, there was another common link to both situations—Katherine. That thought sent Vic running across the parking lot toward the door into the center.

He fumbled for his key to the night lock on the gate, then took a maddeningly long time finding the keyhole in the shadows from the overhanging roof of the one-story building. Once he was inside, the silence of the corridors bothered him even more than the eerie howling of the wind outside had done. He raced down the hallway toward Katherine's office and skidded on snow-damp boot soles around the corner that led to her door. Though the lights were on, her office was empty. Where was she?

Vic listened. The building continued to be as silent as

the grave, and he wished that comparison hadn't come to mind. He considered calling out her name, then decided against it. If she was in trouble, he might be of more help to her with the element of surprise on his side. He was about to return to the main hallway and check the rooms on either side of it when he heard footsteps at what sounded like the opposite end of the long corridor he'd been about to enter. Whoever belonged to those feet was definitely in a big hurry, and headed in Vic's direction. He backed up and flattened himself against the wall on the far side of Katherine's doorway from the hall corridor. The shadows were deeper here, so he might not be seen right off. That was about the only advantage he'd have. His gun was back in the secret compartment of the lamp stand at home. He wished he had the weapon on him now.

Maybe he could pretend he did. Vic reached into his jacket and pulled out the equipment-locker key, which he'd stuck in his pocket this afternoon on his way out the rear door of the gym for lunch. Afterward, he'd been waylaid by Mariette Dugan. Otherwise, he would have gone back to his office to hang this up, the way he usually did, by the oblong of wood attached to the key. That piece of wood was what he had in mind at the moment and the possible instant of shock and surprise he might be able to create with it. He held the wood oblong out in front of him but not far enough to extend beyond the shadows from the corner.

"Stop, or I'll shoot," he shouted in his most commanding voice as the footsteps reached the opening into the corridor directly across from him.

"Vic, it's me."

He recognized Katherine's voice.

"I'd appreciate it if you didn't shoot me," she said,

peeking around the corner from the hallway. "Do you think you could manage that?"

Vic felt like all kinds of a fool as he dropped his hand to his side.

"Sorry," he said. "I thought you might be an intruder."

"You have a habit of meeting me with a gun in your hand."

"Except that it's not really a gun this time."

He walked out of the shadows and held out the block of wood with the key hanging from it where she could see them. Katherine had emerged from the corridor with obvious caution. She stared at the piece of wood for a moment before the smile began to crease her face. Then she started to laugh.

"If you'd turned out to be a really bad guy, I could have locked you up with the old volleyballs and gym mats," Vic said. "If you ever smelled those mats, you'd know what a tough punishment that might be."

Katherine was still laughing, choking a little as if to stop herself. She leaned against the wall with one arm and clutched herself across the stomach with the other. Her laughter subsided some but didn't stop.

"Are you all right?"

She nodded as he reached out to steady her by taking her arm. She didn't resist when he led her inside her office.

"I'm sorry," she managed to splutter just before she sank into her chair behind the desk. "I can't seem to stop laughing."

"You probably need some rest. What's been going on here lately is enough to make anybody a little hysterical."

She'd looked as if she was about to set off into another wave of giggles before Vic said that. Now, the merriment was fading fast from her eyes.

"I'm not hysterical," she said, "and I don't appreciate your saying I am."

"Look," Vic said. "I don't want to fight with you. It seems like we've been doing that all day."

"That's a bit of an exaggeration."

She appeared to have composed herself.

"Not an exaggeration by much," he said. "This morning you were accusing me of being the kind of creep who would take advantage of an unconscious woman."

She didn't respond to that. Instead, she looked away from his gaze and moved a stack of file folders from one side of her desktop to the other.

"Do you really think I could do that?" he asked.

"I don't know what to think," She continued to fuss with the papers on her desk.

Vic stepped across her narrow office from the doorway to the desk in one stride and leaned his palms on the edge of the desk with his face not far from hers. Wasn't this what he'd done this morning, too? He couldn't remember, and he didn't care.

"Look me in the face and tell me you believe I'd do something like that to you or anybody else," he said. "Tell me that's what you think about me and I'll walk out of here and never bother you again."

She raised her gaze gradually to meet his, but she didn't say anything right away. He suddenly wondered if maybe he shouldn't have given her such an easy out. What if she told him that was exactly what she wanted, for him to walk out of here right now and leave her alone for good? The thought sent a chill through him as cold as the winter wind outside the darkness of her office window.

"I don't," she said quietly.

"What?" he asked, still a little shaken by how terrible the idea of losing her altogether made him feel.

"I don't really believe you would do something like that."

He gazed back into her blue-gray eyes. They told him she was speaking the truth. What flashed through him then was as different from the cold chill of a moment ago as it could be. What flashed through him was a hot rush of desire. He stepped away from the desk and settled into the chair next to the doorway. He didn't dare stay close to her. He was afraid she might be able to detect the intensity of the heat he was feeling or at least see it burning in his eyes.

"Good" was all he said.

"What are you doing back in this place, anyway?" she asked. She'd started fiddling with those file folders again. This time she looked as if she was actually about to do some work on them. "I thought we were alone here."

"We? Is somebody else here?"

"Sprite's in the playroom. I was just down there checking on her before you accosted me with that deadly weapon of yours."

Vic managed a smile at his own foolishness.

"What were you in such a hurry about, anyway?" he asked.

"I didn't want to miss Tooley Pennebaker when she shows up. She should be here soon. She's taking Sprite to a friend's house for the night."

"Do you think that's safe for Sprite?"

Katherine shrugged her shoulders and sighed. "It's about as safe as being with me. Whoever is after Coyote may have broken into Tooley's, but they didn't leave a threatening message like they did at my place. I think Sprite will be safer away from my apartment and from Tooley's. The friend's mother has agreed to take Sprite overnight and to bring her to the Christmas party." At her last words, Katherine's voice and her eyebrows rose questioningly.

"The open house I throw every year," Vic confirmed. "I told you that's why I put up the tree. It's for the kids from the center and their parents and anyone from the center who wants to attend. But that's not important now." He took a deep breath before adding, "We need to get through tonight first, and I think you should stay with me again."

Katherine looked up quickly from her file folders. He could see in her eyes that he shouldn't have said anything about staying together. Maybe she thought that was just about as dangerous as being out there with a stalker after her. He wished he hadn't suggested it. He wouldn't make that particular error again.

"At least let me drive behind you after you leave here," he said. "Just to make sure these jokers don't follow you home."

He didn't think he was anywhere near as dangerous as whoever had torn up Tooley's place and broken into Katherine's apartment. At least, not dangerous where personal harm to Katherine or her property was concerned. Being alone with her would create another kind of danger. There was no mistaking the resistance in Katherine's expression. She opened her mouth, probably to give him an argument about following her. The knock at the window came before she could say what she had on her mind. She and Vic both turned to find Tooley Pennebaker gesturing at them through the glass. Katherine motioned in the direction of the main door to the center.

"I'll let you in," she said.

Tooley nodded her understanding and headed in the direction of the entrance. Katherine moved from behind the desk.

"We'll be back in a minute," she said as she left the office.

"I'll be waiting."

Vic intended to keep his word about that. He also intended to follow Katherine home tonight whether she wanted him to or not.

Chapter Fifteen

Katherine didn't want Vic to follow her. She'd told him she would be all right on her own, even though she wasn't at all certain that was true. She had to weigh what could be more dangerous to her, the chance that she'd be revisited by the animals who slashed Daniel's portrait or the possibility of ending up somewhere alone with Vic Maltese. In her office earlier she'd felt drawn to him. He'd leaned over her desk again, just as he'd done in the morning, but this second time there'd been no shield of anger to protect her. This time there was only Vic, inches away, and that irresistible urge she felt to move even closer. A magnetic attraction, that's what it was, as if she were being drawn inevitably to him by a power she was helpless to resist.

She'd been more vulnerable than usual this evening to start with. She couldn't remember the last time she was unstrung enough to give way to a fit of giggles. Of course, he had looked wonderfully ridiculous at the time, brandishing a scrap of wood and calling out, ''Halt or I'll shoot,'' like the hero in a bad western movie. She couldn't help but chuckle to herself even now as she angled into the parking place she was so pleased to find at this hour near the edge of Washington Park and not far from her building. What a sight he'd been, that broad-shouldered, intimidating man with his dark good looks and leather jacket, reduced to holding the villains at bay with a locker-room key. The remembered image brought with it a flush of affection so tender she was all but overwhelmed.

Katherine grasped the handle and pushed the car door open, hoping a blast of cold air would snap her back to her senses before she had to deal with Vic in person again. She stepped onto the running board and down from the tall vehicle. The almost incessant sharp wind was deflected to some extent by the old, broad trees that lined this access road to the park. The trees were bare of leaves so they didn't block entirely the light from the pole lamps that lined the road. Still, it was far more gloomy than bright here, and there were moving shadows everywhere. She locked the car as hastily as she could manage with fingers that trembled, probably not just from the cold.

She looked around for Vic. She'd last noted his low, distinctive headlights behind her just before turning into the parking lot. She could make out no sign of either him or his car now. Maybe he'd meant it literally when he said he would follow her home. He'd shadowed her safely to her block, and then he'd driven on. Maybe he felt the same trepidation about being alone with her as she did with him. She'd recognized a confused play of emotions in his eyes more than once when he looked at her. Suddenly, Katherine wished she had asked him to accompany her to her front door. She would feel a lot more secure right now with Vic by her side.

She thought about calling his name, but instinct kept her from doing so. Instead, she hurried back along the access road toward the turnoff she'd taken in the Cherokee from State Street into the park. Ordinarily, she would have mushed over the snow mounded lawn space in a shortcut between where she'd parked on the access road and the sidewalk that bordered the park. She was taking this longer way around because there were fewer deep shadows here. She wished that made her feel more secure.

Katherine hurried out onto State Street, still scanning the road behind her in vain for a glimpse of Vic. He was nowhere to be seen. In fact, there was no one to be seen. She was alone on the street. There wasn't much nightlife in this part of Albany, not even so close to Christmas Day. She was reminded of that fast-approaching event by colored lights in a number of windows of the buildings across the way.

Though this side of State Street was populated only by trees and their inhabitants, the opposite sidewalk was lined with buildings dating mostly from the last century. Brick fronts and Gothic stone graced tall, narrow structures attached to one another all the way down the block. Katherine loved the decorative detail painstakingly wrought by craftsman of another, less rushed era than her own. She especially enjoyed looking at the way so much of the wrought-iron entry rails, window gratings and even fire escapes had been twined with greenery and red bows in keeping with the season, as Dickens would say. However, she didn't slow her pace to appreciate any of that tonight as she targeted her building, across the road and halfway down the block, and hurried directly toward it.

Katherine unlocked the street door with caution. She would have liked to think this lock afforded some protection from intruders, but she was all too aware how untrue that was. Admittance would be easy to manage for just about anyone. Hitting two or three of the several apartment buttons outside almost always resulted in a responding long buzz, which opened the front door to the building. At this time of year that was more likely than ever. The frequency of gift-package deliveries, house and party guests running in and out, not to mention the general spirit of the goodwill season, had everybody's guard down. She wondered if that was how the intruder or intruders had gotten into her apartment the night before. While she picked her way up the one flight of stairs to the second floor, being careful to keep to the carpeted center where her steps would make little sound, she wished she could feel half as carefree as her neighbors.

She had made the turn around the banister on the first floor when she saw it. Her front door was ajar, just a crack but enough for her to notice. She ventured closer to the entranceway, even as she tracked backward in her mind till that morning, trying to remember if there could be a chance she'd forgotten to lock up before leaving for the center. She was so regular in her habits she couldn't imagine such a lapse. Yet, her extra errands with Sprite had made that morning so much less than regular, she couldn't be sure what she'd done.

She'd worked late tonight on the thick file of applications for the Most Needy Cases Fund in preparation for distributing the huge donation that had come in that afternoon. She might be bone-tired from those long hours, but she wasn't stupid. She wasn't going to walk into what could be trouble again.

She had approached to within a couple of feet of the partly open door. She began to back away from it now, without moving her eyes from the crack between the bottom of the door and the jamb. She was listening, too, for anything that might signal danger. Still, at first she wasn't sure she had really heard the sound, faint as it was from behind the door. Then, she heard it again and froze where she stood, barely breathing, as her memory raced back to her stepson Daniel in his narrow bed before the doctors came to take away his discomfort. What she was listening to tonight was what she had listened to with such torment then, the sound of someone moaning in pain.

Her first thought was of Vic. Could he have parked closer to the building than she was able to manage and had himself buzzed in here to run unaware into a violent intruder? The possibility brought a thin cry to her throat. She clamped her lips tight to keep from breaking the silence of the corridor. A third moan, slightly louder, shattered her caution and sent her bolting through the door into the dimly lit entryway to her living room. Even in the gloom, she immediately made out the body slumped on the floor in front of the fireplace where she'd found Daniel's slashed portrait on the mantelpiece the night before.

Katherine ran to the form on the floor. Her rational mind told her this wasn't Vic. The shape was far too small. Still, she knelt down with an unexpectedly fervent prayer for his safety in her heart. She'd been blocking the light from the open door into the hallway before she knelt down. Now, that light fell upon the head of the person on the floor. Katherine gasped at the unmistakable tumble of red curls and the matting of darker red close to the scalp.

"*Megan*" was Katherine's anguished whisper, barely audible to her own ears beneath the sudden, insistent blare of the door buzzer being rung over and over again by someone in the building entryway below.

VIC HAD BARRELED into Katherine's apartment and found her kneeling over Megan on the floor.

"Where am I?" Megan asked after she'd come to, to find Katherine and Vic on either side of her.

Megan's voice was so soft and shaky Vic could hardly hear what she was saying. He thought maybe they shouldn't let her talk, but there were things he had to know. His naturally suspicious nature had been working overtime ever since he saw the scene in Katherine's apartment. He was on his way toward putting together a picture of what was going on here. Megan might be able to fill in some of the blank spots. Vic had the feeling that, if he didn't finish painting that picture real soon, more people than just Megan could be attacked, or possibly even worse.

"You're in Katherine's apartment," he said. "Try not to move around. We don't know how badly you may be hurt."

"My head," she whispered. "Somebody hit me on the head."

"Did you see who it was?"

Megan tried to shake her head, but Vic wouldn't let her.

"Lie still," he said. "An ambulance is on the way."

"Okay," she murmured, sounding like she might be ready to pass out again.

He didn't like to see Megan so weak. Most of the time, she was about as lively as anybody he'd ever known. He had to make sure she got back to being that way again. Now that she was awake, he'd do whatever was needed to keep her that way. He knew how important it was that a person with a head injury stay awake.

"Whoever hit you," Vic said, "was he inside or outside Katherine's apartment when you got here?"

Megan sighed, as if she might be barely up to staying awake, much less answering questions. Vic felt like a heel for doing it, but he wasn't going to let her off the hook.

"Think hard, Megan. Was the guy inside or outside?"

"It may not have been a guy," she said. "I don't know about that. I do know he, or she, was inside the apartment."

She closed her eyes, looking like she might have tired herself out.

"Don't fade on me now, Megan. How did you get into

Katherine's place? Did the person who hit you open the door for you?''

''Key,'' Megan murmured. ''Had a key.''

''Who had a key?''

''Me.''

''I'd given her a set of keys,'' Katherine told him. ''She took care of my plants when I went to Chicago a few months ago.''

Megan sighed again, more deeply this time, and closed her eyes.

Moments later, the ambulance arrived. The technicians transferred Megan to a stretcher, and Vic and Katherine followed in Katherine's Cherokee.

She pulled to a stop at the entrance of the emergency wing of Albany Medical Center on New Scotland Avenue and jumped from her side of the car. He followed her inside to the admissions desk, where she gave information to the on-duty nurse.

Down the long corridor off the admissions area, Vic noticed the technicians from the ambulance. The last thing he saw before they disappeared through two, large swinging doors was Megan's blood-matted red hair in stark contrast with the whiteness around her.

KATHERINE HADN'T BEEN inside a hospital since the day Daniel died. She stood at the desk now answering questions, but her mind was far away in Chicago a year ago or more. The details were different—this was a larger place and more public than the specialized facility where Daniel spent his last hours. But too much of the rest was similar, especially the swarm of medical professionals bustling up and down hallways, always with blank or sober expressions on their faces. Even the sight of the woman at this counter, with her manner that was more efficient than friendly, chilled Katherine to the bone. She forced herself to answer what she could, but she was having a hard time with it.

Then, thank heaven, Vic appeared at her side and took over. She listened distractedly as he reported that Megan had been attacked after she let herself into Katherine's place. She'd forgotten Megan had keys to both the street door and the apartment itself since the time a few months ago when she'd had to go back to Chicago to clear up some legal details regarding her divorce. Her marriage had been in trouble even before Daniel's illness, and by the time of his death, what was left of her relationship with her husband had long since died.

Katherine turned away from the admission desk and the woman with the frosty expression. She tried to turn away from her painful thoughts, as well. As much as possible, she kept her mind away from the past and the hard, heartbreaking scenes that had happened in places like this. Now, she could feel all of those memories threatening to surge up inside her with the force of a flood powerful enough to drown her in its depths. That was why she didn't object at first when Vic, who had finished with the interrogation at the hospital desk, took her by the arm and steered her back through the automatic sliding doors, out of the emergency room and toward the parking lot.

"Where are we going?" she had the presence of mind to ask at last, as the chilly night air snapped her back to some semblance of sensibility.

"We have to get out of here."

She tried to stop her forward movement by planting her feet solidly beneath her, but Vic kept on pulling her along. He was too strong to resist. Even the deep-treaded, hard-rubber soles of her hiking boots couldn't sustain a foothold against his obvious determination.

"I have to stay with Megan," she protested, continuing to resist despite the futility of her efforts.

"There's nothing you can do for her now. I've given them as much information as she gave me. I don't think she knows any more than that. I told the admitting nurse to call the center in the morning for the health-insurance details. She said they would do that. Now, it's up to the doctors."

"I can't just leave Megan here," Katherine said, her voice loud enough that a couple on their way out of the lot turned to look.

Vic stopped and turned to Katherine, putting an arm around her shoulders, acting every inch the concerned husband trying to calm a distressed wife. For a moment, Katherine let her thoughts linger on that fantasy.

"You have to listen to me," he said in a tone so serious, even desperate, that she couldn't help but do what he asked.

"I'm listening," she said.

"I told that nurse exactly what Megan told me, that she was attacked, hit on the head, by somebody waiting in the dark inside your apartment. What do you think is going to happen next?"

Katherine stared up at him as he leaned down toward her with fierce intensity in his dark eyes. She wasn't quite sure what he was asking. The hospital was still having its effect on her senses.

"I don't know what you mean," she said.

"I mean that in very quick time this place is going to be knee-deep in cops. I just reported a case of criminal assault. The law says the hospital has to call in the police. We shouldn't be here when they come."

"Why not?"

Katherine was suddenly aware of questions about Vic crowding through the haze of her confused thoughts and troubled emotions. What was there about contact with the police that upset him so much that he seemed willing to do just about anything to avoid it?

He leaned closer. "I've been putting a lot of things together about what's been happening to you and to the Bellaway kids these past few days. I've got a strong suspicion we could be up against some very bad guys here."

He'd lowered his voice, as if to prevent anyone else listening in. She could hear the urgency in his words, but she didn't exactly understand what he was saying.

"What kind of very bad guys?" she asked.

"The kind that don't like to leave loose ends around when it comes to the police being involved."

"Are you talking about street gangs?"

The center had its share of problems with gang activity, and the situation had been escalating over the past year. Still, she couldn't think what gangs might have to do with all of this.

"Not the kind of gangs you're talking about," Vic said.

Why was he being so mysterious? "What other kind of gangs are there?" she asked with mounting exasperation. "Are you talking about mobsters or something like that?"

She'd meant that as sarcasm, but the way Vic was staring down at her now suggested she'd accidentally hit upon close to what he considered the truth.

"You've got to be joking," she said.

"I've never been more serious in my life."

Katherine was about to laugh and scoff some more, but something in his eyes kept her from doing that.

"Mobsters may not be exactly the right way to put it," he said. "Let's just say I've got reason to believe these are some extremely dangerous people who will do whatever they have to do to get what they want."

"Vic, what is going on here?"

"What is going on is that we have to get in your car and leave this place before the cops arrive. Otherwise, there could be real trouble, and it just may end up getting those two kids hurt even worse than has happened to them already."

Katherine stared back at him. She had no doubt he believed the things he was saying. She could feel the strength of that belief in his grip on her arms, but it all sounded so fantastic to her. She didn't know what to think.

"You have to trust me," he said, leaning so close she could feel the warmth of his breath on her cheek. "I know this may come across to you as crazy talk, but it isn't. Believe me, there's a lot more to it than that."

She sighed and stopped resisting his hold on her.

"All right. I'll believe you," she said, "but only this one time, and you'll have to prove to me that what you're saying is true."

"Sure, sure," he said. "Now we've got to get out of here while we still can."

He was already pulling her along again toward her car, and, no matter how skeptical she might be about what he had just told her, she was following.

Chapter Sixteen

Katherine didn't even pay lip service to a protest against Vic coming along with her this time. She didn't know what to think about his claims of archvillains being involved in the frightening events of this week. Whatever level villains they might be, she now understood without question how stupid it would be to risk running into them on her own. She let Vic drive her car back to her place. No matter how stubborn she might be about self-reliance, even she had to admit that the hospital experience had her too unsettled to be safe on the road right now. Besides, she was deeply tired. Still, she didn't intend to sleep at her apartment. She was only stopping there to pick up some things. She'd decided that even before Vic found the note. She was on the phone to the hospital at the time.

"The emergency room nurse says Megan is conscious. She has a mild concussion, so they're keeping her there a couple of days for observation and to do some tests, but they think she'll be okay after she gets some rest."

Katherine had called out most of that from the bedroom where she'd used the telephone to contact the hospital and was now packing a suit bag. When Vic didn't answer, she walked back into the living room. She guessed what he was holding in his hands as soon as she saw it. The note looked a lot like the one she'd found on her mantelpiece the night before. What he had *on* his hands was something more of a mystery to her. He was wearing black leather gloves. She'd seen him bare-handed more than once outdoors in these past, very cold days. Yet here he was in her over-heated living room with gloves on.

He must have noticed the direction of her stare because he said, "I don't want to contaminate the crime scene."

Katherine didn't like to think of her living room in such terms, but the dark stain that didn't fit the pattern of her carpet made the truth of his words all too unavoidable. She also didn't like to think about how readily Vic's mind appeared to work like a criminal's, or maybe a lawman's. She grabbed at that straw.

"Were you ever in law enforcement?" she asked.

He was examining the note when she said that. He looked up at her with a look in his eyes that she wasn't sure how to interpret. Then he flung his head back and laughed. The sound was a relief after the tension of the evening. Too bad the moment didn't last.

"Me, a cop?" he said when he had finished laughing. "Not hardly."

There it was again, his utter disdain for the police. What was that all about? She wished she was more certain she really wanted to know the answer to that question.

"Speaking of cops, they should be here soon," Vic said. "If Megan's conscious, they're probably talking to her right now, or maybe they're already on their way to check out where she got attacked. We need to make ourselves scarce."

"I don't know if that's the right thing to do."

Actually, she was certain it was not.

"Katherine, it's like I said back at the hospital. You have to trust me on this one."

Vic was staring at her as earnestly as he had back in the hospital parking lot. She could feel his eyes working their influence over her. She wondered how hard she should resist. Part of her didn't want to resist at all. She knew from the way his gaze made her insides quiver that the part of her advising nonresistance didn't necessarily include her brain.

"Do you have a place to stay?" he asked.

She wished his question didn't arouse in her a sudden pang of disappointment that he hadn't immediately suggested she sleep at his place again. Of course, after what she'd as much as accused him of this morning, she shouldn't be surprised.

"I called a hotel after I called the hospital," she said.

She didn't have any close friends in Albany other than Megan. Katherine's time here had been spent mostly working. That was the way she'd chosen to heal the wounds left by Daniel's death. There'd been little time or inclination on her part for making friends. Perhaps Vic understood that because he didn't comment further.

"Which hotel did you call?" was all he asked.

"The Omni," she said. "It's the only one I know."

She'd stayed there when she'd come from Chicago to interview for the job at the Arbor Hill Center.

"Sounds good," Vic said with a nod. "Let's get going. I'll follow you down there in my car."

Once more, she didn't object to his offer. She also didn't object to his urging that they hurry their departure. This place where she had once felt so comfortable and at home was not either of those things for her right now. She couldn't keep her eyes from straying to the stain on the carpet or a chill from shivering up her spine when she did.

"Just one thing before we go," she said. "I want to read the note."

"Sure," Vic said. "I found it up here over the fire-place."

He gestured toward the mantelpiece as she reached for the paper in his hand.

"Don't touch it. I don't think the cops will find any prints, but you don't want yours messing the thing up any-way."

Again, he was talking like a person who knew a lot about crime. Katherine would have liked to tell herself that was probably because he watched a lot of detective shows on television, but somehow she couldn't imagine such an ac-tion-oriented man spending much time in front of a TV set. She moved close enough to him to read the note he was holding by its edges in his gloved fingers. She couldn't mistake the way her throat tightened just from standing next to him. Maybe some of that was because of what she'd been thinking about his troubling attitude toward the police. Nonetheless, she was honest enough with herself to admit that the anxiety Vic made her feel didn't all have to do with his obvious knowledge of things criminal. She forced herself to focus on the paper he held in his hand.

"We warned you once. You should have listened," it said.

"What do they mean?" she sucked in a scared breath. This note struck her as being as sinister as the last one. She was grateful she hadn't brought Sprite home with her, and glad she'd decided not to stay here herself.

"I don't know for sure, but we have to get out of here," Vic said, as if he might have been tuned into her doubts. "This note is exactly what I'd expect from the kind of guys I've been telling you about, and they've got friends every-where. You don't want your name on some police blotter right now. It's bad enough that they have your address and maybe know you took Megan to the hospital. We need to stall them for a while to keep them from getting any closer. That'll give us enough time to figure out how much we should tell them.''

''Vic, I don't like the sound of any of this.''

''I don't like it either,'' he said, and she could tell he meant it. ''But it's not just us we have to think about. We need to sit down and figure out what's best for those two Bellaway kids. We've got to try to find Coyote, too. We may end up telling the cops everything, maybe not. If we stick around here much longer, we won't have a choice.''

One thing he was saying struck Katherine as definitely true. She had to give herself some time to think.

''My bag is in the bedroom,'' she said, then hurried to get it.

Minutes later they were out of the apartment and on their way down the stairs to the street. They'd left the note on the mantel and the door slightly ajar, just as it had all been when Katherine first arrived home earlier this evening. Vic assured her the police would find the marks a lock pick had made on her door latch, just as he had in his brief inspection. She wished it would be that easy for someone, including herself, to detect and analyze the markings all of this was making on her heart.

IT OCCURRED TO VIC that he was too tall a guy to be spending so much time on tiptoe, but that was what he had to do if he was going to stay around Katherine for any length of time. Five minutes into any conversation with her, he was bound to find himself up on his toes, picking through every sentence he said as if it were made of rusty nails and broken glass. One false step, and he could end up with gaping wounds, or at least in need of a tetanus shot, from tromping down too hard on the wrong spot. He wasn't used to such delicate dancing. He wondered how long it would take for him to get so tired of the trouble it took that he wouldn't care to bother anymore. He knew he wasn't there yet. He only had to look at her and, all of a sudden, he was ready and willing to put up with almost anything as long as she'd let him stick around.

So, when she told him she intended to spend the night in a hotel, he didn't make much comment in response. He knew exactly what he'd like to say, of course. His usual bulldozer self would have come right out with it, too, telling her how there was nothing in the world he'd rather do right now than join her in that hotel room for tonight and any other night she'd let him be there. Then, she'd take off at a run down Capitol Hill as fast as her hiking boots could carry her. In this weather, he'd be left with snowflakes on his face instead of egg, but it amounted to the same thing. That's why he was keeping his mouth shut for this duration anyway.

He had managed to ask if he could follow her down here to the Omni in his car, making a point not to be pushy in the way he said it. Maybe that's the reason she'd agreed without any fuss, or maybe the events of this evening had her so upset she didn't want to be on her own just yet. He'd seen the way she looked in the hospital, with her eyes round and scared, darting from one end of the place to the other. He had put two and two together then, with what she'd told him about her stepson dying after a long illness. Hospitals must have pretty bad memories for her. He'd rushed her out of there partly because of that. He'd only talked about avoiding the cops because he didn't want to make her even more uncomfortable by bringing up those bad memories of hers. Besides, what he'd said about the police was true.

However it had come about, he was happy to be here now, standing in the lobby of the hotel while the automatic door slid open and shut behind him at regular intervals, letting guests in and out on gusts of frigid night air. Katherine was at the registration desk. It would be more discreet of him not to go up there with her while she checked in. Discretion was something else he didn't usually give much thought to, but she seemed to have him in unfamiliar territory in general. Like the fact that, despite all of what had been happening at the center to both of them and to people they cared about, the only thing Vic found himself able to focus on right now was the way wisps of Katherine's hair fell forward across her cheek as she looked down to sign the hotel registration form.

"Can I carry this up for you?" he asked, when she'd walked back over to him with the small folder containing her room key card in her hand.

He was referring to the bag she'd left on the lobby floor next to him while she went to register. He'd seen her shake her head *no* to the bellman when he approached at the desk. Vic expected she'd respond to his offer in the same way.

"I'd appreciate that," she said.

He was so stunned, that she had already walked away to the right, toward the elevators, before he grabbed her bag from the floor and hurried to catch up. He followed her past two lobby restaurants and the hotel gift shop into an open elevator car and watched as she pushed the button marked fourteen. They didn't speak as the car rose or when the doors opened at the fourteenth floor and she checked the wall signs to find the direction of her room. He waited awkwardly behind her as she unlocked the door to her room. Awkwardness was another territory where he had spent very little time.

Vic hefted the suit carrier bag over the threshold into a long living room with a window the width of the wall at the opposite end. The curtains and drapes had been pulled aside to show the state capitol building on the crest of the hill across the way. Lights illuminated the steeply pitched roof peaks topped by metal spire points that had always made Vic think of something more native to Asia than this massive, gray granite building above the Hudson. The view was impressive all the same.

"This is quite a layout," he said as he put the bag down inside the door, which had swung shut on its tight hinge springs when he let go of it.

A spiral staircase near the window wall led upward to what he assumed must be the bedroom. The bag should probably go up there, but he wasn't about to suggest that.

"It's really more than I need," Katherine was saying in response to his comment about the room. "This is where they put me when I came to Albany to interview for the job at the center. There was some kind of convention in the hotel then, and this was all they had available. I imagine they have lots of empty rooms tonight, with the legislature out of session for the holidays and all. I just thought I'd feel better in some place where I'd been before."

She had her back to Vic. He could tell from how fast she was talking and the way she went on and on that she must be nervous, probably because he was still here.

"I'll go now," he said, backing toward the door, and it was the most difficult thing he'd ever done in his life. He didn't want to go. He didn't want to leave Katherine. But he knew in her vulnerable state, he couldn't insist that she let him stay. "My phone number's in the book if you need me."

She turned to face him then, more abruptly than he would have expected.

"Don't go," she said. "I need you now."

Her face was as wide open to him as the space of window glass behind her. Her eyes were clear and looking directly into his. He saw all her fear and her yearning, too, and he recognized the feelings because they matched his own.

Vic walked toward her, stepping carefully and slowly for fear of shattering the fragile moment that hovered in the air above the rose-colored carpet between them.

KATHERINE TURNED and walked away before Vic reached her. She heard him halt, or maybe she felt him do it, behind her. He must be wondering why she had asked him so pleadingly to stay but now walked away from him. She was wondering herself. She wasn't sure. She stopped at the wide window and looked out at the Gothic stone of the City Hall building, St. Peter's Church to the left and the Capitol Building beyond, all solidly planted as if they could stand forever. She wished she felt the same. She knew what she wanted, but she still had doubts about whether what she had said to Vic right now was really true. Did she, in fact, need him? Was he the trouble she suspected he might be? She definitely didn't need any more trouble.

She took three steps to her right and found the long cord to the curtain's traveller rod high above at the top of the window, which rose from this lower level to the upper one. She pulled the cord and drew the gauzy curtain closed across the scene outside. The determination she carried with her at all times, to always think her actions thoroughly through in order to protect herself against the kind of hurt she'd suffered in Chicago, was suddenly as obscured as the view of Capitol Hill beyond this curtain. Maybe, if she stood here a while longer weighing the pros and cons of what she had in mind to do, all would become clear to her. On the other hand, if she turned around, she would be lost.

A voice inside her, unfamiliar but compelling, cried out. *That is exactly what you want,* it said, *and what you need—to be lost.* Katherine turned around.

Where she stood was mostly shadow. The light from the one lamp she had turned on as she came through the door didn't reach this far. She wondered what Vic could see of her. She could certainly see all of him, and the sight actually took her breath away. He had stopped, just as she had felt him do, several feet from where she was now. The pool of light from the lamp touched the thick darkness of his hair and caught almost blue accents there. She couldn't exactly see his deep-set eyes, but she could guess how they were looking at her all the same. The glint in Vic's eyes had been a constant image in her own mind's eye for what had begun to seem like forever.

His trademark close-fitting jeans stretched tight along his right thigh as he cocked his hip in that direction in a posture also typical of him and not lacking in arrogance. In any other man, that attitude would have left her cold. Vic left her anything but cold. The challenge of his stance was received, fast as a telegraph message, direct to her belly, and she tightened there, that tightness clenching farther down her body with every shallow breath she took. He, of course, had on his leather jacket as well. He reached upward in a movement she hadn't expected, grabbed the zipper loop and pulled it down in a single, rapid gesture. A gasp escaped her throat, as if it had been her own clothing he was zipping off.

On trembling legs, she stepped out of the shadow cast by the spiral staircase and into the area of semi-brightness where Vic stood. He remained a few feet away from her and made no attempt to approach. Still, his presence so dominated her senses that he might as well have been filling up the entire room and pressing hard against her from all sides. She was also keenly aware of herself as not quite herself. That engulfing presence had entered into her, perhaps through her parted lips. She felt herself surrender to a will more deeply her own than the surface determination that had held every part of her in check for so very long. The relief which accompanied that release was profound, and experienced in her body as a rush of warmth.

She had unbuttoned her long coat in the lobby downstairs. She shrugged it off her shoulders now, and it fell in folds of heavy wool around her feet. She barely heard Vic's gasp as the coat descended to the floor. She recognized that gasp as the mate to her own, an instant ago. She parted her lips further, as if to speak, but understood then that no words were needed, at least not about what they were both feeling. The two of them, though they might not think alike about a lot of things, were at this moment sharing exactly the same emotions, the same powerful awareness of each other in every fiber of their bodies. The silence was taut and filled with the promise of what was sure to happen between them.

In silence, she moved to the staircase and put her foot on the first step, then the next and the next. He didn't rush to her or make any other abrupt movement, which might have shattered the charmed hush between them. She continued up the spiral. She didn't need to see him there, any more than she had needed to see him before she'd turned around to face him in front of the window below. His image was a bright picture in her mind as he followed her up the staircase to the bedroom of this suite she must have meant all along to be reserved for two rather than just one.

He was suddenly behind her then, where she had stopped next to the bed. His strong hands gripped her shoulders, but gently. Without a word, she turned to face him and lifted her face toward his. She had pulled her hat off in the lobby below. His fingers twined into the mass of her hair, and his mouth met hers. The kiss that followed was long and deep, and Katherine was not aware of herself breathing through any of it. She leaned against him, absorbing his warmth and his strength. At last, he lifted his lips from hers and stared down into her eyes.

"I want you more than I have ever wanted anything in my life," he said.

His voice was husky and even deeper than usual. Before she could answer, or even know if she had thoughts enough left in her head to put words together, he had swept her up in his arms and was carrying her the short distance remaining to the bed. Katherine had never been lifted off the ground in that way, so swiftly or with such command. She tensed for a moment at the newness of being so totally taken charge of. Then, in the next instant, she gave herself up to all of it—the strength of his arms, the scent of his jacket against her cheek, the softness of the bed beneath her as he laid her down on it.

He stood above her and stripped off his jacket first, then his sweater. There was only one low-level ceiling light lit near the doorway that led to the fifteenth-floor corridor. She could see him all the same, not in her mind's vision now, but real and entirely beautiful, standing over her. The power of his torso enthralled her, and the tightness inside her became even more intense as she anticipated touching him across the broadness of his chest and down the muscles of his arms, which hardened now as he clasped his belt and pulled the buckle loose. He would be disrobing her with just as much urgency very soon now. She could hardly wait for that moment to come.

Chapter Seventeen

Vic woke up and knew immediately where he was. The feel of the place and what had happened in it had followed him into his dreams and surrounded him now as bright morning sun streamed through the filmy curtains over the tall, wide window of the duplex suite. On another morning, he might have flung his arm up to shut out the light or groaned and pulled the pillow over his head. Facing the dawn of a new day hadn't always been his favorite thing. Now, Vic faced the brightness and smiled to himself. Today would be different from those other mornings. Except that...

He had turned slowly from the window. He was still at least partly caught up in the dream of last night, a dream that was almost too wonderful to be true. He had stretched his arm across the pillow, as if to take hold of that dream once more in the morning light. Except that Katherine was gone.

Vic sprang fully awake and upright in the same instant. He was alone in the bed, and for a moment he wondered if he could have imagined last night after all. Maybe he'd fantasized about Katherine so much and pictured so vividly how she would look beneath him with her halo of hair spread out against the pillow that he'd finally convinced himself the vision had to be real.

Not a chance, he told himself with relief as he drew in his next breath. Katherine had been in this bed, all right. He could smell her still everywhere around him. He'd heard how scents can remain in the memory, but this was more than that. Her sweetness rose from the sheet as he tossed it away from his naked body. Too bad she wasn't actually in those sheets herself.

He leapt out of bed, propelled by disappointment and something more. He'd have to call that other feeling exasperation. She'd run out on him. She'd made love to him through most of the night. Then, she'd crept out of bed while he was still asleep and left him without so much as a goodbye. He knew exactly what it meant when a guy did that to a woman. He figured it meant just the same when the situation was reversed. He'd been the one-night stand this time. He should probably be glad she didn't wake him up on her way out of here. He didn't know if he'd have been able to stand hearing her say the most obvious brush-off line of all, "I'll call you sometime."

In the old days, his temper would have carried him straight over the top as soon as he realized Katherine was gone. Lucky for him, and for whoever might be in the room next door, he'd worked on that explosive side of himself. Otherwise, he'd be kicking the bedside table right now instead of just standing here, clenching and unclenching the fists he'd clamped resolutely to the sides of his thighs. Besides, kicking furniture wouldn't be a very good idea, at least not as long as his feet were as bare as the rest of him. All the same, he'd like to vent his frustration somehow. Vic considered punching the pillow, but he couldn't do that either, not as long as he still remembered Katherine lying there.

He tore his gaze away from the memory of that sight and sensed a similar tearing in his heart. He could hardly believe how deserted he felt. He picked up the hotel bathrobe at the bottom of the bed and pushed his arm into one of the terry-cloth sleeves. It occurred to him that this robe hadn't been there the night before. He and Katherine had inhabited every inch of this king-size bed from top to bottom and side to side before they finally fell asleep. He would have noticed a bathrobe placed so neatly on top of the also neatly folded quilted spread. Katherine must have left the robe here for him.

"How considerate of her," he said aloud. "She thinks to leave me something to put on but doesn't care enough to stick around till I wake up."

Unless...

He shoved his other arm through the remaining empty sleeve of the bathrobe. Maybe Katherine had only gone downstairs. He'd temporarily forgotten that this fancy hotel room of hers had two floors. He hadn't heard so much as a whisper of sound from below. Still, she could be down on the lower level. Maybe she'd used the bathroom down there so she wouldn't wake him up. She'd thought to leave him the bathrobe. Maybe she was being just as thoughtful about letting him sleep undisturbed. If she had the bathroom door closed, he might not be able to hear her from way up here.

Vic hoped almost desperately that scenario would be true as he hurried halfway down the spiral stairway. One glance told him he was more likely than not thinking like a fool. The living room of the suite was as empty as the hollow that had begun to echo inside him. He continued to move down the staircase all the same, but more slowly now. He'd check the bathroom just in case, but he'd already resigned himself to what he would probably find. Unfortunately, he didn't manage to resign himself enough to prevent another stab of disappointment when the bathroom turned out to be as empty as the rest of the place.

"I suppose I'll be checking the closets next," he said to himself, feeling exactly like the jerk she'd set him up to be.

He was trying not to let it register too deep just how much he hated being in this situation when the buzzer rang at the door a few feet from the bathroom. The sound set his heart dancing in his chest. Katherine was at the door. She'd only gone down to the lobby for a newspaper, or to the health club for a morning swim, or whatever. He didn't care where she'd been. He only cared that she was back. He had his wits about him just enough to pull his robe closed and tie the cloth belt across the front on his way to open the door.

"We're looking for Katherine Fairchild. Is this her room?"

The question came in the few seconds it took for Vic to absorb the disappointment of not finding Katherine at the door. Meanwhile, his mind was doing its best to click through the changes it had to make before reacting to the man and woman in uniform standing on opposite sides of the hotel suite's doorway.

"Is Ms. Fairchild on the premises, sir?" the female officer asked.

Vic didn't feel much like talking, but what was left of his common sense told him he'd better come up with something to say to the policewoman's question.

"Mrs. Fairchild isn't here," he said.

The words were already out of his mouth before he realized he had called Katherine by her previously married title. Too late to take it back, even though he could feel this situation getting harder to explain by the second. He'd guess the lady cop might be thinking the same thing because, while he was speaking, she'd been checking out what he had on—or maybe what he didn't have on. He didn't kid himself for a minute that she was sizing up his masculine charms. He'd bet a year's salary she was busy taking notes. He could almost see them written down in her pocket pad even now.

Unidentified male wearing bathrobe with hotel monogram and clutching front of same, on alleged premises of subject said male refers to as Mrs. Fairchild. Said male possibly of suspicious character. Risk of concealed weapon negligible in his present attire.

"Do you know Ms. Fairchild's current whereabouts?" the policewoman was asking.

Her partner had positioned himself opposite her and at an angle from the other side of the doorway. He peered into the room behind Vic, who thought about stepping to his left to obstruct the shorter man's view, but decided against it. He was very much aware of how vulnerable he had to look standing here in this damned robe. He was also very aware of how dumb it would be to provoke these officers into taking advantage of that vulnerability. They had the drop on him in more ways than one.

"No, I don't know where Ms. Fairchild is right now," he said.

He didn't add that she'd taken a powder before he even woke up, though that infuriating fact was still on his mind.

"Could we step inside for a moment, sir?" the policewoman asked.

She said that in a completely noncommittal tone, with no sign of emotion or even curiosity. She might have been asking him if he would please step aside in an elevator or on a crowded street, as if they were nothing more than two strangers who just happened to be in the same place at the same time. Only, this situation was anything but that simple.

"How did you find out Ms. Fairchild was staying in this hotel?" Vic asked.

He was finally getting his head together enough to realize he had to be careful how he handled this unexpected visit from the law.

"She called Albany Hospital this morning to inquire about the condition of her friend." The policewoman checked her pad which she had, by now, taken from the pocket of her down-filled police jacket. "Ms. Moran told us that Ms. Fairchild was staying in this hotel temporarily."

Her partner gave her a quick look then, as if he thought she was telling more than she should. Vic's mind started clicking again in the meantime. Katherine had called the hospital this morning, maybe from right here in this room while he was upstairs asleep. That made him more infuriated with her than ever, though he wasn't exactly sure why.

"Could we step inside, sir?" the policewoman asked again.

"Do you have a warrant?"

Vic asked the question almost automatically, just the way he would have done if the cops had shown up on his doorstep at home. He still didn't want to give these two an excuse to roust him. He didn't intend to give them access to anything more than they could see from this doorway, either. Not if he could help it, anyway.

"No, we don't have a warrant, sir," the female officer said.

"Then you'd better go and get one."

Vic started easing the door shut while he was saying that. The policewoman had been standing a foot or so back from the doorway, obviously giving herself a margin of safety from the suspicious character in the bathrobe. She took a step forward now and placed her left hand with the pad in it against the door to keep it from closing all the way. Vic could see the firearm she carried in a snap-top holster at her right side. Her right elbow was close to her body, between him and the weapon. Still, he could see that the holster snap was undone.

"Could you give me your name, please, sir?" she asked in a tone that was more demand than question.

He continued pressing the door shut against the resistance of her hand.

"I'm just a friend of Ms. Fairchild's. You don't need to know my name," he said. "I have to go now."

Vic pushed the door shut the rest of the way then and was relieved to hear the automatic lock engage. He listened what felt like a long time, but the officers didn't knock again. If they talked the situation over between them after Vic closed the door, they must have walked off some distance to do it because he didn't hear even the sound of muffled voices from the hallway. He kept listening until he was sure the cops had to be gone. He wished he also felt sure they wouldn't be popping up in his face some time again soon.

COYOTE BELLAWAY was worried about the police, too. They didn't know where he was. Nobody knew that, but they could find out if he wasn't really careful. That's why he'd kept himself on the move. He'd thought a long time about where would be the best place to hide. Miss Fairchild's house was what he came up with first, except he didn't know her address. He had gone to Mr. Maltese's last year for his Christmas party. Coyote never forgot a place he'd been to already, or how to get back there either, but he didn't think he wanted to stay at Mr. Maltese's. He still wasn't too sure if he could trust the man. So, he'd been spending time in a building a few blocks away from Tooley's apartment. It felt good to him to have a roof over his head and a place to sleep indoors instead of out in the snow.

He'd been worried at first that he wouldn't be able to get inside. There was one place, though, that people tended to get careless about when it came to closing up their houses. The basement windows, especially in the back of the building, could get forgotten. Maybe one would be cracked open to keep the basement from going musty. Then, since nobody was down there at the bottom of the house much, that window might stay unlatched. Sure enough, Coyote had found one he could push in and climb through.

He didn't have much in the way of furniture or other stuff, and he'd never been out of Albany in his whole life, but he pretended he was camping out. He let himself daydream for a while about a cabin in the woods, where he and Sprite and their mother and maybe Tooley could all live together. Then he stopped. Daydreams about things that weren't going to happen could make a guy sad. Being sad just slowed him down, and he didn't have time for that.

He'd come here in the middle of the night when the snow got heavy and the wind was too cold for the cardboard boxes on the roof across from Tooley's to keep him even sort of warm anymore. He'd already decided to get out of there anyway when he saw the police all over the place in the afternoon. Then he'd started figuring out where he should go and ended up coming here.

He'd shimmied through the basement window and looked around, using the penlight he always kept in his pocket. He kept a jackknife in there, too, but the most important blade was broken. He'd tried three or four times to save up for a Swiss Army knife, but the money always got spent on something else. The penlight was what he'd needed when he came here, though. He'd found an old, dusty couch and sat down on it and next thing he knew he was waking up there with the light coming through the basement windows. He felt bad about sleeping so late when he should have been on the alert. He felt bad about spending a whole day stuck in this basement.

He also felt bad about losing track of Sprite. He knew Miss Fairchild had taken an interest in his sister, and he had a feeling she'd make sure Sprite was okay. Still, she was his sister and he was supposed to take care of her, but how could he do that when he didn't know where she might be? Coyote had been worrying about that off and on ever since he got here. But he knew he had to stay inside, where he'd be safe, until he could figure out a plan.

He wished he had a father around to help him outsmart the bad guys. But his father had taken off what seemed like so long ago. Thinking about that reminded Coyote of how his mom had told him he was the man of the family now. He didn't feel like he was old enough for that, but he knew he had to do it anyway. Which meant he had to find Sprite and make sure she was all right. She'd be getting out of school for Christmas vacation today. She might be out of there already. She'd go to the Arbor Hill Center, then on to the party Mr. Maltese was having.

He didn't like to think about it being almost Christmas. Thinking about it might start him daydreaming again, and he couldn't do that now. He had to get over to the center and see if he could catch a look at Sprite. The man of the family couldn't waste his time on daydreams.

Chapter Eighteen

Katherine didn't realize she was humming along with the carols until she actually began singing the words to "O Come All Ye Faithful." The sound system had been playing Christmas music since shortly after she arrived at the center. Maybe that was why she'd been close to giddy in her meeting with the Board of Directors this morning. At least, she could blame the carols if anyone happened to notice how unusually exuberant she was today.

It turned out that nobody did notice, after all. They were too preoccupied with speculating about who the generous person with the big donation to the Most Needy Cases Fund might be. The story had been in last night's newspaper under Mariette Dugan's byline, just as she'd said it would be. And, just as she'd also said, Mariette had dubbed the center's benefactor Secret Santa. Curiosity about the contributor's identity was running rampant from the center's kitchen to the conference room where Katherine had barely managed to arrive on time for the special board meeting called to discuss allocation of the half-million-dollar gift.

With everyone's attention directed elsewhere, she'd allowed herself a few precious moments to relive the details of her night with Vic. She hadn't wanted to leave him asleep in the hotel room that morning, and she'd had to drag herself from the cozy warmth of the bed they'd shared. She wondered what it would have been like to wake up together, to continue where they'd left off the night before. Still, she'd given a grateful sigh of relief that she'd checked her answering machine for messages that morning. She'd never have been able to explain her absence at the emergency board meeting. Instead, she'd left a note explaining her absence to Vic.

She tuned back in to the conversations at the meeting, where everyone still speculated about who the Secret Santa could be. That question didn't matter anywhere nearly as much to Katherine. The answer she cared about was the one to her prayers for the children and families she wanted to help, and that answer had arrived in the form of this amazing gift. As far as she was concerned, the check came from heaven, or a piece of heaven in somebody's heart, anyway. Now, all she wanted to do was hand out a holiday grant to every single person who'd applied for one. The directors were, unfortunately, in a more sensible mood than Katherine this morning. They had insisted on sticking to the customary practice of verifying the financial circumstances of each applicant. She supposed they were right about this, except she suspected that anyone who put themselves through the embarrassment of asking for charity probably truly needed it. She was thinking particularly of the Bellaway children and Tooley Pennebaker and how hard they struggled just to get by. Maybe that's why Katherine said what she did when the police arrived.

"Yes, I'm Katherine Fairchild" was her answer to their first question. "What can I do for you?"

Of course, she knew what they were here about, but she hadn't yet decided how much she'd tell them.

"We're investigating the assault on your colleague Megan Moran," the female officer said. "We understand that attack took place at your residence at…'' She checked the small notepad she'd taken from the pocket of her blue shirt. ''Four-forty-one State Street, apartment 2A.''

''That's my address,'' Katherine said.

''Do you think the assailant could have been after you?''

The other police officer, a man older than his partner, had asked that question from behind her, where he'd been standing, keeping the area outside Katherine's office in view and periodically glancing toward the adjoining corridor as if he might be expecting a criminal to approach from that direction.

''The possibility has occurred to me,'' Katherine said.

She and Vic had talked about that. Still, hearing it said out loud again sent a shiver trembling through her.

''Do you have any idea who might want to harm you?'' the male officer asked. ''Maybe a boyfriend you broke up with?''

The female officer looked pained for a moment. ''My partner means we're wondering if you've had any disagreements with anyone lately who might be angry enough to attack you.''

''No old boyfriends. I can assure you of that,'' Katherine said.

She'd understood instantly why the other female officer appeared uncomfortable with having her partner assume that any trouble a woman ran into, especially violent trouble, would most likely have something to do with her love life.

''Your friend, the one who got hit on the head, could have interrupted a thief in the midst of going about his business,'' the male officer chimed in again. ''Except this doesn't look like robbery to me. I was at your place, and the usual goods a robber takes are all still there.''

He'd turned his attention from the adjoining corridor and

was staring at Katherine now. She could tell by the un-
flinching expression in his eyes that he wasn't going to
move away from his spurned-lover theory without a lot of
convincing. She considered encouraging them to go on
thinking that. The problem there would be the possibility
of Vic's name becoming involved. Whatever else she told
these two police officers, Katherine knew she had no intention of mentioning Vic. But Coyote had never turned up
again, and she was worried about the child's safety. It was
time to involve the police. She took a deep breath before
speaking.

"We've been having some problems here at the center
involving two children named Coyote and Sprite Bellaway," she began. "Maybe you'd like to sit down. This is
a rather long story."

The female officer took the chair across from Katherine's
desk. Her partner stayed in the doorway, again dividing his
attention between the corridor and what Katherine had to
say. By the time she'd finished, she'd told them about Coyote's grant application, his night on the mats in the equipment room, his sister Sprite's claims about a man in a black
car who was after Coyote, the break-in at Tooley Pennebaker's, the slashing of Daniel's portrait in Katherine's
apartment, and the fact that Coyote was still missing. She'd
told them almost everything. The parts she left out had to
do with any mention of Vic Maltese.

"Are you anticipating another break-in, Ms. Fairchild?"
the female officer asked just when Katherine had hoped the
interview was at an end. "Is that why you're staying at the
Omni Hotel?"

Katherine was taken more than a little by surprise.

"How do you know that?"

"Ms. Moran told us."

Katherine came close to breathing an audible sigh of relief but stopped herself.

"We went there looking for you before we came here," the male officer added.

Katherine's relief was short-lived.

"You went to the hotel?" she asked.

"Yes," he answered. "We spoke to your friend."

He was staring at Katherine again. She had to force herself not to look away from his gaze.

"What was your friend's name?" he asked.

Katherine took a moment to steel herself before replying, so she wouldn't give in to her usual strictly law-abiding instincts.

"He's just a friend," she said and stood up from her desk. "Now, if you're finished asking questions, I have to get back to my work."

She was fairly certain they couldn't force her to give them Vic's name. She hoped they wouldn't ask her too many times because she wasn't sure she could keep on holding out. She thought about telling them she had to call her lawyer. The problem was the only lawyer she'd ever had was the one she'd hired in Chicago to handle her divorce. Fortunately, the police appeared to be giving up on her. The female officer rose from the chair and tucked the pad down into her shirt pocket while her partner continued to watch Katherine but took a step backward out of her office.

"We may be in touch with you again," the policewoman said. She pulled a business-card case from her coat pocket, took out a card and put it down on the edge of Katherine's desk. "If you think of something further you'd like to tell us, you can call me at the number on this card."

"I'll do that," Katherine said without either picking up the card or looking at it.

She really didn't intend to cooperate, not if cooperation involved jeopardizing Vic. After the police left her office, she watched the parking lot from her window, waiting for them to emerge from the building and drive away. All the while, she was praying they wouldn't come across Vic on their way out. She hadn't seen him yet. In fact, she'd been wondering earlier why he hadn't called her or stopped in to see her if he'd come into the center. In that note she'd left on her side of the bed this morning, she'd asked him to call her here at the center when he got up.

She was relieved to see the two police officers striding across the parking lot toward their car. Katherine ducked back from her window so they wouldn't catch her in the act of spying on them. She headed out from behind her desk and through the doorway that led to the center's main corridor. She was past the reception office when she saw Vic come out of the gymnasium farther down the hall. A thrill shot through her at the sight of him, and she had to stop herself from calling his name. He had his back to her, and he wasn't alone. Vic and the man he was with had their heads together in conversation and didn't appear to notice Katherine. His companion turned, and she saw him more clearly for a moment before he leaned toward Vic again.

In that instant, she dropped her hand and closed her mouth. She also grabbed the doorknob of the office she'd been about to pass, turned the knob and stepped inside.

She held the door open a crack and peered through the opening to watch Vic and his companion. They still stood in what looked like an intimate conversation down the hall. Vic was doing most of the talking, actually, while the other man nodded and seemed to be listening very carefully. That man's appearance was what had made Katherine want to disappear from view. He was as tall as Vic and almost as broad. He also had similar thick, black hair, but that was where the similarity ended. Vic was handsome and strong-featured. This man had strong features as well, but the impression they left was not an attractive one. From her first glimpse of him, Katherine was certain she was looking at a dangerous man.

She watched from behind the office door and wished she could hear what this man and Vic were saying to each other. She didn't like to think that Vic had such friends. She was telling herself that they could be less than that, maybe only acquaintances, when Vic reached up and patted the other man on the back. In response, he gripped Vic around the shoulders in a friendly bear hug. Katherine sighed. She was about to close the door quietly and wait out of sight till the two had left the corridor. Before she could do that, she saw the large man with Vic look quickly down the corridor just as she eased the door shut.

Katherine pressed her back against the closed door. She was breathing hard all of a sudden, as if she'd run the length of the corridor outside at least a couple of times. She didn't question why she was so winded. She recognized her reaction as fear and shock at what else she'd seen when Vic's companion glanced down the hallway. She'd seen his hand move reflexively inside the front of the long, dark coat he was wearing and onto the hand grip of the gun in a holster he wore underneath his arm.

KATHERINE FELT GUILTY about laying her personal problems on Megan when she was flat on her back in the hospital, but their telephone conversation seemed to gravitate that way without much help from Katherine.

"If they don't let me out of here soon, I'm going to start using bedpans for frisbees," Megan said, sounding every bit her usual, irrepressible self. "You'd be surprised how close I can get one of those things to somebody's head without actually making contact. There's a floor supervisor here who'd make a perfect target.''

Katherine laughed, despite the tension that had her sitting so stiff in her chair the cold outside might have frozen her there.

"I can tell you're definitely on the mend," she said.

"My doctor will be in here this afternoon for one more check before they'll release me."

"I feel just terrible that this happened to you at my place."

That was the absolute truth, too. Katherine hadn't stopped feeling guilty since the moment she found Megan on the floor. It didn't help to know that Megan had stopped by to visit her when she'd happened upon Katherine's intruder. The attacker had struck too quickly for Megan to get a look at whoever it might have been.

"I feel just terrible that this was probably meant to happen to you instead of me," said Megan in a much more serious tone this time.

Katherine didn't want to dwell on that.

"Do you think the doctor will let you leave when he sees you this afternoon?" she asked.

"He'd better do just that, or I intend to cut a swath through this place wide as Santa's sleigh with all his reindeer attached, including that changeling Rudolf."

Katherine laughed again.

"So tell me what's bugging you," Megan said. "That laugh of yours sounds about as tinny as me singing 'Jingle Bells.'"

Katherine hadn't intended to go into detail. She'd counted on Megan's wonderful humor to ease the anxiety all by itself. Now, she found herself pouring out the whole story, including the night at the hotel, though she didn't go into detail there. Megan, who was maybe the most outspoken person Katherine had ever known, remained discreetly without comment on the hotel part of the story.

"What do you mean when you say the guy Vic was talking to looked dangerous?" Megan asked instead.

"It's hard to answer that in concrete terms. When I saw his face, I got this feeling." She paused to remember that moment. "His eyes. The feeling I had about him came from seeing his eyes."

"What about his eyes?"

She thought for another moment. "They had no compassion in them," she said.

"I hear you." Megan didn't respond with the skepticism Katherine had half expected. "You say that this guy and Vic looked like they were buddies?"

"They hugged each other."

"I see. Though I actually don't know that I can see Vic Maltese hugging another man. I wouldn't have guessed that was on his macho agenda, if you know what I mean."

"I know what you mean," Katherine replied.

She'd hoped Megan would make the worrisome aspect of Vic's behavior go away. Instead, she was taking the incident in the center corridor as seriously as Katherine had.

"The most effective way to deal with this situation would be to come right out and ask Vic about it," Megan said.

"I don't think that's a very good idea."

Especially not after last night, Katherine added silently.

"I figured you'd say that."

Katherine didn't respond. She was wondering what she actually would consider a good idea. As she pondered the answer to that, her gaze wandered to her office window and her view of the parking lot.

"Megan, I'll call you back later," she said hastily.

Megan was asking, "What's going on?" as the telephone receiver dropped back into its cradle and Katherine grabbed her coat and ran for the door.

KATHERINE HAD NEVER tailed anybody through traffic. She was only half convinced she should be doing it now. She'd seen Vic headed for his car and taken out after him more from instinctive impulse than because she'd made a reasoned decision to do so. He'd had his head bent down, almost hunched between his broad shoulders, in a posture she'd never seen on him before. What she knew about him told her he wasn't on his way to pick up a cup of coffee and a doughnut. He had a goal he was after and, in light of what had been going on here lately, Katherine wanted to find out what that goal might be.

They'd spent the night together, and it had seemed wonderful and right and even necessary at the time. But how much did she, in fact, know about Vic?

He dedicated his life to helping kids, especially boys in trouble. That was certainly admirable, she admitted, keeping the black Trans Am in sight as it turned left from Livingston Avenue onto North Pearl Street. She was also keeping in mind what Megan said about the charitable impulse and how it could sometimes come from a dark place in the psyche. Katherine was well aware that her own similar inclination had a lot to do with her need to heal. She wondered what Vic might have to heal, or to hide.

She glanced to the right toward the brick facade of Hope House. Those words above the door inspired a silent prayer in her heart, except that she wasn't quite sure what she should be praying for. That Vic wouldn't turn out to be a criminal? That she and Vic would... What? She definitely had no idea how that particular prayer should end. She'd settle for the catchall plea that everything would come out all right for everybody when all of this was finally finished. She didn't care to think about how real the possibility was that this prayer would not be answered.

She was driving through a street of deserted-looking industrial buildings and vacant lots where the crabgrass was hidden by snow. She watched the Trans Am but kept a safe distance back, with a car and a plumber's van in between. She was glad for the presence of so many four-wheelers like hers on the road. She'd also not taken time to wash the Cherokee lately, so it was covered with a coating of dried mud splashes and road salt. The more nondescript the vehicle, the better. She didn't want Vic seeing her back here. It didn't seem likely he would with the other vehicles between them, especially not on this late morning, which had suddenly turned very gray, but she told herself she needed to have some kind of story fabricated to explain the coincidence if he did spot her.

The Trans Am turned left on Loudonville Road, and Katherine followed. Where was he going? They were headed out of the city. The wind blew harder as the Cherokee mounted an overpass, and the tall vehicle shuddered against the blast. She pushed the dashboard heater indicator closer to maximum output and wished she hadn't decided to wear a dress today. She'd done that because she wanted to look more attractive than might have been the case in slacks or a skirt and sweater. She'd done that because of Vic, of course. Even before they went to the hotel, she'd packed this outfit, including her impractical knee-high black suede boots with the too-precarious heels, with Vic in mind. How foolish that seemed now. Something longer, with enough material in it to fall in folds around her ankles and keep her from turning frigid altogether, would have been a much wiser choice.

Vic veered right off Loudonville Road onto the bypass

at the rear of Albany Memorial Hospital. Katherine stayed on his tail, but she was thinking about Megan lying in another hospital on the opposite side of the city. She was going to be all right, but that might not have been the outcome. A blow struck just a little more forcefully and to a slightly different spot could have left her brain damaged, her life drastically changed, the important work she did perhaps ended forever. Could Vic have had anything to do with that attack? Big black cars with scary men in them, professional break-ins, a small boy on the run from what Vic had hinted could be gangsters. And what was his connection to all of that? How much did he know that he wasn't willing to tell anyone, especially not the police he so obviously preferred to avoid? Why had he been behaving so cozily with a man who looked like an outlaw and carried a gun?

Katherine hit the power button on the car radio in the hope of distracting herself from the troubling questions that had grown to inescapable prominence in her mind. She sighed when Christmas music poured out of the speakers and pushed the button to turn the radio off again. She couldn't help remembering how she'd been singing along to a Christmas carol at the center such a short time ago. That thought filled her with the sadness of loss, the same kind of loss and sadness she'd vowed to shield herself from, no matter what. She didn't feel strong enough to face an experience that echoed with the suffering she'd gone through when Daniel died, even if those echoes were only a fraction as powerful. Grief was grief, and she'd already dealt with about as much of that as she could stand. Yet, here she was putting herself in the way of more.

Speaking of where she was, what were they doing on their way into Loudonville? She'd followed the Trans Am beyond the Albany city limits toward one of the most exclusive communities in the Capitol District. Large, impressive homes lined the road on either side. She'd assumed Vic would drive straight on through, toward some less imposing neighborhood beyond this very privileged one. Then, he turned left onto a lane marked Crumitie Road and left again after a few blocks. He wasn't on his way through Loudonville as a shortcut to somewhere else. He was driving into the residential heart of the township.

There was no traffic here, and Katherine had to be more careful than ever to remain undiscovered. She wished her interest in Vic's destination, and his behavior in general, didn't come from such a close and personal place in herself. She wished she didn't care so much about him. Meanwhile, she kept on praying everything would turn out all right, though she wasn't exactly certain what all right might be.

Chapter Nineteen

Coyote wasn't sure exactly what made him crawl into the back of Miss Fairchild's car in the first place. The parking lot at the Arbor Hill Center was cold, and too open to be safe for hiding. He had the idea of waiting near the center till nobody was around, then sneaking inside to look for Sprite. School was out today for Christmas. He couldn't find her at Tooley's place, so he thought Sprite might turn up here. He knew he was grabbing at straws, like they say, but he couldn't think what else to do. While he was waiting, he'd ducked down behind Miss Fairchild's car to get out of the wind. That's when he saw a big guy coming out of the center. He wasn't the man Coyote'd been running away from, but in a way this guy reminded Coyote of that man in the black car who'd dumped what could have been a body in the alleyway on Broadway.

They both were big men across the chest and shoulders and looked like they could knock a boy down by just thinking about it. They walked very straight and didn't bend their necks when they turned their heads. They made Coyote think of two blocks of wood. They made him afraid, too. Being scared was probably the real reason he slipped around Miss Fairchild's car right then and tried the back door. He should have guessed she'd leave it open. She'd be the type to trust everybody. He could almost remember when he'd been that type himself.

He could even remember when he wasn't scared of hardly anything. These days he was afraid pretty much all the time. So he climbed into the back of Miss Fairchild's car and held on to the door without closing it all the way shut because that might make too much noise. He peeked up and saw the man who looked like a block of wood get into a big, dark car of his own that made Coyote shiver from more than being cold. He ducked his head down then and didn't peek over the bottom of the window of Miss Fairchild's car again till what seemed like a long time later when he heard an engine rumbling.

He saw Mr. Maltese's black sports car back out of his parking place very fast and spin around to leave the parking lot with a squeal of tires. A huge puff of exhaust smoke almost hid the car inside as Mr. Maltese speeded out onto the street. Coyote was so busy watching that he almost didn't notice Miss Fairchild herself on the way to the car where he was hiding. He ducked down onto the floor and dragged the blanket from the seat over him just in time. Good thing he'd pulled the car door shut already, or she might have gotten suspicious and checked the back seat. She didn't do that, though, as far as he could tell. She got in the car and took off out of the parking lot almost as fast as Mr. Maltese had done.

Now, here Coyote was, still under the blanket on the floor between the front and back seats of Miss Fairchild's car. She'd driven a pretty long time over roads that were bumpy sometimes. She'd turned a few corners, and he'd lost track of what direction they must be going after a while. Finally, she pulled over to the side of the road and turned the car off. Coyote waited a couple of minutes after she got out of the car before poking his head up very slowly and carefully from behind the seat. What he saw made him slip back onto the floor again while he tried to figure out where they were.

Coyote was sure he'd never been in this place. He didn't even know where it could be. He didn't think they'd driven far enough to be all the way to another city like Troy, but what he'd seen just now—big houses with wide lawns and very tall trees—sure didn't look like the Albany he was used to. He'd heard about where rich people lived. He hadn't been to any of those places in person, till now. He wasn't going to get out of this car here, that was for sure. He'd be spotted straight off for not belonging. He was in enough trouble already without asking for more.

He did peek up over the bottom of the window again. The car was parked next to a high wall with bare vines all over it. Branches from big trees reached over the wall. Then he saw Miss Fairchild. She was at the far end of the wall from where she'd parked the car. What she was doing made Coyote's eyes open extra wide.

She'd taken hold of one of the tree branches hanging over the wall and was trying to hoist herself up on it by walking her feet from stone to stone. She didn't make it very far before she slipped and bumped into the wall. Coyote couldn't see her face, but he'd bet it hurt when she hit the stones. He'd just about decided he had to get out of the car and try to help her when he saw somebody come around the corner of the wall.

The man walked up behind Miss Fairchild and grabbed her arm. They talked for a minute, and Coyote saw her try to pull away, but the man didn't let go. He led her away after that, back around the far corner of the wall and out of sight. From the way Miss Fairchild was being pulled along, Coyote could tell she was in trouble. No matter how much he wanted to stay here hiding in the car, he knew he had to do his best to find out where they were and what was happening to this nice lady who did so much to help so many people.

VIC HADN'T BEEN here in a long time. Still, the minute he stepped through the door, he was straight back in the middle of it all again, just as if he'd never left, and wondering if his reason for coming was really important enough to put himself through this. Nothing had changed much, at least not in terms of his feelings about this place and what it stood for as far as he was concerned. Those feelings were as uncomfortable and agitated as ever, especially when the woman he saw in his thoughts every day came hurrying through the double doors from the living room with her arms open wide to embrace him.

"Victor, I am so glad to see you," she said.

The wideness of her smile shone with the truth of her words, and her eyes were bright with tears. Vic kept his gaze level and over her head so he wouldn't have to see the joy in her face as she ran into his arms.

"I'm glad to see you, too, Ma."

He felt tears of his own fill his throat. He hugged his mother until she pushed herself out of his arms and gazed up at him. As he looked at her, he noted with surprise that her blue-gray eyes were almost the same shade as Katherine's.

His thoughts drifted to the evening before and to the sight of Katherine, eyes wide and shining and hair spread out on his pillow. He smiled to himself, remembering his hurt when he thought she'd left the hotel without a word to him, and then his overwhelming happiness when he'd found her note, which had slipped beneath the edge of the bed. He'd called the center, only to learn she was already in the board meeting, and by the time he'd arrived, she was busy in her office. He'd had the pleasure of watching her unnoticed for a moment, then had headed down the hallway with more energy than usual as he went to work.

He hoped his mother, who was still gazing at him, couldn't read his mind.

"You are so very handsome, my son," she was saying with such obvious pride Vic was afraid she'd have him blushing soon. "I've missed you."

She said that simply, without any accusation in her voice. He felt a pang of guilt all the same.

"I've missed you, too, Ma."

She could have jumped on that with both feet just by asking why, if he missed her so much, he didn't ever come to see her. She didn't do that. She wasn't the kind of mother who tried to make her children feel bad. She also wasn't the kind of woman who whined or complained. Katherine was like his mother in that way, too.

"Your father also misses you."

Whatever softness and sentiment Vic had begun to feel cut off sharply when his mother said that.

"I don't miss *him*," he said.

His mother closed her eyes for a moment, probably because his words had hurt her. He'd had to say them anyway.

"Still, you've come here to ask him for something," his mother said.

Her manner was more subdued now than when she first came hurrying toward Vic.

"What makes you think that?" he asked.

"You always hold your head a certain way when you are going to ask your father for something. You have a defiant expression on your face. It has always been the same."

"I've hardly ever asked him for anything."

Vic heard himself sounding like every belligerent, rebellious kid there ever was. He wanted her to understand he was more than that, but he didn't know quite how to do it.

"I know all too well that you have come to your father for very little in your life, which makes those occasions all the more vivid to me," she said. "As I say, I can tell that this is one of those few times."

She'd been like this for as long as Vic could remember, able to read him with almost scary ease.

"Why don't you come inside and sit down," she said.

He hesitated.

"Victor, your father isn't here now," she added with a shake of her head.

She turned and walked away from him, back to the double doors, which she pulled open. Vic had no choice but to shrug and follow his mother.

The foyer was pretty much unchanged from what he remembered, except for a fresh coat of paint on the woodwork and a lighter shade of wallpaper in what he figured was probably silk brocade. After all, Gabriel Maltese never settled for anything but the best. The living room, on the other hand, had undergone a complete transformation. The original mahogany panelling had been replaced by light-colored surfaces. The heavy drapes were off the windows. Even the furniture, formerly large antique pieces, was all different and much less old-fashioned and imposing. The only object in the room that wasn't white or pale-toned was the tall, floor-to-ceiling live evergreen tree in the bay window that looked out onto the vast lawn. Its boughs were hung with the glass angels he remembered from his childhood.

"What's this, Ma?" he asked, referring to the decor. "Your California period?"

She laughed, and he was suddenly aware of how much he'd missed hearing her do that.

"Your father," she said. "One day he decided we needed to brighten things up around here. You know how he is."

"I know how he is."

His mother must have chosen to ignore the sharp way he said that because she kept on talking. "He gets an idea in his head, and immediately we have a project on our hands. He's even more that way these days, since he retired."

Vic stifled an exasperated groan. She talked about his father as if he'd been a regular businessman going off to the office every day, instead of what he really was.

"Besides, it isn't true that you know how your father is," she was saying. "You don't know much about him at all, especially not now."

"I don't want to get into that," he said, unable to hide his impatience.

"I know you don't," his mother answered with a smile that couldn't help but soften him some. "Sit down with me and we'll talk about what you did come here for."

She'd taken a seat on a long, off-white sofa upholstered in fabric with a pattern of small flowers. Vic couldn't imagine his father picking out furniture, or anything else, with flowers on it. His mother patted the cushion next to her and smiled up at him. She'd always been beautiful, and in the bright daylight of this room he could see that she was beautiful still. She probably colored her hair to cover up the gray, but she never would have talked about such a thing. Her skin was as smooth as it had ever been, and she didn't wear much makeup. She was dressed as he always remembered her, in simple, well-made clothes that came from the best stores, but were never flashy or deliberately expensive-looking. It had occurred to him many times that she was way too elegant to be called "Ma," but she seemed to love him doing it all the same.

"Sit with me," she repeated.

"I don't know…" he began.

"Sit."

Vic shrugged once again and sat down on the long sofa.

"Now, what is it you need your father to do for you?"

"Ma, I think that's something I have to talk about with him, not you."

"Why is that?"

Her eyes were completely clear, as if she'd never had a secret or could never tell a lie. He'd felt that about Katherine's eyes, too, though he hadn't really known it till this minute.

"Why is it you don't think you can talk about the same things with me that you could discuss with your father?"

"Ma, this is business."

She laughed again. "You act as though you think this is some kind of Hollywood movie where the wife keeps herself deliberately ignorant of her husband's professional involvements."

Vic stared at his mother. He always had thought something just like that.

"I know you don't approve of some of the people your father has associated himself with over the years," she said. "Maybe I didn't entirely approve myself, but I love your father and I support whatever he does or whatever he may have done."

"Ma, he's a…" He didn't want to say the word.

"You think your father is a gangster." She supplied the word for him. "He is not. He simply knows people who know things."

He breathed a heavy sigh. This was why he didn't come here. He was ashamed of what his father had done with his life, how he had made the money that bought this house, and the one in Colorado, and the one in Barbados. Vic was ashamed, and nobody else would even admit there was anything to be ashamed of. He made a move to stand up and leave, but his mother took his arm to stop him.

"I sense that you want to know things yourself now. Why don't you tell me what they are, and I will speak to your father."

Vic usually knew exactly what he had to do. He wasn't so sure about that now.

"I would guess that your question must be of great importance to you," his mother added. "Otherwise, you would not have come here."

Once again, she had read him accurately. There was more at stake here than his differences with his family, even his feelings about his father. By the time the knock sounded at the double doors, he had told his mother most of the details of the situation with Coyote and his suspicion that professional criminals of the organized variety might be involved. He needed to find out specifically who those criminals might be and what they were up to. As his mother had said, his father knew people who knew things. If anybody could dig up the information Vic was so desperate to find out, that somebody was Gabriel Maltese.

"Come in," Vic's mother said in response to the knock.

Vic might have been disgusted by the palooka who came through the door and how typical he was of the kind of guy Vic's father had to keep around him for protection, but Vic wasn't thinking about that now. He was too startled by who the palooka had in tow.

"Katherine!" Vic exclaimed. "What are you doing here?"

THAT WAS MORE QUESTION than Katherine was prepared to answer at the moment. Before she answered anything, she had some questions of her own.

"What are *you* doing here?" she said, not bothering to be polite about it, despite the presence of the very distinguished-looking woman sitting next to Vic.

"I used to live here," he said.

"I suppose you must have had his job then."

Katherine indicated the brawny groundskeeper, or whatever he was, who had escorted her in here.

"I was a little closer to the family than that," Vic said in a slightly amused tone that made Katherine want to punch him right in the nose. "In fact, I'd like you to meet my mother."

The woman on the long sofa stood up, as Vic had done when Katherine first came in.

Katherine smiled and said, "How do you do," because she was too stunned to respond any other way than with the automatic courtesy she'd been taught from childhood on.

"Mother, this is Katherine Fairchild. We work together."

Vic still sounded amused.

"I'm so pleased to meet you," the elegant woman said with a radiant smile as she came around the sofa with her hand outstretched to greet Katherine. "Won't you come in and sit down?"

Katherine was searching for signs of resemblance between the two faces in front of her. She supposed there could be a few, mostly around the mouth and in the way they were both smiling now, though Vic was wearing more what she'd call an irritating grin.

"Come, Miss Fairchild. Sit down," Vic's mother said again and took Katherine's arm to lead her into the room.

When she moved to follow, her right leg smarted and she flinched from the pain.

"Are you all right, my dear?" Vic's mother asked sounding truly concerned. "Are you hurt?"

"She was trying to climb over the back wall and she skinned her knee," Katherine's brawny escort explained.

Vic's mother gazed down at Katherine's torn stocking and the bloody scrape underneath, then looked up with a confused expression. Katherine was feeling the same, and embarrassed as well. She couldn't help being grateful when Vic stepped forward to what she hoped would be her rescue.

"I told Katherine about the gardens at the back of the house, Mother," he said. "She couldn't wait to see for herself."

Katherine smiled in what she meant to look like agreement.

"If you'll excuse us for a moment," he went on before she could babble some kind of response about her alleged interest in the gardens, "I'm going to take a look at her injuries."

"Yes, you must do that," his mother said. "I'll send in a pair of stockings to replace those torn ones. The downstairs bathroom is beyond the staircase."

"I remember how to get around this place," Vic said with an edge in his voice that made Katherine all the more curious about what might be going on here.

However, after he had supported her by the arm while she hobbled across the marble floor of the foyer of this very grand house and they were out of earshot inside the equally grand bathroom, he was the one to begin the questioning.

"How did you get here?" he asked.

"I followed you."

"You trailed me all the way from the center?"

"Yes, I did."

"Why?"

He'd seated her on a chair in front of a dressing table with three mirrors, each offering a separate view of her flushed face.

"I wanted to find out more about you," she said.

He laughed. "Well, I guess you're doing that. Aren't you?"

She didn't know what to say. The mirrors had already told her she looked as bewildered as she was feeling.

"I'll bet this place comes as a real shock to you," he said. "Not what you expected from me. Right?"

"Right."

She knew it might be more diplomatic to tell less than the whole truth, but she didn't feel like being diplomatic just now.

"You probably had me pegged as coming from the wrong side of the tracks."

Katherine only sighed in response to that one. Then, she gasped. Vic had lifted the leg she'd hit against the stone wall onto his lap as he knelt on the floor in front of her. His touch seared through the thin material of her torn stocking. That was what caused her to gasp. Fortunately, the sound was covered by his next remark.

"I see you have these silly boots on again," he said.

She felt the blush begin in her already red cheeks. He'd reminded her of why she'd dressed this way that morning, because she wanted to look sexy for him. Now, all of that and her foot in his lap struck her as very out of place. She pulled her leg away.

"I have to leave now," she said, standing up and doing her best to ignore the sting in her scraped leg.

Vic stood up next to her.

"We need to talk," he said.

"I don't think so."

He backed against the door as she was moving toward it.

"You came all the way here to find out more about me. That's what you just said. Right?"

"That's right. Now, I wish I hadn't done that."

"I think it was a good idea," he said.

Something had changed in his voice, softened in a way that made her stop trying to get past him to the door, at least for the moment.

"Why do you think that?"

"I want to tell you about myself. You deserve to know the truth."

Katherine suspected she should resist the temptation to agree with him. She wished she was that strong.

"We'll talk on the way back to town," he said, reaching behind him to open the door. "We can take my car."

"But I drove here," she said.

"Gus will bring your car to my place."

"Gus?"

"The guy who caught you climbing the wall."

Vic had opened the door. He took Katherine's arm to lead her out into the foyer, but she stood her ground.

"If this Gus drives my car into town, how will he get back here?" she asked.

"Don't worry about that," Vic said. "Guys like Gus are very resourceful."

And what about guys like you? She would have liked to ask, but the maid had arrived with a pair of new stockings, still in their package.

"Why don't we take these with us," he said, relieving the maid of the package. "We'll say our goodbyes now."

Despite her questions and misgivings, Katherine followed Vic toward the living room to take their deceptively polite leave of this bewildering place. She was too eager to hear Vic's story to do otherwise.

Chapter Twenty

What Vic hadn't understood till this very minute was one of the reasons he'd never told this story to anyone. He didn't really know how. He'd wanted to grab Katherine in his arms and kiss her when they were alone in his parents' mansion. He didn't follow through on his instincts, and not because he was afraid she would push him away. She might do that, but he'd try again till she melted against him and returned his kiss with the passion he knew well from last night. He hadn't put his arms around her because he was holding himself back from that closeness, the closeness that would bring him to this minute, when he'd have to tell his story.

The time had come anyway. Maybe it was bound to happen. Maybe all these years of being alone, at least as an adult, had been about knowing this minute would come and putting it off as long as he could. So, why stop putting it off now? Katherine was the answer to that one. He cared about her more than he cared about keeping himself safe from hard-to-handle feelings. He cared about her, and he didn't want to lose her and go back to being alone again. He gripped the steering wheel so hard his knuckles went white. When he began to talk, his voice was husky with emotion.

"We didn't always live in that house," he said, not sure why he'd chosen to lead off with this statement. He could feel Katherine's quiet attention as he talked. "We were in Troy till I was almost twelve."

He took the turn off Crumitie onto Route 9 more slowly than was usual for him.

"I was told later that my father got out of the businesses he was into when we left Troy."

"What businesses were those?" she asked softly.

"Not-so-legal businesses," he said.

Vic saw her nod out of the corner of his eye as he kept his gaze deliberately on the road ahead.

"After Troy, my father supposedly went strictly legit, as the saying goes. Mostly, investing and real estate. He did very well, as you can see from the way they live, but what got him his start was the money he made in the rackets."

"What kind of rackets?"

"Gambling, for the most part," he said. "That's what I was told anyway when I got old enough to put two and two together, around eleven or so. Hints of things I didn't really want to believe. By the time I was sixteen, I had a pretty clear idea what was going on."

"You said your father had…" Katherine hesitated. He could imagine how hard she was trying to pick just the right words. "You said he'd changed his line of work by then," she began again. "What made you think he'd been doing something illegal before that?"

"He still had a lot of the same friends. They'd come around the new house, especially at this time of year. My mother puts on a big Christmas Eve party every year. It would be wall-to-wall mobster city in there. Even a kid like me could figure that out, especially with the way they had their palookas lined up outside the house supposedly to guard the limos but really to keep an eye out for cops or reporters.''

''Are you sure that's what was going on? Maybe they were only wealthy businessmen with bodyguards.''

Vic glanced out the side window. They were driving past some very expensive real estate right now, high-class houses lived in by high-class people. He could understand why Katherine might have a hard time putting this kind of neighborhood together with the idea of career criminals. What he was saying had to come across to her as way too far-fetched to be true.

He shrugged as he turned his attention back to the road in front of them. ''I know what those guys were about no matter how crazy it may sound,'' he said. ''They were hoods in high-priced suits, nothing more, nothing less.''

''How can you be so certain of that?''

He could tell she was trying to help him out, doing her level best to give him a way off the hook. Her caring and concern for him struck him in a place very close to his heart.

''I know you want to make all of this easier on me,'' he said, ''and that's very nice of you. But, the truth is, I can be sure I'm right about my father because he proved to me that I was.''

''How did he do that?''

''By what he didn't say the day I confronted him with what I suspected about his history.''

Vic had stopped taking advantage a long time ago of opportunities to crawl off the hook of the truth about his family. Still, he would have preferred to find at least a little of the escape artist in himself right now. The thought of this classy woman hearing the real scoop about the down-and-dirty background he came from was almost more than he could stand.

"What was it that your father didn't say to you?" she asked.

He sighed. "First of all, he didn't say I was wrong about the things I was accusing him of. He also didn't say I was right. That's my dad straight down to the ground. Don't explain, don't complain. He used to say that a lot. He has some very strong principles…for a crook."

He could hear the bitterness in his voice, and how fresh that bitterness sounded, even after all these years.

"Was your father ever convicted of any of these crimes you suspect him of committing?"

"Not convicted. In fact, he was never even formally charged. He had big-time connections in high places all over Rensselaer County. The cops didn't dare lean on him too hard. Still, they had their eye on him. They'd have loved to catch him at something, I'm sure, but he was too smart to get caught. That's also my dad straight down to the ground. He's a smart guy through and through, and he knows how to take care of business."

That was why Vic had gone to Loudonville today, though he didn't like admitting it even to himself. Today he needed the help of somebody who could take care of business.

"Do you know these things for absolute fact?"

"I found out for an absolute fact when I got a little older and was stupid enough to start asking around about joining the police force myself. Lucky for me, I guess, a cop I knew clued me in before I could make a total fool of myself by actually putting in an application to the police academy. He told me that, as long as I had the last name Maltese, I had about a snowball's chance in hell of getting into a station house for anything except maybe to stand in a lineup."

"Maybe you should have put in that application anyway. That policeman friend of yours could have been wrong."

Vic kept his eyes trained on the road ahead. The last thing he needed right now was to look over and see the sympathy on Katherine's face. He was having a hard enough time listening to it in her voice.

"I'm better off where I ended up. Working at the center, I mean," he said. "I don't have to be proving myself to everybody all the time."

"Except maybe to yourself."

"Why do you say that?" he asked as they headed onto North Pearl Street.

"Because I can hear you doing it right now. I can hear you being ashamed, as if you were the one who did something you should be punished for. I think you ought to let up on yourself a little."

"The apple doesn't fall very far from the tree. Or maybe it's the acorn. Isn't that what they always say?"

"They say a lot of things. More often than not, they aren't worth listening to. I say you are a good man."

Vic had pulled up at the stop sign where North Pearl Street meets Livingston Avenue. They were back in the city of Albany now, only a few blocks from the Arbor Hill Center. Maybe that was why he'd suddenly become aware of the tightness of his throat and of his fingers on the steering wheel. He was back in his own territory. Loudonville might be only a few miles down the road, but it was really a universe away as far as Vic was concerned.

He'd been right about how much it would bother him to tell this story. The words had left him in a rush, leaving a dark place of hurt behind. What he hadn't anticipated was that, along with the hurt, came release and relief.

More than that though, he knew it was what Katherine had just said that made him feel freer inside himself than he had since he couldn't remember when. He turned to look at her and saw proof of her belief in him shining out of her beautiful eyes. He wondered what he'd done to get so lucky.

He didn't want to return to the center just yet, didn't want to be separated from Katherine at all. And, in spite of his tangled emotions where his family was concerned, he had the troubles of another family to worry about, too. Katherine readily agreed to a detour to Tooley's neighborhood to look for Coyote. Though they spent the better part of an hour cruising the streets, they found no sign of the boy. Obviously, Coyote was too street-smart and too scared to come out of hiding. When Katherine said she'd informed the police about the situation, Vic told her she'd made the right decision.

As they made their final trip past Tooley's apartment building, he looked at his watch and swore. He'd completely forgotten what day it was.

"I have a favor to ask of you," he said when Katherine looked at him in concern.

"What would that be?"

"I told you about the open house I have every holiday season. The party's this afternoon, and I could use some help putting it on."

"This afternoon! Aren't you cutting last-minute planning a little close to the last second?"

Vic laughed and was relieved to hear he still could.

"I'm not quite as bad as all that. The food's taken care of. Sandra Thomas, from the center, caters for me every year. The part that isn't quite nailed down yet is the decorating. I need a hand with that before people start showing up."

Katherine reached across the seat and touched his arm.

"My hand is yours," she said.

His heart leapt so hard, and so unexpectedly, in his chest that he had to brace himself against the impact. He might have sat there grinning goofily at her all day if a horn blast from behind hadn't reminded him he had to make a right turn and take them both home.

THE PROBLEM of Coyote and Sprite Bellaway stayed in Katherine's mind even as she helped Vic decorate for the party. It was still with her as they greeted his guests at the door.

She would never have guessed she'd end up hostessing Vic's holiday open house, but here she was doing exactly that. She was glad she'd worn a dress and high-heeled boots today, after all. A few minutes in the bathroom, some Mercurochrome, a bandage and Mrs. Maltese's donated stockings took care of the damage she'd done to her knee during her ill-fated attempt at wall climbing. Remembering that awkward scene, and how much she'd been frightened at first by the huge and fierce-looking man who apprehended her behind the Maltese mansion, also made her think about what Vic had revealed to her while they were driving back to Albany. The man who had gripped her by the arm and all but carried her into the grand, spacious house that turned out to be Vic's family home certainly did fit the stereotype of a mobster muscleman. So had the old family friend who had come to the center to say hello to Vic.

Vic's mother, however, had been another story entirely. She didn't fit any of those stereotypes at all. She was, in fact, the kind of gracious and elegant woman Katherine had always hoped she herself would grow into someday. Mrs. Maltese also very obviously adored her son. It was difficult to imagine her ever doing anything that might jeopardize his well-being in any way. Still, Katherine knew that Vic could be correct in his suspicions about his father's back-

ground. From what she understood about Vic already, she
could tell—or at least she believed she could tell—he
wasn't the kind of man who would have tormented himself
for half his life over a delusion.

The thought of that torment, and the imprint of it she
had seen earlier in his eyes, made Katherine all the more
determined that this should be the most joyful holiday party
he had ever given. She rose to that challenge with a sparkle
she hadn't realized she still possessed. She'd believed that
the capacity for high social spirits had been burned out of
her by the sadness of losing Daniel. Instead, today she
found herself greeting each newcomer with a bright smile
and a heartfelt happy-holiday wish. Each time she went to
the door, too, she hoped to see tiny Sprite Bellaway standing outside. The family friend she was staying with had
planned to bring the little girl to Vic's party.

Katherine and Vic didn't have much time at all to talk,
though she saw plenty of him as he mingled with his guests
and often sent her a devastating smile. She poured punch
and chattered while she made certain every guest was stuffing himself or herself from the trays and bowls and chafing
dishes of good food, which Sandra Thomas kept full to
brimming. That went on all through the late afternoon, till
at dusk, Santa Claus appeared carrying a bulging bag over
one stooped shoulder.

Katherine hadn't known there would be a Santa at the
party. Apparently, the kids from the center hadn't, either.
Their surprise and delight were wonderful to see as a cheer
went up, followed by cries of, "What's in the bag, Santa?"
Katherine had no idea who Santa might actually be. He
brought to mind the Secret Santa of the newspaper articles
along with a rather wild thought. What if this was the same
person? She was telling herself how absurd that had to be
when Santa looked up from his gift-distributing to favor

her personally with a particularly hearty, ''Ho, ho, ho.'' She knew instantly then that Santa was none other than Vic Maltese himself. She'd have recognized those eyes under any disguise. There wasn't a hint of torment in them now. Suddenly, Katherine realized, with a pang of warmth, which travelled directly to her heart, that the joy in Vic's eyes was the best present Santa Claus could possibly have given her.

Even Mariette Dugan showed up for some eggnog. She had a photographer in tow, of course. Mariette didn't strike Katherine as a woman who was ever one-hundred-percent off the job. The photographer set about at once snapping shots of Vic in the Santa suit. Katherine didn't believe for a minute that Mariette's motives were either sentimental or charitable. She would use these photographs to promote her Secret Santa story and squeeze just a little more play out of the series before the day after Christmas made it old news.

Katherine actually hoped the big contributor's identity wouldn't be revealed. There was more magic to the generous gesture while it remained anonymous, as if the spirit of the season had been the real benefactor who brought so much relief and happiness to so many people who truly needed those unexpected gifts. She'd heard several reports of how just about every staff person at the center had been happily busy all day making phone calls, handing out money orders, delivering food baskets and wrapping presents. Part of Katherine regretted missing out on the fun of spreading so much joy and goodwill, but she reveled in the new knowledge she had of Vic and in the closeness she'd felt between them as they'd silently scoured the neighborhoods earlier. Besides, she knew that being at Vic's side today was the most important, and the happiest, holiday duty she could possibly perform. She was thinking about how special that experience had turned out to be when the phone began to ring. Vic, as Santa, was still being mobbed by children under the tree so Katherine answered the call.

"Could I please talk to Mr. Maltese?" a young boy asked at the other end of the telephone line.

Katherine recognized the voice at once. The child had never been far from her thoughts all day.

"Coyote, is that you? This is Katherine Fairchild. Where are you?"

There was silence from Coyote for a long moment, and Katherine was afraid he might be about to hang up the phone.

"Mr. Maltese is right here," she said. She gestured at Vic, but he didn't appear to notice her over the clamoring of the children who surrounded him. "We both want to help you. Please, tell me where you are. We'll be happy to come for you if you need us to."

The silence continued, but for only a moment this time.

"I'm at the cathedral next to the Plaza," Coyote said. He sounded like he might be shivering from the cold.

"You mean the cathedral near Empire State Plaza?"

The expanse of marble concourse and tall state office towers across State Street from the Capitol Building was referred to by just about everybody locally as the Plaza. The Cathedral of the Immaculate Conception wasn't far from there. Katherine had gone inside once just to sit for a while and feel the peace of the place.

"That's where I mean. Next to the Plaza, just down the street from there," Coyote said. "I hitchhiked here from that huge house you drove to this morning. I was hiding in the back of your car. I saw that big guy drag you away, but I never did find out where he took you. When I went to get back in the car, the same guy was driving it away so I hid till he was gone. Then I got out of there as fast as I could.''

Katherine could hardly believe what she was hearing. Coyote Bellaway had stowed himself away in the back of her car? She'd had no idea he was there. She would have liked to question him further about why he'd done that, but finding that out wasn't what really mattered now. She could hear Coyote's fear in his voice, and his exhaustion, too.

''Go to the front of the Cathedral, by the steps,'' she said. ''Mr. Maltese and I will be there very soon.''

''Come as fast as you can, please.''

''We'll be right there,'' Katherine said, and hung up the phone.

She signalled to Sandra Thomas, who was just passing by with a tray heaped high with cookies.

''We need you to take over here, Sandra,'' Katherine said. ''Vic and I have to attend to an emergency situation involving one of the children.''

Sandra nodded and immediately launched herself into the swarm of children surrounding Vic.

''Santa has to go now,'' she boomed. ''His sleigh is double-parked. But, Mrs. Santa sent these just for you guys.''

The tray of cookies distracted the children long enough for Katherine to drag Vic away and tell him quickly why the party had to be over for him for now. He followed her immediately, without even so much as a parting, ''Ho, ho, ho.''

Chapter Twenty-One

They made it across town to the Cathedral in record time, even with Vic taking the time to change out of the Santa Claus suit.

"My guess would be that Coyote is trying to be as inconspicuous as possible," Katherine had said. "Being met by a man in a red suit stuffed with pillows might defeat that purpose."

Vic had to agree with that logic. But he definitely didn't agree that there was any logic at all to having Katherine come along on this little adventure. He had no idea what might turn out to be waiting at the other end. What if somebody had intimidated Coyote into making that phone call to Vic's house? What if this was a setup? With those possibilities in mind, and maybe some worse ones too, Vic had stopped by the hallway cabinet on the way out of his house and retrieved his gun from the hidden compartment there.

"What's that for?" Katherine asked.

Naturally, she'd refused to credit his objections to her coming along to meet Coyote. Naturally, she was also watching every move Vic made. He wouldn't have put it past her to follow him upstairs so she could make sure he didn't sneak out the bedroom window when he was supposed to be changing his clothes. They were better off that she hadn't, of course. The thought of getting Katherine into his bedroom and keeping her there was very tempting even for a man on a mission of mercy. Maybe too tempting to resist.

"Why are you taking a gun?" Katherine repeated, not allowing him to avoid the question as he would have preferred to do.

"Just in case," he said, figuring she'd give him an argument for sure about carrying a firearm. He was more than a little surprised when she didn't.

The cathedral stood at the top of a steep hill. Two roads bordered a triangular park across the street from the church and converged at the bottom of that park to form a single road down the hill all the way to the Hudson River. Two Gothic spires thrust high into the night sky above the sandstone face of the old building which had commanded these heights for almost a century and a half. Vic could see why the boy might choose a place like the cathedral to hide. This holy fortress looked like it could stand against any enemy, especially the ungodly ones. He took Katherine's arm as they crossed the street.

Vic looked around in every direction. He knew he couldn't depend on the powers of the church alone for protection. He had to keep a sharp eye out for more earthly demons. Down Eagle Street across Madison Place and on the same side of Eagle as the cathedral the Executive Mansion loomed. This was the residence of the governor of New York State, and this area was called the Mansion Neighborhood because of that huge old house. The governor's residence was lit up now with spotlights set all around the grounds, as if to shield it from the residents of some of the much smaller and less impressive buildings advancing toward the mansion up the hill. By comparison, the cathedral struck Vic as much more vulnerable and exposed the way it jutted right out onto the street with nothing but a cast-iron fence to hold back the dangers of the world.

"Where do you think he could be?" Katherine asked. "He said he'd wait by the front steps."

Coyote was nowhere to be seen. In fact, the streets were deserted. Last-minute holiday shoppers would have no business in this neighborhood. They'd be crowding the malls on the outskirts of the city tonight.

"He probably decided he should keep out of sight," Vic said. "Maybe he's inside."

He climbed the few stone steps to the wide doors. A wreath of evergreen boughs tied with a wide red ribbon had been hung above each of the three entrances. Vic tried the handles to each of the sets of double doors, but all of them were locked. He turned and shook his head at Katherine as he walked back down the steps.

"Not here," he said, gazing around again.

"Maybe he got scared and ran away."

"Maybe."

Vic scanned the front of the cathedral again. Large pots containing even larger pine trees had been set at each side of the stone steps. Coyote could have hidden behind one of them, but he wasn't there.

"Let's check the park across the street," Vic said.

He hooked his hand around Katherine's arm as he made his way to the curb.

"I wish you hadn't insisted on coming along," he said. "I don't like the feel of any of this."

"I care just as much about Coyote as you do," she said with a tug at his hand as if to pull away from him.

Vic tightened his grip on her.

"That has nothing to do with it," he said. "I don't know what we might be walking into here."

The stark truth of that sent his free right hand darting

into his jacket pocket, where it encountered nothing but his car keys. He had told himself that guns weren't always the answer to a problem, though some of his father's former associates believed they were. The thought had been enough to make Vic decide to leave the gun in the car until he could scope out the situation. His fingers closed around the car keys as he stopped walking and turned to face Katherine. He could see the resistance in her eyes even before he began to speak again.

"There could be trouble here tonight," he said trying to make his voice convey the truth of that. "I don't want to take the chance that you might get hurt. I think you should wait for me in the car."

"Absolutely not," she said, pulling harder against his grasp on her arm.

Vic dropped the car keys back into his pocket and took hold of her other arm as well. He pulled her so close she could hardly avoid looking up at him.

"All I'm asking is for you to sit in the car while I scout things out and make sure there's no real danger."

She stopped pulling away from him and stared up into his face. In the light of the bright streetlamp he could see the sadness come into her eyes. He would have taken her into his arms if she hadn't raised her gloved hands and placed them both flat against his chest.

"I was forced to sit and wait and do nothing while Daniel died," she said. "Please, don't ask me to sit and wait and do nothing again."

The tremor in her voice resonated in Vic's heart. For an instant, he could see her sitting in a hospital corridor, anguish shadowing her lovely face, her hands clutching each other in her lap. He could imagine how helpless that would feel, and how unbearable. He dropped his hands from her arms and reached up to brush a stray curl away from her cheek. The thought of anything happening to her out here made his fingers tremble, and he had to take a deep breath before he could speak.

"If you're coming along, you have to be very careful," he said.

She nodded. "I will be."

"And let me take the lead."

He was ready for an objection to that when a sound behind them made him put that last request into action and shove her protectively behind his wake. He spun just in time to see one of the wide church doors slowly opening.

"It's me," a boy's voice called from behind the opening cathedral door.

Coyote's head emerged a second later. Vic breathed a sigh of relief. Before he could think whether or not he should stop her, Katherine had darted out onto the curb and across the sidewalk. She reached Coyote just as he was letting the door to the church close behind him. She crouched down to his height on the top of the stone steps and wrapped him in an embrace.

"Thank heaven you're safe," she said. "We've been so worried about you."

Vic half expected Coyote to pull himself out of her arms. Boys his age had a way of doing that when it came to physical gestures of affection or concern, but Coyote didn't pull away. Instead, he did quite the opposite. He wrapped his own arms in their pitifully thin jacket as far around Katherine as he could reach. In that one movement, Vic could see, plain as day, the ordeal this little boy had been through and how glad he felt that he was no longer on his own. Vic walked up the steps and put his arm around Coyote, too.

"Everything's going to be fine now, son," Vic said.

He glanced up at the cathedral doors and said a little

prayer that he would turn out to be right. He also found himself wishing he really could be a father to Coyote, and to Sprite as well. He was sure he'd be able to do a better job of protecting them than anybody else had managed so far. Tooley Pennebaker tried her best, and the mother was too sick to do anything. The children's father had disappeared long ago and most likely wasn't coming back. Vic had been a kid on his own at too young an age himself. He still remembered how lonely, and how scary, that was. He said another small prayer that Coyote and Sprite might be spared that loneliness and fear. His second glance at the cathedral brought another thought suddenly to mind.

"How did you get inside?" he asked Coyote. "The place was locked up tight when I tried the doors."

"I found another way in."

Something in Coyote's voice, a hint of guilt, told Vic the boy had broken into the church. He probably knew a lot about how to break into places. Vic couldn't help but wonder what other talents for deception Coyote might have developed. A kid had to master a lot of not-so-nice skills when it came to surviving on his own out in the world. Vic also couldn't help but wonder how much of what Coyote had done and led them to believe so far might be a product of those deceiving ways. Vic would have liked to push that grim thought out of his head, but he had to be realistic about what might or might not really be going on here.

"Let's get going," he said as he stifled a sigh and straightened up.

He left his hand resting on Coyote's shoulder, but it felt more tentative there now. Katherine stood up too. She'd pulled off her gloves and was smoothing Coyote's cropped hair away from his dirt-smudged face with her fingers, but she was looking at Vic. He caught a glimpse of the question in her eyes before he turned away. She must have heard the note of suspicion in his voice. He'd heard it there himself.

"Why don't we take a little walk and talk a bit?" she said.

Her suggestion let Vic know his guess had been right.

KATHERINE FELT GUILTY about keeping Coyote out in the cold, but she had detected the doubt and distance that came over Vic all of a sudden and knew those doubts needed to be cleared up. Her instincts told her there was no better time than right now for that clearing up to begin. The police would be involved soon. They would certainly have to be called in, the minute she and Vic got Coyote back to Vic's place. In fact, they should probably take the boy directly to the police station now. She didn't want to do that, at least not just yet. There was no telling what would happen to Coyote's story once he had to tell it to a policeman. The best chance they had of finding out the unvarnished truth was to go after it right now.

Coyote shrugged in answer to her suggestion that they take a walk, but he didn't say anything. She hoped that wasn't a sign that he intended to clam up now in the face of questioning. As if to confirm that fear, he slipped away from her touch and headed down the church steps onto the sidewalk. He turned left toward Madison Avenue. His bouncy stride had carried him halfway to the corner before Vic called out with some urgency in his voice.

"Hey, wait up, kid. Let's stick together here."

Katherine saw Vic glance furtively around as he hurried on ahead to catch up with Coyote. She glanced around, too, but saw nothing that looked even remotely like danger. Vic and Coyote were at the corner by then. Vic unzipped his jacket and took it off then slipped it over Coyote's shoulders. Katherine was as warmed by that gesture as Coyote must have been. Vic might have his doubts and suspicions, but he still cared about the boy. She was relieved to see that because she cared so very much herself, about both Coyote and Sprite. Suddenly, she realized, in something of a flash, how important it was to her that she and Vic feel the same way, especially about this one thing. She hurried to catch up with them as they rounded the corner.

"I thought we might walk the other way, back down the hill," she said as she joined them. "We might find a coffee shop or a restaurant to go into where it's warm."

She didn't know of any place like that in the direction they were headed.

"I like the Plaza," Coyote said. "I spend a lot of time over here."

Katherine had grown wise enough in the ways of street kids since she came to the Arbor Hill Center to understand that Coyote might actually mean he'd have lots of places to run away from them and hide again once he was on familiar ground. On the other hand, he might also mean he'd feel safer where he knew his surroundings. He had certainly experienced precious little safety lately.

"All right," she said. "We'll walk this way, but let's stop for a minute first and sit down."

She headed toward a low wall just beyond the fenced-in cathedral grounds where a driveway led to a parking lot for Empire State Plaza visitors. The much-acclaimed architectural marvel was a popular tourist attraction in the daylight hours. By this time of night, and two days before Christmas, the buildings were closed and the streets were deserted. Katherine sat down on the low wall. The much higher wall of the State Museum, a tiered building that always reminded her of an Egyptian tomb, loomed to her back and shut out some of the wind.

"Coyote, we need for you to tell us what exactly you've

been running away from,'' she began as soon as they had joined her.

She drew Coyote down to sit next to her on the wall, but Vic remained standing. She understood he would want to be in a position to watch both them and the street.

''I been running away because of something I saw that I'd be better off if I hadn't,'' Coyote said very fast, as if letting go of a burden he'd been carrying too long.

Katherine had been concerned that he might not be willing to talk and they would have to pry the story out of him. She could tell now that wasn't going to be the case. She felt her own relief as he hurried on.

''I saw a guy dump a bundle in an alleyway off Broadway. I went there to mail my letter to you about the fund money. I was in front of the post office near the corner of Livingston when the car pulled up down the street and this big guy got out.''

''Is that the black car Sprite told us about?'' she asked.

''Yeah. That's the kind of car it was,'' Coyote said nodding.

There was something in the quality of Vic's silence that let Katherine know how skeptically he was listening to what Coyote had to say. She hoped Coyote wouldn't read that skepticism and stop talking.

''What happened then?'' she asked.

''The man opened the trunk and took out a long bundle. I think it was wrapped in a rug, but the paper didn't say anything about a rug, so the big guy must have taken that away with him.''

''What paper are you talking about?''

''The *Chronicle*,'' Coyote said matter-of-factly, as if she should have been expecting him to follow the local news while he was on the run. ''I been looking for copies in wastebaskets ever since that night, just so I could see if they wrote about what happened. It was in there the second day, how they found the guy right in that same alley where I saw the black car pull up.''

''What guy did they find?'' Vic asked.

Katherine could see that Coyote had Vic's full attention now. She wished the expression on his face didn't reveal quite so obviously how little he believed of what he was hearing.

''They found a guy named Gilford Vogel. The paper said he worked for a place in Troy that did import stuff. I don't know what that means, but it said he was a bookkeeper there.''

Katherine guessed that Coyote was providing as many details as he could because he wanted them to think he was telling the truth.

''They had the whole story right there,'' Coyote went on. ''The paper said the cops think it was a robbery, but I know it wasn't. I saw who put the guy there. I even saw his face. That's why he's been after me ever since.''

''What else did the *Chronicle* say?'' Vic asked, his disbelief more apparent than ever.

''They told about the guy. Mr. Vogel,'' Coyote said. ''How when they found him he was stone-cold dead.''

Chapter Twenty-Two

What Coyote was saying had to be too fantastic to be true. Yet, Katherine found herself believing him. Then, he yelled out, "The man from the black car. There he is."

Those words shattered Katherine's belief. The child had now obviously brought his fantasy to life in an attempt to convince the adults he wasn't making things up. She found that so sad and touching she would have taken Coyote into her arms again, the way she did back on the cathedral steps, to reassure him everything would be all right now. Except that Coyote was already running away. He'd shoved his sleeves into Vic's jacket as they were walking up the hill. That jacket flapped around the small boy's legs as he dashed off the low wall and straight across the four-lane road toward the other side. Fortunately, there were no cars coming at the moment. Unfortunately, Katherine could now see that Coyote had concocted his fantasy to create a distraction and allow him to run away yet again.

She could tell Vic was just as discouraged by Coyote's deception as she was. She'd heard Vic sigh loudly when the boy first claimed to see the notorious and maybe imagined man. She'd glanced upward for an instant at Vic then. He'd been staring off toward the looming marble towers of the Plaza with a resigned expression on his face as he shook his head. Then, Coyote ran off and Katherine cried after him, "Coyote, wait," with her hand upraised. But he didn't wait. He didn't even turn around. A figure appeared from the parking lot.

"Vic," she cried out, but he had already joined the chase in pursuit of the large man in the black coat who was obviously after Coyote.

Two cars drove by in quick succession then, and Vic had to wait for them. Katherine gasped as he stumbled to a halt at the very last minute to keep from running in front of the second car. The driver hit his horn with a loud blast. Vic charged off again when the car had passed, but the man in the black coat was far ahead by now. Coyote was farther ahead still and had disappeared over the barricade that blocked the steps to the Plaza mall. The mall area was kept closed to the public at night, but only low, metal guardrails blocked access. Coyote scrambled over them easily and was out of sight.

Katherine's suede boots with their high, narrow heels, which had been so perfect for hostessing Vic's open house, were nothing but an impediment now. She hurried as fast as she could manage after the parade already in Coyote's wake. She stumbled several times in her haste but managed not to fall. She thought about calling the police, but decided they might not arrive in time to give Vic the help he needed. She'd have to do her best to provide some of that herself.

She ran to the Plaza Mall and struggled over first the guardrails at the bottom of the steps and then a second set of rails at the top. By that time, Vic had caught up to the bigger man somehow, and the two of them were grappling along the marble walkway that bordered the mall. Skyscrapers towered overhead. Maple trees stripped bare of leaves by winter lined the walkway. To the left, the long reflecting pool had been pumped dry to prevent freezing and cracking in the frigid months. Vic and his opponent veered dangerously close to the edge of that pool, locked in a battle grip from which lunging arms and fists emerged to land blows whenever and wherever they could. Coyote was nowhere in sight.

"Vic, watch out for the edge," Katherine screamed as she ran toward the struggling men.

She was too late with her warning. They were already toppling over the rim and rolling into the snowy pool bed a few feet below the level of the mall. Vic landed at least two solid punches, the second to the jaw of the big man, who staggered backward with a grunt. Katherine was about to pull off her coat and jump down onto the pool bed herself when Vic glanced her way.

"Stay back, Katherine," he yelled.

She was startled by the strangled sound of his voice. He was out of breath. She wasn't surprised that fighting a man so much superior in bulk would have Vic combatting exhaustion as well. What happened next did surprise her, and not happily. The big man took advantage of Vic's moment of inattention by wrapping huge arms around Vic's chest from behind and squeezing visibly hard. Katherine knew she mustn't listen to Vic's insistence that she stay out of this fight. She was unbuttoning her coat and dragging at the sleeves when a boy's voice rang out behind her.

"Let go of him!"

A well-aimed chunk of ice hurtled through the air past Katherine. She turned to find Coyote a few feet behind her, armed with several chunks of ice and snowballs. She heard a grunt of pain and looked back at the two in the reflecting pool. Coyote's ice missile had hit its mark. The big man stumbled backwards a step, holding the side of his face. A second chunk struck him on the top of his head, and he winced again. Katherine remembered Vic mentioning his work with Coyote on his pitching skills. Those efforts were definitely paying off now. Vic didn't waste the opening Coyote's attack created. He was after the bigger man in a shot, pounding and pummelling him till he went down on one knee in the pool bed. Still, the man was a powerfully built opponent. Vic would need help. Unfortunately, another glance back at Coyote revealed that he now had on only his own thin jacket.

"Where is Vic's jacket?" Katherine cried out.

Coyote looked at her for a moment as if he didn't understand what she was asking.

"Where did you leave Vic's jacket?" she repeated. "I have to find it."

"Back there."

Coyote gestured toward the stand of barren trees at the edge of the walkway. Katherine hurried in that direction with her half-unbuttoned coat flying behind her. Overhead, lights illuminated the mall, but the tree-lined area was still very much in shadow. She strained to see into the darkness. She thought she might have spotted a clump that could be the jacket. She prayed she was right and that Vic's gun would still be in the pocket. She feared that Coyote's snowball barrage and Vic's pummelling would hold this mountain of a man at bay only temporarily. She was headed toward what she hoped would be a more decisively effective weapon when a woman's voice rang out, echoing in the emptiness of the long mall and against the marble buildings.

"Let him up right now, or I kill the kid."

Katherine spun around and looked immediately at Coyote, expecting him to be in the clutches of whoever had shouted those cold, impassioned words. Coyote was poised with his arm raised to throw another snowball, but there was no one with him. Katherine followed his transfixed gaze down the marble walkway in the direction of the opposite end of the Plaza. The mall lights reflected in the pale blond hair of the tall woman walking toward them.

"Lacey Harbison," Katherine breathed, recognizing the woman who'd visited her office two days before.

Even more shocking than this woman's unexpected arrival was the presence of the child she was gripping by one arm and pushing along in front of her. Sprite's small face was white against the night. Her eyes were huge and terrified. Katherine leapt forward, ready to drag the child away from the woman. Then she saw the gun pointed at Sprite's head and backed off.

"Let him up out of there like I told you," the Harbison woman shouted.

Back in the pool bed the two men had stopped struggling to stare at the blonde with the child. Vic had apparently managed to overpower the bigger man after all. He was lying flat in the pool bed with Vic on top, clutching the other man's throat. Katherine watched with a sinking heart as Vic released his grip and rose slowly to his feet. The big man labored to his knees. She could hear him gasping for breath.

She could also hear Sprite sobbing softly and longed to run to her.

"You all right, Cuda?" Lacey Harbison asked. The big man nodded in reply. Maybe he was so winded he couldn't speak yet. Nonetheless, when he finally rose to his feet, looming even larger and broader than Katherine had previously registered, he'd regained enough strength to lunge at Vic, who stepped quickly out of reach.

"We've got no time for that now. Get up out of there," Lacey Harbison said, gesturing with the gun still frighteningly close to Sprite's bare head. "Where's the other kid?"

Katherine's glance darted to the spot where Coyote had been standing only a moment ago. He was gone. She scanned the walkway and back among the trees, but he was nowhere in sight. Once again, he'd managed to slip away. This time Katherine was grateful for the street-learned craftiness that allowed him to disappear so skillfully.

"He's gone," the big man Harbison had called Cuda growled as he hauled himself out of the pool bed. "I'll find him."

"No time for that now," Harbison barked in a tone that left no doubt who was truly in charge. "We've still got this one." She yanked hard enough at Sprite's arm to make her cry out. "I think we'll be able to make a deal for the other brat. Either that or this sweet little girl ends up good and dead."

The cultured tone and charming smile Lacey Harbison had put on in Katherine's office had vanished now. Even in this imperfect light she could detect a glint of viciousness in Harbison's eyes. She looked as if she would be entirely capable of following through on the threat she'd just made. Katherine clenched her fists at her sides and willed herself to stay very still. Vic remained standing in the reflecting pool. He wasn't moving either. She guessed he had also recognized the potential for heartlessness in Lacey Harbison.

"We'll be in touch with you tomorrow," she said, glaring at Vic. "You be sure to be home when we contact you."

The big man named Cuda had joined her by now. He grabbed Sprite away from his accomplice. Katherine saw Vic flinch at that, but he stood his ground. He obviously knew as well as Katherine did that they'd better not make any kind of move while Harbison and Cuda sauntered away with little Sprite, still terrified and at gunpoint.

Katherine barely noticed when Coyote materialized beside her out of the shadows cast by the trees. Vic's jacket was draped over Coyote's arm, but there was no use going for the gun in the pocket now. All the three of them could do was watch helplessly as the three others disappeared from view beyond the massive Christmas tree at the State Street end of the mall. The multicolored lights twinkling from the branches of the tall hemlock mocked the sudden hollowness in Katherine's heart and the holiday joy she could no longer feel.

Chapter Twenty-Three

Sandra Thomas and her crew had cleaned up so well Vic could hardly tell there'd been a party here yesterday. He could find no trace of anything like a good time inside himself either. He walked from one room of his house to another as if he were shuffling in and out of a nightmare where everybody looked perfectly normal but nothing, in fact, was. Worst of all was the sadness in Katherine's eyes and how bravely she tried to hide it, especially when Coyote was around. She didn't fool Vic for a second. She'd already had one child torn away from her in her life. Vic had grown so close to her in these past few intense days that he could feel the depth of her sorrow.

Tooley Pennebaker had been with them since shortly after he, Katherine and Coyote got back from Empire State Plaza. He had sent a cab to pick her up and bring her here to join in the long wait with the rest of them, as he knew she would want to do. As it turned out, she'd already known that something had happened to Sprite, though she had no idea the child had been abducted. According to her friend, Sprite had been fretting about looking for Coyote, and when Sprite had vanished from in front of their home where she was staying, the friend's mother thought the little girl had left to search for her brother.

Tooley stayed the night in one of his guest rooms. Katherine and Vic agreed that Tooley shouldn't be alone during this ordeal. No one had slept much. They wandered up and down stairs and drank cups of coffee, which was the last thing any of them needed. They all looked pretty worn out this morning, as Megan Moran had been quick to point out with her usual bluntness when she arrived an hour ago, head bandage and all.

And, of course, there were the cops. They'd been here all night too, asking questions, taking down statements, setting up electronic connections to Vic's phone line. He had to hand it to all of them for trying as hard as they did to stay out of the way and be as inconspicuous as possible. Still, nobody, particularly not Vic, could forget for a minute that his house was under constant surveillance, his telephone was tapped and there was a makeshift police command post set up in his dining room. For someone who'd tried to avoid cops most of his life, Vic certainly had brought a carload of them down on himself today. Strangely enough, he was glad to have them here. Anything that would help get Sprite back was okay with him. He only wished he could do more to help.

"It's driving me crazy, sitting here not knowing what to do," Tooley said, echoing Vic's thoughts and shaking her head slowly.

Megan sat down next to Tooley and put her arm around the woman's shoulder.

"It's up to the police now," Megan said. "We have to let them do their jobs. They'll get Sprite back. I know they will."

"I don't know what I'm going to do then, either," Tooley said, sounding very close to tears. "I thought I could take care of these kids and do my job plus overtime hours, too, but I know now that I can't. I promised their poor mama I wouldn't let them go into foster care, but I talked to her doctors just last week and it looks like she's going to be in the sanitarium for a long time. Even when she gets out, she won't be strong enough to take care of those children. Lord knows I want to keep my promise to her. I just don't know how.''

Almost before he realized he was going to say anything, Vic stepped forward and put his hand on Tooley's shoulder.

"You don't have to worry about any of that," Vic said. "I'm going to help you."

Tooley and Megan both looked up at him expectantly. All of a sudden, Vic knew exactly what he wanted to say. He'd never been so sure of anything in his life before, except maybe how much he had come to care about Katherine.

"I'd like Coyote and Sprite to come here and live with me," he said.

Tooley shook her head again. "How're you going to manage that on your own? You'll have most of the same problems I did."

Before Vic could respond, the phone rang. The room went suddenly still except for the echo of that first ring, while they all waited for the next. He had his instructions from the police. He was to let the phone ring three times, then pick it up. He was at the phone with his hand poised over the receiver before the second ring could sound, and Katherine was at his side.

"Hello, this is Victor Maltese," he said when it was finally okay to answer.

"Vic, it's your mother."

Her voice on the other end of the line was almost the last one he would have expected to hear.

"I can't really talk right now, Ma," he said. "There's a lot going on here."

"I know exactly what is going on, son," she said.

Vic wasn't surprised to hear that. His father had friends who kept him informed, from both sides of the law. As soon as the Maltese name appeared on the police blotter last night, somebody from downtown would have called Gabriel to tell him exactly what was what.

"I'll be there soon myself," his mother went on. "I wanted to call you first to let you know your father is already on his way."

Vic began to count to ten. He felt Katherine's hand on his arm, as if she'd seen the way his jaw had tightened. He stopped counting. Her touch soothed him more than a row of numbers ever could.

"Look, Ma. This isn't the time…" he began, more calmly than he would have thought possible right now.

"This is precisely the time," she said. "You must take my word for that. It is time for us all to be together as a family."

There was a sternness in her voice that Vic had heard very seldom in his life. He understood how futile it would be to disagree. He'd save that for his father.

"All right, Ma. I'll expect him. Thanks for calling."

Vic hung up the phone and stood stock-still as a heavy weight of dread settled over him. This was on its way to becoming the worst Christmas Eve Day on record. At the same time, it could very possibly be the best day of his life. He felt the warmth and closeness of Katherine next to him. He had no right to the joy her nearness gave him, but he couldn't help what he felt in his heart. Suddenly, he realized that no one could ever help that.

KATHERINE'S PULSE had quickened when Vic offered to have Coyote and Sprite live with him. She had known how much she cared about the Bellaway children for some time now—the same way she knew now how much she'd come to care about Vic. She would have staked her life on the certainty of all of that. Now, she knew how he felt about Coyote and Sprite, too. She wished she could be equally sure what he felt about her. She exasperated him sometimes, she realized, till he looked like he was ready to start tearing out his gorgeous, black hair. Maybe they could get past that now, and the children would bring them closer together still. Katherine was praying so hard for this to be true and to get Sprite back unharmed, that she jumped when the phone rang.

They'd all been waiting for a call from the man called Cuda or from Lacey Harbison. The policemen seemed surprised that call hadn't yet come. When the phone finally rang, Katherine had seen the officer with the headset in the dining room signal thumbs down and shake his head after listening for a moment. The call wasn't about Sprite, after all. Still, Vic sounded upset as soon as he started listening to the voice on the other end of the line. Then Katherine had realized he was talking to his mother and understood his agitation.

He had ended the conversation, but still stood with his hand on the receiver. She could tell by the way his dark brows knitted together in a scowl that he was unhappy about something. She could feel tension in the muscles of the arm he had around her.

"What was the call about?" she asked quietly.

"Almost the last thing in the world I want to hear right now."

Her breath caught in her throat. Could this be bad news about Sprite after all?

"My father is on his way here," he added.

Her relief was profound, but she understood that Vic wouldn't share that feeling.

"He probably wants to be here to support you through this bad time," she said, choosing her words carefully. "How did he know what was going on?"

There'd been no reports in the papers or on the broadcast news. Mariette Dugan had been here earlier, but the police had sent her away. She was probably hanging around somewhere close by. Still, she'd been given nothing definite to report as yet.

Vic shrugged. "My father knows what's happening to me almost before I do. I didn't move far enough away to stop that. Maybe I should have done what you did, put half the country between myself and my past." He glanced at her quickly. "I'm sorry. I shouldn't have said that."

"You should say exactly that because it's true. I don't mind hearing it now, either, because all of that is changing for me."

"In what way?" he asked.

She could feel him gazing down at her.

"I'm starting to put the past behind me and think about living for the present and the future," she said.

She looked up into the warmth of his dark eyes, and he touched her cheek with his fingers.

"Could be it's time for me to do the same thing."

"Could be," she said.

Katherine was thinking very much in the present, about how she would like to kiss Vic now, a gentle kiss to give comfort to them both, if only there weren't so many people in the room. Before she could decide whether she might forget about audience and act on that thought anyway, the doorbell rang. Megan went to answer it, and her squeal a moment later could not have been mistaken for anything but joy.

"It's a miracle," Megan trilled from the foyer.

A tall, very distinguished-looking man appeared in the

archway to the living room. His hand was firmly in the clutch of none other than little Sprite Bellaway.

"I brought her back to you, son," the tall man said to Vic. "It is the very least I could do."

THE HOUR that followed was as miraculous as the sweet child's return had been.

Gabriel Maltese revealed his role in Sprite's rescue. The kidnapper was a man named Barricuda Taft, sometimes referred to as Cuda. He and Leta Hatcher, alias Lacey Harbison, had siphoned off a considerable amount of gambling-operations money from some people even more dangerous than themselves then tried to cover up the theft by killing the bookkeeper, Gilford Vogel, who found the discrepancy. Mr. Maltese's contacts from his former life had tracked Cuda down during the night. Gabriel himself had persuaded the pair to turn themselves in, rather than face the much harsher judgment of their criminal colleagues.

An even more startling revelation came when Vic's mother arrived and told everyone, over her husband's protests, that the Secret Santa who'd made the huge donation to the Most Needy Cases Fund had been none other than Gabriel Maltese. As Vic had said earlier, Mr. Maltese kept close tabs on everything his son was doing, including this program at the Arbor Hill Center. That, and how deeply Gabriel's heart had been touched by Katherine's interviews in the *Chronicle,* had moved him to make the generous gift. At that news, Vic reached out to embrace his father.

Katherine was at Vic's side all the while, tears coming to her eyes, joy filling her heart. She knew it would take more than money for Mr. Maltese to earn his way back into Vic's life. She also knew the journey had begun.

They would be a real family some day, and soon. She could feel it. The people in the room were a family al-

ready—Katherine, Vic, his mother and father, Coyote and
Sprite, their mother, Megan and Tooley, too.

Katherine and Vic stood watching the excited crowd in
his living room. He wrapped an arm around her to move
her a few steps to the archway into the hall.

"Were you serious when you told Tooley you wanted
Coyote and Sprite to come live here?" she asked.

"More serious than I've ever been, with one exception,"
he told her, looking deep into her eyes. "But I won't do it
alone," he added in a voice so calm and certain, she knew
what his words implied.

"No, you won't do it alone," she echoed, answering his
unspoken question.

He put his arm around her shoulders and hugged her
closer to him.

They moved back into the living room as Vic's father
lifted Sprite up to hang a sparkling glass angel, which Mrs.
Maltese had brought from another tree in Loudonville, on
one of the highest branches.

Coyote reached for Katherine's hand.

"Way to go, Sprite," he cried out more happily than
Katherine had ever heard him sound.

Just for an instant, as the angel came to rest against the
fragrant bough, Katherine imagined she heard Daniel's precious voice. Her heart soared at the joy in his tone as he
said, "Cherish the love you find in one another at this
blessed time of year, and forevermore."

They're brothers by blood, lawmen by choice, cowboys by nature.

THE COWBOY CODE

The McQuaid brothers learned justice and honor from their father, the meaning of family from their mother. The West was always in their souls, but now it's the past they have to reckon with. And three women hold the keys to their future.

Don't miss this exciting new series from three of your favorite Intrigue authors!

McQUAID'S JUSTICE
Carly Bishop
January 1999

A COWBOY'S HONOR
Laura Gordon
February 1999

LONE STAR LAWMAN
Joanna Wayne
March 1999

Available at your favorite retail outlet.

HARLEQUIN®
Makes any time special ™

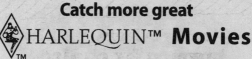